ELLE GRAY

BLAKE WILDER

FBI MYSTERY THRILLER

THE
HOUSE
ON
THE HILL

PROLOGUE

Gerald Ford Elementary School; Denver, CO

B RIDGET KELLER PULLED THE CAR TO A STOP IN THE DROP-off lane in front of the school. As her son Cole opened the car door, she quickly reached into her purse and pulled out some cash.

"Cole, honey, here," she said. "This is for lunch. Make sure you feed your sister."

"I will, Mom."

"More than just a candy bar."

Cole flashed her a devious grin. "But that's all she wanted."

"Cole—"

"All right, all right," he relented with a laugh. "I'll make sure she gets something to eat."

Lyssa sat in the back seat grinning at the exchange. She had a mischievous look on her face, so Bridget turned around and fixed her with a serious expression.

"I mean it. Real food. Not candy," she insisted.

"I don't think what's in the cafeteria can be called real food, Mom," Cole quipped.

"Do your best," she replied. "I'll be sure to make your lunches tomorrow."

The car behind her honked its horn and Bridget had to bite back the irritation that flashed through her. She reminded herself that she was blocking the drop-off point, though, and needed to get a move on.

"All right, you two. Have a good day at school," she said. "I'll see you this afternoon. Love you both."

"Love you," they replied in unison.

Cole and Lyssa climbed out of the car and Bridget watched them head toward the front doors. For a moment, she felt a brief flash of nostalgia. It didn't seem all that long ago that they were little kids, running around the house in their diapers, laughing and roughhousing with each other. But now, Cole was eleven and already in the sixth grade. And Lyssa, in fourth grade, had just turned nine. Where was the time going?

The car behind her blared its horn again and Bridget waved at him. "Yeah, yeah, yeah," she muttered to herself. "I'm going. Jesus, keep your shirt on."

She dropped the minivan into gear and pulled out of the half-circle-shaped drop-off driveway and onto the street. She had a lot to do today and decided she needed a little liquid fuel before she got to it. Bridget stopped at the Starbucks drive-thru, got herself properly caffeinated, then headed off to her first stop to drop a few things off at the dry cleaners.

It took most of the day to knock everything off her to-do list, and by the time she got to the grocery store, it was almost 1:30. She had forty-five minutes to get the shopping done before she had to pick up the kids from school. Bridget smiled to herself. She liked it when everything seemed to fall right into place. She enjoyed being efficient.

Bridget pulled a bleach wipe out of the pack in her purse and wiped down the handle on the shopping cart. That done, she threw the wipe away and headed into the store. Bridget knew the layout of the store by heart and had already divided her shopping list by section so she could make one quick, efficient pass through the market. She always managed to get everything she needed in one fell swoop.

Her husband, Brad, was the polar opposite. Most of the time, he never even bothered to make a list. He ran from aisle to aisle, having to double back to grab something he'd forgotten. It was somewhat endearing, but she hated shopping with him for that very reason. Brad was one of the most sought-after architects in all of Colorado and ran a very prestigious firm. But in truth, he was a bit of a hot mess. At least when it came to grocery shopping. She couldn't count the number of times she'd had to send him back for something he forgot.

Bridget made her way through the produce section, stopping to pick up some apples. As she put some Granny Smiths into a bag, she felt the hair on the back of her neck stand up and a chill sweep over her.

It was odd. She couldn't quite place it. She was putting a bundle of green onions into a plastic produce bag when she realized what it was: she felt like she was being watched. There were three women—two of them she'd seen before—and a pair of men in the produce section with her, but none of them seemed to be paying any undue attention to her.

And yet, that feeling of having eyes on her persisted. It seemed to grow thicker even though not a single person she could see had so much as glanced at her. She wasn't a paranoid woman by nature, but once in a while, she had the feeling of being watched. It seemed to be happening more frequently over the last six months. She thought about mentioning it to Brad a few times, but he probably would have said she was being silly. And truthfully, most of the time after that feeling faded, she thought she was being silly too.

"Hey, Mrs. Keller."

Bridget let out a yelp of surprise and spun around, her heart hammering a staccato beat in her chest. She put her hand to her heart and, when she saw who it was, let out a relieved laugh.

"JJ, sorry," she said, breathless. "You surprised me."

"I'm sorry about that, Mrs. Keller. I totally didn't mean to scare you."

She shook her head and waved him off. "Nothing to be sorry about. I'm just getting jumpy in my old age."

"You're hardly old," he replied.

JJ had been a sophomore in high school when he started working at the store and was now a twenty-year-old sophomore in college. And he'd flirted with her shamelessly the entire time. Bridget couldn't lie—she kind of liked the attention from a younger, good-looking man. But she was fifteen years his senior, and though technically not old, she sometimes felt like a dirty old woman for enjoying the attention he lavished on her.

"You ready to leave that husband of yours and run away with me?" he asked.

"And where would we go, JJ?"

"Bali? Fiji?" he mused. "A country without an extradition treaty for when they accuse me of kidnapping you?"

She laughed softly. "That's really tempting, JJ. You never know. One of these days I might just take you up on it."

He smiled. "I'm waiting for the day," he replied. "You finding everything okay?"

She nodded. "Yeah, I'm good, thanks."

"Okay, you need anything, you just give me a shout."

"I will. Thanks, JJ," she said, her eyes still darting left and right.

"Hey, are you okay?"

"Huh?" she asked, turning her gaze back to him.

"You look a little freaked out about something," he told her. "You okay?"

"Oh, yeah," she replied. "I'm fine. Just… a lot on my mind today."

He looked at her for a long moment, as if trying to decide if he believed her not. She offered him a smile she hoped looked more reassuring than it felt. JJ looked around the department and frowned, apparently not seeing anything out of place, then turned back to her. He still didn't look convinced but offered her a gentle smile.

"Well, if you need anything—anything at all—just let me know." He flashed her his patented megawatt grin.

"I will. Thanks again."

He gave her a nod then walked off, still looking around as if trying to spot the source of her discomfort. The chill persisted, but Bridget did her best to shrug it off. She needed to finish up with the shopping then go get the kids. This little interlude had cost her time. And as much as she hated inefficiency, she hated being late even more.

After dinner that night, Bridget finished up the dishes then walked into the living room. Cole was watching something on TV, laughing along with whatever was happening while Lyssa sat cross-legged on the couch playing games on her tablet.

"All right, you two," Bridget announced. "Time to get ready for bed."

She was met with the usual groans and pleas for ten more minutes. Bridget laughed to herself. She learned long ago how to play this game with them. Now, she told them twenty minutes before their bedtime so when they pled for ten more minutes, she could magnanimously grant them that small indulgence—and still get them to bed on time. It had taken some time, but Bridget had learned to play the game with them very well.

She puttered in the kitchen for ten minutes, then stepped back into the living room to inform them their time was up. The kids grumbled and moaned, as usual—they couldn't give Bridget a win by giving in too easily, of course. But this time they got up and headed for their rooms to get ready for bed. They were good kids, and Bridget felt lucky to have them.

As they brushed their teeth and put on their pajamas, she finished closing up the house, making sure the doors and windows were all locked up tight. They lived in a good neighborhood, but Bridget didn't believe in taking anything for granted. She was careful by nature. Always had been. She suspected she always would be. It was just how she was raised. Her mother was almost obsessive about making sure the house was buttoned up at night, and Bridget supposed it must have rubbed off on her.

She stepped into the front room and shut off the television and the lights. She stood at the large picture window and looked at the neighborhood that lay beyond the glass. Their home sat atop a small hill at the end of the street, the elevation giving her a beautiful view at night. The lights of the neighborhood twinkled in the darkness, and the moon hung high overhead, casting the world outside in a soft, silvery glow. She loved standing at the window at night and watching all the lights sparkling in the dark. It almost looked like the stars in the velvety blackness of the sky above, both views seeming to stretch out to infinity.

But that small smile on her lips faded as her skin prickled and the hair on the back of her neck stood up again. That feeling of being watched washed over her again. It was stronger than it had been at the store. Much stronger. It was nearly suffocating. Bridget took a step back from the window, her heart thundering so hard in her chest, it was difficult to breathe.

She quickly turned out the lights and headed back to Brad's office at the back of the house. Bridget pushed the door open to find her husband hunched over his laptop, banging away at the keys, his brows furrowed in concentration. A soft smile touched her lips as she looked at him, and the fears that had held her in their grip loosened, letting her breathe once more. Brad had always had that calming effect on her. No matter how tense things got, she always felt comforted in his presence.

They'd met just after she'd graduated from college and had fallen in love almost immediately. He was working for the government, doing urban planning for the Department of Housing and Urban Development, and she was planning on going back to get her Master's. Bridget had always wanted to be a university professor, but she'd gotten pregnant with Cole, and her priorities changed. Eventually, Brad left HUD and opened his own firm. He seemed happier working in the private sector.

"Hey," he said, looking up from his computer at her. "You all right?"

"Yeah, I'm fine," she replied. She wished it didn't feel like she was trying to convince herself.

Brad closed his computer and stood up. With a gentle smile on his face, he crossed the room and took her in his arms. He gave her a soft kiss and looked into her eyes.

"What's wrong?" he asked. "You're so tense."

"It's nothing," she shook her head. "Just my paranoia kicking in, I guess."

He cocked his head. "Paranoia?"

"Yeah, just silly stuff."

He smiled. "Like what? Like the kids are eating candy bars instead of their lunches?"

She sighed. "No, not that. It's… I've felt like I'm being watched lately."

Brad took a step back and his expression quickly sobered. He licked his lips and his body tensed. Bridget had expected him to laugh and make her feel silly like he did whenever he thought she was acting like a goof. But his reaction was serious and was freaking her out.

"You said lately," he said, his voice tight. "How long have you felt like you were being watched, Bridget?"

"I don't know. The last couple of weeks or so, I guess. I just figured you'd say I was being paranoid and silly—"

"Get the kids and pack a bag, Bridge," he cut her off. "We need to go."

Her eyes widened. "What are you talking about?"

"Now, Bridge. Get the kids and pack a bag. We need—"

The sound of the front door crashing inward cut off his words. He looked at her, and for the first time since she'd known him, Brad looked terrified.

"Oh, God. It's too late," he said.

Pete Malvern and his wife Sherry walked their dog down the street early Saturday morning. It was sunny, and the skies were blue, but there was a system coming in. By nightfall, they were predicting severe thunderstorms, so they wanted to get some exercise in before it hit. They were passing by the Keller's place. Pete stopped and looked up at the house that sat on the hill.

There was a time when Pete had thought anybody who bought that house had to be pretentious. He knew it was silly and irrational, but he'd always hated that there was a house in their neighborhood that sat, quite literally, above the rest. He knew it was just a house and that whoever bought it had no idea the sort of lot it sat on, but it still seemed sort of elitist to him. But when the Kellers had moved in, he found that he was wrong. Brad was a good guy. He was levelheaded. No good on the grill, but a friendly neighbor. His wife, Bridget, was lovely. Smart, dedicated to her family, and just a kind person. And their kids were just angels. They weren't just good neighbors; they were good friends.

"Hey, have you talked to Brad or Bridget lately?" Pete asked his wife.

Sherry shook her head. "No, I was supposed to get together with Bridget for brunch, but I never heard from her."

"Huh," Pete said. "When was that?"

"About a week ago."

Pete looked up at the house, searching for any sign of life. But there was nobody at the windows, the kids weren't in the yard, and their cars were still in the driveway.

"Yeah," Pete said. "I've sent Brad a few texts, and he hasn't gotten back to me."

"I thought it was weird. Bridget's usually really responsive," Sherry said.

Pete looked from the house to the gate at the bottom of the driveway. The newspapers were all stacked up in front of it—at least a week's worth. As he thought back over the last week, he tried to remember whether he'd seen the Kellers at any point and realized he hadn't. That was more than a little unusual. They were busy people, always coming and going, and the fact that Pete couldn't recall seeing them at any point over the last week worried him.

"Maybe they had to go out of town suddenly," Sherry offered.

"Yeah," Pete replied. "Maybe."

They walked on, but he wasn't convinced. Something seemed off to him, and his concern grew with every step. Something was wrong. He could feel it.

CHAPTER ONE

Office of Senior SSA Maximillian Stone; Quantico, VA

I STAND IN THE OPULENT OFFICE OF ONE OF THE MOST HIGH-ranking agents I've ever met, looking at the wall of photos and citations that detail a truly extraordinary career. There are pictures of him with two presidents, various congresspeople and dignitaries, as well as a few celebrities. There's one of him with Brad Pitt, who played Stone in a movie about one of his more notorious cases. But there are several photos of him with regular people—first responders and families. Those photos have a more prominent place on his wall, telling me he is most proud of those.

Maximillian Stone is a legend. His cases and methods are taught at the Academy and he is one of the Bureau's most revered figures. He might even surpass Eliot Ness as the most celebrated law enforcement agent of all time. Stone started as a profiler—one of the first in the field—and took down three of the country's most prolific serial killers almost single-handedly. He has foiled bombing plots, taken down bank robbers, smashed human trafficking rings, and rescued more abducted children than I can even remember.

As I said, the guy is a legend. And at just fifty-eight years old, he's still got plenty of years left in the tank. More than one Director has tried to draft him into the ranks of executives in DC, but Stone has refused every call. He wants to remain in the field—or at least as close to it as he can get. So rather than let him retire, the Bureau created a rank and gave him his choice of assignments. Because his experience and expertise are so valuable, they basically let him do whatever he wants to do. He's spent a lot of time working with and training profilers but still enjoys hunting the more flamboyant serial killers.

I don't think even the word legend does the man justice—which makes me wonder why I'm standing in his office. I'm kind of starstruck, honestly. I'm nowhere near this guy's level, so why he called asking for me to come to Quantico to see him is a mystery. I tried to get ahold of Rosie the entire day after I got the call but couldn't reach her. Still can't. I've called so often and have sent so many texts already, I'm feeling like an obsessive girlfriend. But it's not like Rosie to go radio silent like this, so I'd be lying if I said I'm not feeling a sense of foreboding about all this.

I mean, Stone isn't with the Office of Professional Responsibility, so I'm not afraid that somebody filed a complaint against me. I haven't done anything wrong, so OPR has nothing to look into anyway. And he's not with the Director's office, so I'm not here to receive a citation or promotion. Not that I'm looking for those things anyway. The simple fact that I'm here at all with no explanation and that I can't reach Rosie is what has me on edge. What could they possibly want with me here?

Even so, I can't deny the fact that Max Stone even knows my name—and asked for me personally—seriously charges me up.

I hate to sound like a fangirl, but I have admired Stone's career from afar and have tried to emulate his methods. Some of them, anyway. Being who I am and as independent as I tend to be, of course, I put my own spin on things. But then, that's how Stone got to where he is—by doing things his way. And like him, I like to think that I get results.

"SSA Wilder, thank you for coming all the way to Quantico."

I turn to see Maximillian Stone come through the office door, striding with a sense of purpose. He's a tall man—six-two or six-three—with blonde hair and icy blue eyes, wide shoulders, and an athletic build. Even at fifty-eight, he looks fit enough to take on assailants half his age. With his strong jawline and chiseled features, he reminds me of Captain America. He's definitely got the stereotypical all-American good looks you'd see on military recruiting posters. All he needs is a red, white, and blue spandex suit.

He stops before me and extends his hand. I give him a firm handshake, and we both take a moment to size each other up. He's wearing a nicely tailored, navy-blue suit with a red tie slashed with blue stripes and a crisp white shirt beneath a blue vest. A red pocket square completes his outfit. I notice, though, his suit isn't a designer brand. It looks like something off the rack he had tailored. That fits with what I know of his personality. He's not about status or celebrity. Stone is all about the substance rather than the style.

Still, the man just has a presence about him. I mean, it could be his mystique and what I know about the man and his career, but standing in front of him, I find myself in awe.

"I appreciate you taking the time to come out to meet with me," he says. "I know you're a busy woman. Please, have a seat."

I move over and sit in one of the plush chairs situated in front of a large desk which is a large piece of polished oak sitting atop a black support structure. It's plain and functional. There is a laptop, several neatly stacked files, a couple of photos of his family, a marble nameplate, and a box of challenge coins sitting on the desktop. Like the man himself, his desk has few frills.

"Thank you, Senior SSA Stone," I say. "But I have to admit that I'm not sure why you wanted to meet with me."

"Please, call me Max," he replies. "And I wanted to meet with you because I thought we should get to know each other… since we'll be working together. This is an introduction and a conversation I thought best had face to face."

I clear my throat and try to keep the expression of confusion off my face. But I feel like I just got blindsided by a bus.

"W—working together, sir?" I ask, hoping it comes out more like a question than a sputter.

He frowns and sits back in his seat, his expression darkening. "You don't know."

"Know what, sir?"

"Max. Please," he tells me. "I don't like all this forced formality or standing on protocol. It doesn't work for me. I like to keep things looser and more… free-flowing."

"Fair enough," I reply. "But what is it I'm supposed to know?"

He mutters under his breath and looks off. I can see he's frustrated, but I know it's not with me. On the one hand, the idea of working with somebody as legendary as Max Stone is thrilling. It puts a fire in my belly. On the other hand, the fact that I've not been informed that I'll be working with him snuffs that fire and puts a quiver of worry there instead. Something's going on, and nobody's seen fit to tell me. And I get the feeling that whatever it is, I'm not going to like it.

"I'm sorry, Blake," he says. "I really thought somebody told you."

"Obviously not. So, please, feel free to enlighten me."

He sighs and leans forward again, folding his hands together on his desktop as he looks at me. I can see him trying to organize his thoughts. He's carefully choosing his words, which tells me I'm really not going to like whatever bomb he's about to drop on me.

"New presidential administration means changes at the top," he says. "You're aware there's a new Director of the FBI?"

I nod. "I've been keeping up with what's going on. From what I understand, Director Holland is a pretty celebrated agent. I heard he's a good pick."

Stone nods. "He's a good man. A friend. The Bureau is in very capable hands," he says. "But every new Director likes to put their own stamp on the Bureau. Holland is no exception. So, there's some shuffling and reorganization happening."

"All right," I say slowly, not liking the direction this seems to be headed.

"SAC Espinoza has been promoted to ADIC in New York effective immediately," he explains. "I'll be taking over the Seattle Field Office."

I feel like I just had a bucket of ice-cold water dumped over my head. Rosie hadn't said a word to me about any changes. Certainly nothing about being promoted. This is all coming out of the blue and is throwing me for a loop. I'm not somebody who likes change much at all. But I like it even less when that change is totally unexpected and I haven't had any time to prepare for it.

"Also, your unit is being disbanded. You will be reformed as a special ops unit that I am putting together at the Director's request," he goes on. "And you'll be reporting directly to a Section Chief I'll be naming shortly."

All I can manage to say is, "Um."

I feel like I've been kicked in the gut and had all the air driven from my lungs. My head is spinning, and I can't do anything except stare at him with a blank look on my face. None of this is making any sense to me. My team works hard. We get results. The idea that they'd dissolve my team just boggles my mind.

I shake my head. "I'm sorry, but I don't understand—where is this all coming from?"

"From the top," he says. "I told you, Director Holland wants—"

"I understand that. But why? Why are these changes being made? My team gets the job done. We've broken some big cases—"

He holds his hand up to keep me from going on, and it strikes me as an incredibly condescending gesture. I have to keep from rolling my eyes and saying something I would most definitely come to regret after they pink-slipped me for not being able to control my temper.

"Look, I'm going to be honest with you here. Director Holland isn't a big believer in analytics, Blake," he says. "He recognizes the good work your team has done and thinks highly of you, but he thinks your considerable talents can be better used elsewhere."

"That's … amazing," I remark.

"What is?"

"That is the most sunshine and smoke I've ever had blown up my backside at one time," I say. "It's impressive really."

A wry grin flickers across his lips. He quickly buries it, though, and fixes a stern expression on his face as he looks at me.

"I've heard you have no problem speaking your mind," he notes.

"You heard correctly."

"I respect a person who speaks their piece," he says. "But there's also wisdom in knowing when to hold your tongue."

"I've never played politics exceptionally well."

"I've heard that too."

"Seems like you've done your homework on me," I reply hotly.

"I have. I like to know the people I'm going to be working with," he says. "And I like that you don't play politics and, instead, seem to be all about the job."

"I'd like to know why my team is being dissolved," I demand. "I'd like to know why all the good work we're doing is being—"

"I think you misunderstand me."

Irritation flashes through me. "Perhaps you didn't explain yourself well enough."

"That's entirely likely. I apologize for not being clearer," he replies. "Director Holland isn't a fan of analytics. He sees it as inefficient and little more than guesswork—"

"Guesswork," I growl. "It's solid policing. Statistical data is an effective method of establishing patterns and—"

He holds his hand up again to cut me off, and I find it's getting harder to hold my tongue. I don't appreciate being treated in such a dismissive way. I don't care who does it.

"The Director may not see the value in analytics, but I do. I've watched this program you started flourish, and I see the good it's doing. I personally believe it's an effective model, and that's why I've spoken with the Director and have persuaded him to keep the program going," he says. "But I do agree with him that this program is a regional thing and that your talents would be better used on a bigger stage."

"What are you talking about?"

"The work your team is doing is great for the Seattle area, Blake. And a new CDAU team will continue using the program you started to keep doing that good work," he explains. "But I'm putting together something different. Something national. The Black Cell teams will be rapid deployment units, and we will be working the biggest, highest profile cases all over the country."

The sense of disbelief wars with the anger swirling around inside of me, and I don't know whether to laugh or punch him in the face. I close my eyes and count to ten before responding.

"My understanding is that there are already rapid deployment teams in service," I say.

"There are. But they've become bloated and inefficient, and we're changing how they operate. Our rapid response units haven't been very rapid, I'm afraid," he says. "We need to be lean and streamlined so we can move quickly. I'm certain you understand the need to be at a crime scene as soon after the crime as possible."

"Yes, of course—"

"Under our current model, our teams haven't been arriving soon enough. Some take as many as forty-eight hours to arrive," he goes on. "I don't need to tell you how much can be lost in that amount of time."

He doesn't. Cases, not to mention lives, can be lost in forty-eight hours. I wasn't aware that the Bureau's rapid deployment teams had become so bloated and inefficient. It's inexcusable. But pulling me off my team and putting me under somebody... I can't adequately explain the anger and disrespect I feel right now.

"Blake, you're one of the most talented and passionate agents I've seen in quite some time. You are exactly the type of person I want heading up one of my teams," he says. "I know this change is sudden, but think of the good things that can come of this. Working on a national stage could put you on a path toward the Director's chair if you wanted it. The success—"

"You assume I want the Director's chair," I snap. "You clearly haven't done enough homework on me if you think that's what drives me."

"That's not what I mean. I merely mean that the success you have with my team will allow you to punch your own ticket, Blake. Look what I've been able to parlay some success into," he says.

"Again, though, you assume I'm not content being in the field with my team doing what we're doing," I say.

"You can't work in the field forever, Blake. That was a reality I had to accept too."

"You and I are nothing alike, sir."

"I think if you're honest with yourself, you'd see we're a lot more alike than you want to believe," he counters. "But even if you reject that, age and time make us the same. It's just a simple fact that you can't do at fifty what you're doing now at what... twenty-nine?"

"Thirty-one," I correct him. "So, am I correct in assuming I have no say in this?"

"The wheels are already in motion."

"And what of my team?"

"Your team will still work with you. But you will have a couple of additional recruits," he says. "I'm going to be assigning one more tech analyst and one more field agent to your cell."

"Do I at least get to choose my team?"

"You have chosen your team," he replies. "The two new additions are my picks."

"With all due respect, sir, you have to trust your team. How can I trust somebody I don't even know?"

"You will have to learn to trust them," he says. "Blake, most people would be jumping at the opportunity to lead one of these new teams. What is your hesitation?"

"My hesitation is that I have spent a long time building something, sir," I reply coldly. "And now I'm being told that despite all our success, it's not good enough, and I'm having it yanked out from under me. This feels a lot like retaliation."

"Retaliation? I don't follow."

I look at him closely and don't see any trace of guile or deception on his face. Of course, if anybody were going to know how to appear sincere when lying through their teeth, it would be an agent as seasoned as Stone. So, I can't really take his appearance of sincerity at face value.

"I have to admit, I'm surprised at your attitude, Blake. I was told you were a good team player," he says.

"I am a good team player. It's a bitter pill to swallow, though, to have my team yanked out from under me with no warning and no real good reason."

"Ahh. So, that's what this is about. Ego."

"It's not ego, sir. It's going from leading my team to being subordinate," I reply. "Do you know what that does to my credibility? It will look like a demotion—"

"I was given to understand that you don't much care about how things look to other people, Blake."

"That's hardly the point."

"Listen, this meeting was a courtesy and a sign of my respect for you, Blake. I'm sorry if your ego is bruised, but this is the way things are," he says. "Now, I'll see you in Seattle in a week. Please make sure you've briefed and handed off all your cases to the new CDAU team that will be coming in."

I shake my head and blow out a breath of frustration. All the work I've put in up to this point feels like it means absolutely nothing. All the successes I've had are meaningless. And yet, these men come storming in with their grand proclamations and bigger plans and expect me to just bow down and accept it?

Only in the federal government will they try to make you believe a demotion is actually a promotion and a sign of respect. And that's what this is—a demotion. I'm going from being my team's leader and reporting directly to my SAC to being subordinate to somebody I don't know. Even if he is a living legend. That's kind of the definition of a demotion, no matter how Stone tries to spin it. And I can't help but believe this is retribution for what happened in the serial bombing case between me and former ATF ASAC Ellis Winslow a few weeks ago.

"This is happening. You can either get on board or... not, I suppose," Stone says. "Either way, I'll be in Seattle next week. Thank you for coming in, SSA Wilder."

And just like that, I'm dismissed. As Stone turns to his laptop, I stand and exit his office without another word. There's nothing really left to say anyway. He's taking over, I'm being stripped of my command, and my unit is being reassigned to somebody else.

As I walk down the hallways, all I can think about is getting out of there and getting back to the hotel bar where I plan to have a few drinks. Probably more than a few.

Now I understand what they mean when they say you should never meet your idols.

CHAPTER TWO

The Pulpit; Downtown Seattle

"**W**HY IS IT THAT EVERY TIME I COME TO SEE YOU, you want to come here?" I groan as I slide into the booth.

"Don't get all Catholic on me now, Blake. This place is great," he says.

Paxton Arrington, one of my closest friends, sits across the table from me. When I got back from Quantico, I needed to talk, and he was my first choice. Pax gets me in ways nobody else does. He's also willing to kick me in the backside when I need it. Which is exactly what I need right now. As much as I love and respect

Astra, I'm still not sure what I'm going to say to her about all this. I need somebody with a little more discretion—and a little less restraint. Even if he insists on taking me to a place with such irreverent charms as this.

In a former life, the Pulpit was a Catholic church. The current owners kept the structure the way it was, with its high arched ceilings and stained-glass windows all around. The old pews and other things that were left behind were all repurposed and turned into booths and tables. The polished wood of the thirty-foot-long bar itself used to be pews. At the far end of the bar, where the altar used to stand, is a stage for the bands who play here on the weekends. The waitresses all wear skimpy nuns' habits, and the drinks all have sacrilegious names like, "the Bloody Pope," which is a White Russian with a dash of grenadine.

It's also where Paxton's girlfriend, May, works. He asked me to meet him here because he's picking her up and going on a surprise trip out of town when her shift is over. It's a good thing I got ahold of him when I did, or I'd be stewing over this alone.

"I think that I understand why you went into the private sector," I tell him. "And it's looking pretty good to me right now."

He laughs. "You're not the private sector sort. You're a government lifer, through and through."

I roll my eyes. "God, I wish I wasn't."

He gestures around to the setting. "Not sure prayers still work here."

"It was worth a shot."

He raises his glass to me and takes a sip of his Burning Bush.

"Hey, Blake," May waves as she stops by our table.

"Hey, May," I reply. "How are you?"

"I'm good. Curious about what Paxton has planned though," she chirps. "You wouldn't happen to know, would you?"

"I have no clue," I confess honestly. "He doesn't confide in me about things like that."

"Because Blake can't keep a secret to save her life," Pax cuts in.

"Well, that's not true."

"Yeah, it's kind of true," he says.

"Well, I'm curious and excited," May says with a laugh, then turns to Pax. "I'll be punching out in half an hour. Nice to see you again, Blake. Don't be such a stranger."

"I'll be waiting," he tells her.

She leans down and gives him a quick peck on the lips before hustling back to work. Pax watches her go with a faint smile upon his lips. May is the first woman he's dated since his wife was murdered a few years back, and the fact that he looks like a man in love makes me smile. It does my heart good to see him happy. It's something I didn't think I'd ever see in Paxton again. But he's more resilient than I thought he was.

After Veronica was killed, Pax traveled to a very dark place and seemed to settle in there. He got comfortable with the grief and anger that went along with it. Although he faced obstacles of every kind, he never quit trying to find out who killed his wife. It was a tangled and convoluted path, but he eventually found them. I'm glad I was able to lend a small assist in bringing them to justice, and I think that did a lot to bring him some peace. But I think his relationship with May has done more to heal his heart than anything.

"Looks like things are going well with you two," I note.

He nods. "She's great. I feel lucky to have her in my life."

"You *are* lucky to have her in your life," I tell him. "Don't screw it up."

He laughs softly. "Doing my best to avoid it."

"Do better."

He snaps me a salute and grins. "Yes ma'am," he says. "So, tell me what happened out there? What has you so rattled?"

I take a long swallow of my drink then launch into the story. I tell Pax everything Stone said to me, give him my thoughts, and make sure he knows how pissed I am about it all. The whole time I'm speaking, Pax just sits there listening to me, an amused smirk on his face. And when I'm done, my throat is dry, so I swallow down half of what's left of my drink. Pax still hasn't said a word. He just keeps grinning at me.

"What are you smirking at?" I finally ask.

"Tell me something," he says. "Why did you join the Bureau?"

"You know why."

"Humor me. What made you join the Bureau?"

I sigh and run my finger around the rim of my glass, a frown touching my lips. I take a moment to collect my thoughts before answering.

"Because I want to help prevent people from feeling the loss I did when I was a kid," I say. "Because I want to help protect people."

"Right," he replies. "And don't you think you can do that in one of his… what did he call them again?"

"Black Cells," I reply with an eye roll. "It's all very dramatic, don't you think?"

He grins. "It is. But if there's one thing government agencies love more than their acronyms, it's dramatic names. Anyway, it's beside the point," he tells me. "The point is that you can do those things working for this guy Stone every bit as much as you could under Rosie."

"Stone and whoever he appoints to be the new Section Chief—whom I'll be reporting to now, oh, by the way," I snap.

"Right, okay, so you'll essentially be doing the same job—except on a national level?" he asks. "You'll be helping protect people all over the country, rather than just here in the Pacific Northwest. That about right?"

"Yeah," I admit grudgingly.

"Hey, and for all you know, you might even be able to do some cases over in Cockeysville, Maryland."

I level him with a deadpan glare at the mention of my hometown. "Don't push it."

He still can't wipe the smug grin off his face, but he continues. "And you'll be working the highest profile cases—which could raise your profile and open doors you never even considered at some point down the road?"

I blow out a frustrated breath. "You, of all people, know that recognition isn't why I do this job. I'm not in it for the medals, Pax."

"I know that," he replies calmly. "All I'm pointing out is that there are things you can't even conceive of yet that this could lead to. Look at what this Stone guy is doing. He has a golden ticket to do anything he wants. What if that's you one day?"

"All right, fine," I relent. "Fair enough."

"Great," he replies. "So, then, my personal feeling is that Stone is right. This is about your ego, Blake. You're all riled up because your ego was bruised."

"That's not true."

"It is, though. From everything you've said to me here, you're most pissed off about having to report to somebody new. That you're not the big boss," he says.

"I don't need to be the boss," I protest. "I just—"

"Respectfully, Blake? Yes, you do," he counters. "You always need to be in control. And you hate change. You'll no longer be the one calling the shots, and you hate that. But here's the thing: you and your team are still going to be doing the same job, more or less. But you'll be doing it on a bigger stage. Doing this job means you're going to have a high profile. You have a chance to do some real good, Blake. But you're hung up on the chain of command issues."

"You're making it out to be a lot more simplistic than it is."

He takes a drink and sets his glass down. "Am I? Then, explain it to me. What is it that has you so riled up if not a bruised ego? And trust me—I know ego."

"It's about respect," I tell him defensively. "My team and I are damn good at what we do."

"Which, as I understand it, is why this guy Stone requested you lead his team," Pax points out. "That seems like a big sign of respect to me. I mean, you said this guy is a legend, and if he's asking for you to lead this new initiative, to be the face of it, I'd say that's a major sign of respect for you and your skills."

I open my mouth to reply but close it again, knowing I can't argue the point. As much as I hate to admit it, I see that he's right. Stone is a legend, and I respect him. I should be flattered. I should be honored that he's asking for me. That makes sense. Which means that, yeah, I suppose if I'm looking at it from that point of view, I guess this is about my bruised ego.

"I hate you," I say with a laugh.

"Only when I have to kick you in the ass."

"Yeah, maybe," I say. "The one thing that keeps tripping me up, though, is the timing. I can't help but think that me getting demoted—"

"You're not getting demoted, Blake."

"I'm having my team taken from me."

"Are you though?" he asks. "I mean, unless there's something I'm missing, you're not losing your team. You're just moving offices."

"Let's not forget the two spies that are going to be planted on my team."

"You're an FBI agent, Blake. You're all spies."

"Remember what I said about not pushing it?"

That makes him actually bark out a laugh. "What I'm saying is, if you're not doing anything other than your job, you're not going to have any problem with them reporting on you."

"I don't like having people I can't trust breathing down my neck."

"I get that. But you're freaking out about things that may or may not even come to pass," he shrugs. "What if these two newbies simply want to do the job? What if they look up to you the way you look up to Stone and work hard to impress you? You have the opportunity to mold them into the sort of agent you want to see more of in the Bureau. Right?"

"And what if they're not? What if they're the stab you in the back to get ahead type?"

"Maybe you should give them a chance," he says. "You're worried about a lot of what-ifs right now. That's not like you."

"Yeah, well, this whole situation sucks. It's thrown me a little off-kilter."

"But it's got the potential to be something really good. Put your ego aside and focus on doing the job as well as you always do," he says.

And that's why I wanted to talk to Pax. In less than thirty minutes, he's managed to talk me off the ledge and knock a little sense into me. I appreciate that about him. I'm still not thrilled with the notion of having my command stripped from me and having to report to somebody I don't know. The timing of it all still stinks. But in the bigger picture, I know that Pax is right. And I hate that he is.

"And when did you learn to be the voice of sunshine and rainbows? You're normally the gloom and doom type."

He shrugs. "Things change. Besides, you're dark and angry enough for both of us right now."

I shake my head. "It's just… I spent a lot of time making my unit into something good. I spent a lot of time building credibility with my approach. And now—"

"And now your hard work and your success are paying off. You got the attention of a Bureau legend and somebody you admire, and he's now asked for you by name," he presses. "Your unit will be in capable hands, I'm sure. And you'll be doing something even better, Blake. It is a change, but don't look at this as a bad thing. Look at this as being given the green light to hunt even bigger prey. The way I see it, this is something to be excited about. You're in the big leagues now and playing with some of the Bureau's heaviest hitters. The Director of the FBI knowing your name ain't nothin'."

I let his words rattle around in my brain for a moment and nod. Put that way, it doesn't seem as bad as I've been making it out to be in my head the entire way back from Quantico. It's good to get a little nonemotional perspective from somebody who's not directly involved. The opinion of somebody I respect.

I can't say I'm not still feeling the sting of being reassigned this way. And I can't say I don't still think the Winslow situation doesn't have some role in how this all played out. The timing is just too coincidental to not be connected. It feels like all this has come around simply because I pulled the tiger's tail, and Winslow still has friends in high places.

But Pax is right. Just because things are changing, it doesn't mean it's necessarily a bad thing. And the fact that Maximillian Stone asked for me to lead his new team is pretty cool. Now that I have a little perspective, it shows me that, yeah, maybe my efforts haven't all been in vain and that the successes of my team haven't gone unnoticed.

Looking at it objectively—or as objectively as I can, anyway—the opportunity to work the highest profile cases across the country isn't entirely unappealing. We'll be able to do a lot of good for a lot of people across the country, not just up here in the Northwest. We'll be, to use Pax's words, hunting even bigger prey. And if I'm being perfectly honest with myself, I'd have to acknowledge that it's somewhat... exciting.

"Thanks, Pax. I appreciate you talking to me."

He grins. "Anytime, Blake. You know that."

"Yeah, I do," I reply. "I'm thankful to have a friend like you."

"And I'm thankful to have you as a friend," he replies. "Now, I'm going to take my girl away for a weekend. You go get your head together and get ready for the changes that are coming. I think this is going to be good for you, Blake. I really do."

A soft smile touches my lips. I want to believe that. Having been talked off the ledge now, I think Pax is right. This is going to be a good thing. I think this might benefit my entire team. And he's right; it could lead to more open doors for us than I can even conceive of somewhere down the line. This could be great for all of us.

But I've been wrong before.

CHAPTER THREE

Black Cell Alpha Team Bullpen; Seattle Field Office

"S WANKY NEW DIGS," ASTRA WHISTLES.

"I'll say," Mo adds. "And I love that we have windows and can see the world outside."

"I kind of liked the basement," Rick mentions as he looks around.

"That's because you, my friend, are a cave troll at heart. They're known to love cold, musty dwellings," Astra says with a grin, earning her an obscene gesture from Rick.

Over the last week, I've briefed Astra, Mo, and Rick about the situation, and they all handled it a hell of a lot better than I did. They seem eager to get started, embracing our new mission with a sense of excitement I'm still trying to muster up. We've also moved out of our unit's basement offices and up to the tenth floor.

I have to say that hauling out my last box and turning the lights off on the CDAU was a bit more emotional for me than I'd anticipated. Yeah, I know another team will be coming in and the lights will go back on. But I'm proud of what we built down there. I'm proud of our accomplishments. And walking out of there for the last time hit me like a punch to the gut from Mike Tyson in his prime.

"All right," I say. "Let's get set up."

Unlike our basement dwelling, this bullpen is pretty swanky. Though the design and layout of our bullpen are the same as the one in the basement, the Bureau spent more than a few bucks making this place not just functional but comfortable as well. The workstations are all much nicer and more spacious, the captain's chairs at each station are a bit bigger and plusher, and even the carpeting is nicer and has more padding than what we had downstairs.

There's an office at the back of the bullpen, which I assume is mine, and at the front of the room is a small dais which I'll probably end up falling off because of my perpetual pacing as I think. On the walls at the front are four monitors that are much larger than our old ones, and as Rick fires them up, I can see they're sharper as well.

"Beautiful," he comments as he calibrates the settings. "Can't wait to see these horrific, gory photos of our victims in glorious, crisp 4K."

There's a row of clocks above the monitors—digital as opposed to our old analog timepieces. The bullpen is painted a very soothing shade of blue, and the rear wall of the room has the FBI shield etched into it. We even have a designated kitchen area with all new appliances.

Everything seems new, tight, and professional. There are no bundles of wires hanging down from a busted acoustic tile in the ceiling, no water stains on the carpeting, and no nicks or dings in the furniture and the walls like we had downstairs. Though our old bullpen was a little beat up and shoddy looking, I liked to think it had some character. This place, though nice, seems a bit cold and sterile to me. But as Astra said, it's swanky new digs.

We spend about an hour making ourselves at home and getting our workstations set up. I do what I can in my office, but no matter how many times I arrange then rearrange everything, I'm just not comfortable. I've spent twenty minutes just adjusting my chair height alone. Irritated, I finally get my office to a place I can deal with it, then decide to leave it all alone. Maybe it'll grow on me. I'm just about to head out into the bullpen when Stone and another man I've not met before walk into my office, and I have to guess Stone is introducing me to my new boss.

The man standing with Stone is tall. Six-four at least. He's slender but has an athletic appearance. If I had to guess, I'd say his exercise of choice is swimming. He's definitely not a weightlifter. He's got dark, wavy hair, darker eyes, and skin the color of warm terra-cotta. His smooth, unlined face sports a neatly trimmed mustache and beard that's slightly flecked with gray. He's got the bearing of an academic but also of somebody who's seen a lot. I'd put him somewhere in his late forties or early fifties and of Middle Eastern heritage. If I were forced to be more specific, I'd say Egyptian.

The man is wearing an expertly tailored suit: designer, I immediately notice, not an off-the-rack job like Stone wears. He's got monogrammed cufflinks and a flashy watch on his wrist, though not a Rolex. A quick glance identifies it as a Montblanc, which is expensive, but doesn't have the pretentious label a Rolex tends to carry. It tells me he's got money, and he prefers his tastes a little more obscure. It shows me he's discerning and thoughtful when it comes to his appearance—hopefully, that reflects in his personality as well.

"SSA Blake Wilder," Stone intones. "This is Section Chief Bomani Ayad."

I put on a smile I hope doesn't look as fake as it feels and try to keep myself from bristling. His skin is smooth. Soft. And as we shake hands, I notice his fingers are long and slender, his hands perfectly manicured.

"It's nice to meet you, sir. I'm looking forward to working together," I say as diplomatically as I can.

He gives me a small smile that tells me he knows I'm full of crap. But he nods and makes that silent pact with me to play the game and keep up appearances.

"It's nice to meet you, SSA Wilder," he says. "Your reputation precedes you."

I can't be positive of course, but his voice seems to carry a slight edge to it. A twinge of recrimination. When he says that my reputation precedes me, I get the distinct impression he doesn't mean it as a compliment. Yeah, we're off to an awesome start.

"I thought the three of us should get together and get on the same page," Stone starts.

"Right. Yeah," I reply. "Please, sit down. And forgive the mess, we're just moving in."

The men take the chairs in front of my desk, and I walk around behind it. I drop down into my new captain's chair and have to grudgingly admit that it's a lot more comfortable than where I was parking my backside downstairs. Not that I'll ever say that to these two.

"So," I start. "What do we need to get on the same page about?"

"Well, the first thing is that I want to clarify any chain of command issues," Stone says. "You head your team, of course. But you report directly to Section Chief Ayad."

"Yeah, I kind of figured," I reply. "Nice to meet you, Mr. Ayad." I wish it was.

"Please, call me Bo," Ayad says. "We are going to have five Black Cell teams on this floor, and I'll be overseeing all of them."

"Kind of implied by your Section Chief title," I point out.

He gives me that flickering smile again that looks more feral than humorous. I can already tell that Ayad and I are going to get along about as well as fire and gasoline. The way he looks down his nose at me is already rubbing me the wrong way, and I've known this guy for all of five minutes. Yeah, the private sector is looking a hell of a lot more appealing right now.

"Right. Well, I'll be assigning the cases to your team," Ayad says. "You're no longer required to chase files. And believe me, we'll be putting you to work."

"You're my alpha team," Stone adds. "Your squad will be working the biggest cases that come our way, Blake. Your talents are going to be put to good use."

"That's good to know, sir," I say, trying to keep myself from screaming in frustration. "My team is always ready for a challenge."

"Blake, I'm in charge of the entire Field Office now, but my door is always open to you," Stone says. "I have a lot of respect for you, and I know that it's in large part because of your work that the Seattle FO has become a highly respected hub. I also know it's a big reason why SAC Espinoza is now ADIC Espinoza. I have every faith that you're going to do a lot to get our rapid deployment teams back on track."

Ayad looks away as Stone speaks, and I get the feeling he's saying all this for his benefit. It almost reads to me as if Ayad has already voiced his skepticism about me and putting my team on the big cases, but Stone shot him down. And this little speech seems designed to reinforce that notion. It gives me a small boost of confidence.

"Thank you, sir," I say.

"All right, I'm going to leave you two to get better acquainted. I have some things I need to see to," Stone says. "I want you both to remember, though, the relationship between a Section Chief and his team leads is important. Critical, even. It's imperative you two learn to work and play well together."

"Of course," Ayad says.

I nod. "I agree."

"Good. Then I'll leave you to it."

Stone stands up and walks out. I watch as he introduces himself to the team and exchanges a few words with them. I think Mo and Astra both know who he is; they are in as much awe of the man as I am. I turn to Ayad, though, and the air in my office instantly starts to crackle with tension. I don't have any specific grudge against the man—I don't even know him. But there are those people who come into your life who you know from the start you aren't going to get along with. Bomani Ayad is one of those. We've exchanged but a handful of words so far, but I can tell already this is going to be a long, bumpy road.

Ayad crosses one leg over the other and folds his hands in his lap as he looks at me. I don't know anything about him, but it is clear Stone sees something he likes in the guy. So, because I respect Stone, I suppose I need to give him a chance. After all, my initial read on Pax was that he was an arrogant, condescending blowhard. And while, yeah, he certainly can be those things, if I hadn't taken a chance and gotten to know him better, he wouldn't be one of my dearest friends right now. Not that I think Ayad and I will ever be that tight. It's just the principle.

"So, where are you coming over from, sir?" I ask.

"Counterterrorism," he replies. "Listen, I think we should get something cleared up between us now that ADIC Stone is gone."

"All right," I nod.

"I respect the things you've done, SSA Wilder," he says. "But I don't approve of some of the methods you employ."

"Which methods are those, Section Chief Ayad? Thumbscrews? Waterboarding? Perhaps you object to my use of the Iron Maiden?" I ask, sarcasm dripping off my tongue. "They're controversial, but they're all highly effective, I assure you."

"Sarcasm isn't going to get you very far with me, Agent Wilder."

"And buying into rumors, lies, and innuendo isn't going to get you very far with me either, Section Chief," I snap. "Trust me, I've heard the rumors about my methods, and it's all pure garbage spread by little people."

"So, you don't routinely question suspects without their attorneys present?"

I stare at him for a moment, disbelief on my face. "Seriously? We always question a suspect as long as we can without an attorney present. It's SOP," I say. "But the moment they invoke, we get them a lawyer."

"My understanding is that you push that boundary."

"Then your understanding is a misunderstanding," I reply. "I do things the right way. Always have and always will."

"I hope so. Because in my unit, we do things by the book, Agent Wilder," he says. "I have zero tolerance for those who break the rules or go rogue. I have no use for cowboys in this unit. Do I make myself clear?"

I chuckle softly to myself. All the pretense is gone now that Stone is out of the room and I'm seeing the real Bomani Ayad. He's stern, which isn't a problem. But he seems to be a paint-by-numbers investigator, and that is a problem. The book is fine. It's there for a reason. But there are times when it doesn't always apply. There are times when bending that line and pushing the envelope is necessary to save lives. Ayad is a Boy Scout, and in the world of law enforcement, those types make good middle management, but they make terrible field agents. Any field agent worth their salt has gotten a little mud on their hands from time to time.

I can handle that stringent, by-the-numbers approach though. I can deal with his rigid, unyielding approach to the rules. It's annoying as hell, but I can deal with it. What I can't deal with is the fact that he listens to the rumors that go around about me. That he bases his opinion on me and my methods on watercooler gossip. I wouldn't expect less from a middle manager, but the fact that he's my new boss is a problem. A very big problem.

I lean forward and pin him to his seat with my glare. "And I have no use for people who have heard a few stories and think they know me. I have no use for people without the strength of character or integrity to form an opinion about me based on nothing more than rumor."

"Well, ADIC Stone thinks very highly of you," he pivots. "So, I'm willing to allow you to show me that his opinion is warranted."

"That's mighty big of you."

His eyes flash dangerously, and his jaw muscles are flexing. I can tell he's doing his best to keep himself from escalating the situation any further. But he wants to lash out. I can see it.

"Just remember, I run a clean shop," he reminds me. "I have zero tolerance for rule breakers."

"Yeah, you said that already. Message received."

"Fine," he says as he gets to his feet. "Just make sure you don't step one toe over the line, because rest assured, I will be watching."

"I have no doubt."

He turns without another word and walks out of my office. I watch through the glass wall as he exits the bullpen altogether, and only then, do I get up and walk out to join my team. They're all looking at me expectantly. I frown and look away for a moment as I try to gather my thoughts. I honestly don't even know where to start.

"So?" Astra finally asks. "Going to keep us in suspense? Who was that?"

"Yeah, spill," Rick says. "Who was that guy?"

"That's our new boss," I tell them. "Section Chief Bomani Ayad. We report to him directly now."

"He's got a sour pucker on his face," Mo remarks. "I get the feeling that's a permanent condition too."

Astra nods. "The guy looks like he's got a stick wedged firmly up his backside. I'm not sure how he even walks."

"Carefully," Rick chimes in.

I laugh and shake my head. "Yeah. This is going to suck."

CHAPTER FOUR

Black Cell Alpha Team Bullpen; Seattle Field Office

I'M SITTING IN MY OFFICE STEWING—THE SAME THING I'VE been doing the past two days. My conversations with Ayad have been brief, tense, and totally unproductive. I'm trying to keep an open mind. I really am. But the more I think about this situation, the more I become convinced this is payback for what happened with Winslow.

"You're brooding."

I look up to see Astra leaning against the doorway.

"I'm bored," I tell her.

"Yeah, I'm a little surprised," she replies. "I thought this gig was going to be nonstop action and adventure."

"Stone says they're trying to get a few last-minute logistical things into place before we are fully operational."

Astra walks in and drops down into the chair across from me. She crosses her legs and sits back. Her silver-blue eyes are piercing, and I can see that she's trying to see deep into my brain. Astra has always had that knack—she's always been able to see into me in ways other people can't. Pax might be the only other person, aside from my kid sister, Kit, who can cut through all my barriers and defenses and see into me. I hate it.

"You know this isn't a big deal, don't you?" she asks. "You're making too much of this whole Section Chief thing than there needs to be."

"That's what Pax said."

"He's right now and then," she replies simply. "Blake, I love you with everything in me. You know that don't you?"

I laugh softly. Whenever she prefaces a statement with that, I know I'm not going to like what comes after. And here I thought she'd gone soft and was pulling her punches with me.

"Of course, I do." I brace myself for the blow.

"I say this with love, but you're a bit of a control freak. That and you don't like change," she says. "And this shuffling is hitting you from both sides—it's stripping you of control and is forcing you to change at the same time. So yeah, you're freaking out. I get it."

"Pax said that too."

"Wow. He's a lot smarter than I thought," she said.

"He has his moments."

"So, you don't think this has anything to do with what happened with Winslow?" I ask. "You don't think the timing of all this is coincidental?"

"So, what if it is?" she asks in return. "Does it matter? Nothing around here has changed, Blake. We're still doing our thing. And isn't that what really matters?"

"Yeah, it is. But—"

"But nothing. The job hasn't changed, Blake. The only thing that's changed is we have a new boss, and you're not real thrilled with it. I get it, but that's the long and short of it," she says.

"Damn. You aren't holding back, are you?" I note. "And here I thought you'd gone soft on me."

"Yeah, that's never going to happen," she tells me with a laugh. "I took it easy on you for a minute because you had a lot going on. That grace period is over, and it's time for me to get back to giving you the hard truths."

"Clearly."

"As I said, our job hasn't changed a bit. We've just got different bosses now. No big deal," she shrugs. "And let's not forget that we're working for Maximillian freaking Stone. How cool is that?"

"Well, technically, we're working for Chief Ayad," I reply.

"I haven't spoken with him, but he seems all right."

"Yeah, he's really not," I tell her. "Do not turn your back on that man, or you're going to find a knife in it."

"That bad, huh?"

"Worse," I say through gritted teeth. "Hold that thought."

My office door opens, and Ayad walks in. In the bullpen behind him, I see two people I don't recognize and assume those are my two new team members. Astra and I both get to our feet, and she turns to him.

"Astra, this is Section Chief Bomani Ayad," I say. "Chief Ayad, this is Astra Russo."

She shakes his hand. "Pleasure to meet you, Chief Ayad."

"Nice to meet you as well," he replies. "May we have the room?"

"Yeah, sure," Astra replies.

She cuts a glance at me before she walks out, leaving me with Ayad. I gesture to the chair in front of my desk.

"No need. This won't take long," he says. "I'm just dropping off your two new team members. Take a minute to introduce yourself."

"Sure. No problem," I nod. "Quick question, are we going to get a case any time soon? This is the longest we've ever gone without one."

"Just see to your team and leave the case assignment to me."

I bite my bottom lip to keep the scathing reply from accidentally popping out. There's no need to throw more gasoline onto that fire. Instead, I just give him a snappy salute.

"Yeah. Sure," I reply. "I'll get the newbies acclimated."

"Good idea."

Ayad turns and walks out of my office. He stops to say something to the two newcomers, giving them both a smile before leaving the bullpen altogether, all sunshine and rainbows after being so dark and gloomy with me. The man has more personalities than Sybil. I watch the two newbies mixing with Astra, Mo, and Rick from my office for a couple of minutes. Stone told me they were his picks, but I get the feeling Ayad had some input into their selection, which makes me instantly distrust them. I just hope they both prove me wrong.

Steeling myself, I head out into the bullpen, and conversations cease as I step over to my two new team members.

"SSA Blake Wilder," I introduce myself. "Just call me Blake."

"Lucas Okamura," says the man as he extends his hand. "It's nice to meet you. I've studied your work, SSA Wilder, and I'm very much looking forward to working with you."

Okamura isn't a large man. He's about five-nine and has a lean, athletic build. His dark hair is short, and he's clean-shaven, giving him a bit of a baby face. He's got high cheekbones and a strong jawline. It's obvious he takes care of himself. Okamura is wearing a respectable blue suit with a white shirt and blood-red tie. He strikes me as a man who takes the time to make himself look professional but isn't overly obsessed with his appearance.

Okamura's enthusiasm doesn't seem like pretense, but he seems to be laying it on pretty thick anyway. I can't say that's proof he's here to spy on me and report back to Ayad, but it sets off a warning bell in my head, so I make a mental note to watch what I say around him. He's my new field agent, and on paper, he's got a pretty good track record. Ordinarily, I'd be glad to have a guy like him on my team. Under the circumstances, though, with him being foisted on me, I'm less than thrilled with his posting to my team.

"Glad to have you on board with us," I say, hoping it doesn't sound too stiff, then I turn to the woman standing beside him and give her a firm shake. "And you must be Nina Alvarado."

"Yes, ma'am," she says quickly with a wide, awkward smile on her face. "It's an honor to be working with you, SSA Wilder."

Nina looks to be all of about twenty-three or twenty-four and has the enthusiastic energy of a teenage girl. She's small, no more than five-two with a pixieish build, with long, silky dark hair. Her skin is rich, tawny, and smooth, and her eyes are dark, mysterious pools that give nothing away.

She's obviously trying to hide it, but there's a powder blue streak tucked inside her thick mane, and now that I look, I can just see the corner of a tattoo peeking out from beneath the cuff of her shirt. It's good to note that she's got at least a little bit of a personality. There's a light behind her eyes that I appreciate as well. She's small but formidable—and not just intellectually. I can tell the woman is a scrapper.

The more I look over her, the more I notice that her clothes, unlike Ayad's or even Lucas's, aren't quite so polished to a sheen. They're clean, of course, and they fit well, but they're obviously off the rack—not that I really care about fashion, but more that it seems like she's had the same set of professional clothes for some time now. She gives me the impression that she's very frugal and more concerned with practicality over superficial matters—which is a trait I admire.

I don't know Nina's full story yet as there are pieces of her file that seem to be missing—which is something I will definitely be looking into—but my understanding is that Ayad plucked her straight out of the Academy program and dropped her into my unit. By all accounts, she's a savant with a computer, and her records make me think she might even rival Brody as far as skill and talent go, which is about the highest compliment I can give somebody. She seems to have bypassed all the normal assignments they throw at rookies. She didn't even do a stint in cybercrimes where a woman of her talents should have started. And that is a discrepancy I find a bit troubling.

"*Blake* will be fine, guys," I tell them. "Go ahead and grab a workstation and get yourselves settled in. We should hopefully be getting a case soon."

Astra and I step aside as Lucas and Nina set up shop. She takes a station next to Rick, which makes sense. As our tech analysts, they'll need to work in conjunction with each other. Lucas seems a little more uncertain but sets up shop near Mo and Astra's station—though not too close. As I watch him settling in, I can't help but think he looks like a new kid walking into a classroom on the first day of school and trying to find his place. He seems a little awkward, and it's a bit difficult to watch.

"What do you think?" Astra asks quietly. "Any red flags?"

"Not sure yet. But for the time being, I want to minimize their role as much as possible."

"Good thinking," she replies. "Ayad seems like the kind of guy who'd plant eyes and ears in the shop to keep an eye on us."

I nod. "Especially after his song and dance about doing things by the book and having zero tolerance for agents going rogue."

She laughs. "If he only knew you're probably a little more by the book than he is. You'd have to watch a few tutorials on YouTube to learn how to go rogue."

"Yeah, well, he seems to think I'm some revolutionary or something, out here breaking the law all willy-nilly," I mutter. "Which means he's going to be watching us very closely. It seems like he's looking for reasons to drop the hammer on us."

"Then we'll have to be sure to avoid giving him any."

"Yeah. But in my experience, if somebody wants to come for you bad enough, and you give them nothing, they'll get creative," I reply.

"Well, the one thing we have in our favor is that Ayad doesn't seem like a real imaginative type. He doesn't strike me as an outside-the-box thinker."

"I hope so. I really hope so."

I watch Mo and Rick chatting with our two newcomers, and all at once, I feel the pressure settling down on my shoulders. Like an anaconda, it slithers around my throat and starts to squeeze. Its cold, scaly body grips me tight, slowly cutting off my air.

Ayad's attitude makes me think he's just looking for a reason to sideline me, if not push me out altogether. What I don't know is why. We've never met or worked together, so he's got no valid reason to dislike me other than the gossip. That leads me to believe he's squeezing me at somebody else's behest. Which means the question I need to be asking is not why, but *who* is gunning for me?

And that is a lengthy list.

"God, this is going to suck," I mutter.

CHAPTER FIVE

SSA Wilder's Office, Black Cell Alpha Team Bullpen; Seattle Field Office

"ALL I'M SAYING IS THAT A HEADS UP WOULD HAVE been nice," I say.

"Blake, I had no warning myself. They just called and told me to report to Quantico. When I got there, they filled me in on what was happening. I had no chance to call and tell you," Rosie replies. "I had zero idea this was coming. And I've been on the run ever since. This is the first chance I've had to call you. I hope you know I'd never do you dirty like that."

I look at Rosie's face on my tablet screen and frown. Deep down, I know she'd never do me like that. Rosie can be stern and gruff, but she's a fair woman, and I never had to wonder if she had my back. She always did. But I can't say this whole episode is making me feel any less paranoid about the situation. If anything, it's ramping up my paranoia.

"So, they do all this shuffling under the cover of night," I note. "Seems pretty coordinated to me. Almost like it's—"

She gives me a patient smile. "Before you get that big brain of yours working, field offices all over the country went through similar changes, Blake. Some people were forced out, others were reassigned," she said. "New presidential administrations usually come with big shakeups too. It's just part of the business."

Intellectually, I know that. But coming on the heels of an emotionally charged situation with Winslow, as well as the state of my life the last couple of years, I should be forgiven for being a bit paranoid. I've got more enemies and people looking to take me down than I can count. And knowing the Thirteen still exists in some form and still has members inside the government doesn't help those feelings either.

I haven't heard anything from the Thirteen in a long while, which has already had me feeling a bit on edge before all this went down. As much as I wish it were otherwise, I know they haven't forgotten about me or my sister. You don't get to kick a hornet's nest like that and not get stung. We obliterated their group, but the win wasn't total. And by allowing those elements that remain to draw back into the shadows to regroup, I've given them time to rally their forces to take another run at me.

And a shakeup like this, which seems coordinated, makes me think this was the opening salvo to another offensive.

"I'm going to lay a hard truth on you, Blake. You ready?"

"Do I have a choice?"

"Not really," Rosie replies. "The world doesn't revolve around you, kiddo."

I scoff. "And you think I don't know that?"

"I have to wonder sometimes," she says with a grin.

"Yeah, yeah, yeah. Whatever."

"My point is that not every moving shadow is a monster coming to get you," she says. "And not everything that happens is a conspiracy against you."

"Unless it is."

"Blake, I know you've gone through some things—are going through some things. I know that a lot of powerful people have taken aim at you. I get how that's going to make you jump at every shadow. I get it, Blake. I'm sure anybody in your position would feel the same way," she tells me. "But I also think you've lost some perspective and have allowed what's happened to impact your judgment. The bureaucracy shuffles people around all the time to give the illusion it's doing something. You know this, don't you? You should, since I recall that you were so fond of saying something similar."

I frown but am forced to nod my agreement. She's right. I know that bureaucracies like to make it seem as if they're doing something when all they're actually doing is moving pieces around. To me, it's more like rearranging the deck chairs on the Titanic. I hate to admit it, but maybe I have lost some perspective. She's right—and I suppose that means Pax and Astra are right too.

"Just take a beat and clear your head, Blake," Rosie presses. "It may be difficult for you to see right now, but this is a great opportunity for you. To have the attention of somebody like Max Stone—that's no small thing."

"Yeah, I know," I reply. "I guess I'm just so used to being on the defensive and—"

"And you're always looking for a fight. I seem to recall having a conversation with you about that. A couple of times, actually," she says with a laugh.

A wry grin touches my lips. "Yeah, I remember," I admit. "And I'll work on getting my perspective back."

"Good girl."

"Anyway, Ayad is coming, so I need to see what he wants. Thanks for calling me back, Rosie. I appreciate it."

"I wish I'd been able to call sooner."

"It's all right. And hey, congratulations on the promotion, ADIC Espinoza."

Rosie smiles. "Thank you, Blake. I know I wouldn't be here without you."

"No, you wouldn't, would you?" I say with a grin. "Take care, Rosie."

"You too."

I end the call just as Ayad steps into my office. He's carrying a black file folder in his hand, and I feel a jolt of excitement knowing we're getting our first case. He drops it onto my desk in front of me.

"Review it, then present it to your team," he tells me. "You're wheels up in an hour."

"Yes, sir."

He turns and leaves without another word. I roll my eyes so hard I worry they're going to get stuck like that. But they don't, so I open the file and start to read. Once I've gotten myself acquainted with the facts—as sparse as they are—I head out into the bullpen and take my customary place up on the dais at the front of the room. Astra gives me a smile and nods to the black folder in my hand.

"We finally getting something to do?" she asks.

"We are," I reply.

Astra claps her hands. "Oh, it's like Christmas."

"Thank God," Mo says. "I was thinking I made a mistake and there might be more excitement back in white-collar crime."

"Small minds get bored easily," Rick says.

"Don't mind him, Mo," Astra says. "He's been watching online porn this whole time."

"Only half the time, thank you very much," he fires back.

Neither Lucas nor Nina laughs along with us, looking uncertain instead. They glance at each other, though, and it looks to me like they're both uncomfortable with the crude humor.

"I like to keep things loose here, guys," I tell them. "If you're uncomfortable with the humor, this might not be the shop for you."

"No, it's fine," Lucas says quickly.

Nina nods. "It was just unexpected."

"Good. Then learn to laugh when you can," I say. "Most of the time we're up to our butts in misery and darkness—humor is an effective coping mechanism."

Neither of them says a word in reply. They just sit there looking like rabbits caught in the headlights. Yeah, this is going to be fun.

"All right, we're heading to Denver, Colorado," I announce. "We have a family that's gone missing. Possibly abducted."

"Who reported them missing?" Astra asks.

"A neighbor," I reply. "Friend of the family. Local PD did a wellness check but found nothing to indicate whether they were abducted or left town voluntarily. But they thought it strange nonetheless, so, they kicked it to us."

"Thank God they did," Astra says. "I like our new digs, but I'm tired of looking at the same walls already."

"You and me both," I reply.

"Do we have anything else to go on?" Lucas pipes up.

"Nothing. They preserved the house and haven't let anybody else in, so I guess that's something," I tell him. "We will hopefully be able to pick up some clues there. But as of this moment, we've got nothing."

"What does the family do for work?" Lucas asks.

"Brad Keller is one of Colorado's leading architects; his wife Bridget is a homemaker," I reply. "They've got two kids: eleven-year-old Cole and nine-year-old Lyssa. Both attend Gerald Ford Elementary just a few blocks away from their home."

"And do we know if they've received any specific threats?" Lucas presses.

Lucas is asking good questions. The right questions. It tells me he's a capable investigator and has the right mindset for this kind of work. He's also eager to work and assertive, which would ordinarily be a virtue. In the current climate, though, I want to pull his reins a bit and keep him from sprinting too far ahead. At least until I know whether I can trust him or not.

"Not that we know of," I tell him. "As I said, we're not sure of the disposition of the family. For all we know, they simply went out of town for a bit and just didn't tell anybody. Maybe they had an emergency. There are lots of question marks right now."

"So, we've got nothing to go on. Local PD doesn't even know if they've been abducted," Mo pipes up. "Why are we even making the trip?"

"Because Chief Ayad gave me the special black folder—which is a little on the nose if you ask me. But whatever," I shrug. "But he thinks there's a case here, so we go see if there's actually a case to be had. At least we're getting out of the shop for a while."

"And we get to ride on the private jet," Astra says with a wide grin. "Think they'll have bottle service?"

"Doubtful. Rick and Nina, you're here in support," I say, then turn to Astra, Mo, and Lucas. "Grab your go-bags, kids. We're wheels up in thirty minutes."

"I wanna go on the private jet," Rick whines.

"We'll bring you back some peanuts," Astra cracks.

CHAPTER SIX

Miller Airfield Hangar C-12; Denver, CO

A FTER GETTING OFF THE PLANE, WE WALK INTO THE hangar. Miller is a private airfield at the far edge of the Denver International Airport that contracts with the Bureau. We land, get our cars, and leave from there. It's a lot more convenient than having to fly commercial.

"Why did we not have a jet before?" Astra asks. "I love traveling by private jet."

"Hard to justify the expense of private jets when we were usually traveling less than fifty miles," I tell her.

"Hey, we went to Idaho that one time," Astra says.

"Oregon another time," Mo adds.

"Well, we've got a jet now," I say.

"Yeah, well, if nothing else, this new unit is awesome just for the fact that we have a jet now," Astra beams. "Though we are going to have to work on the in-flight cocktail situation. I like to have a drink when I fly."

"I think that would be against Bureau regulations," Lucas offers.

Astra, Mo, and I all exchange a glance, and though we all try to control it, a laugh bursts from our mouths anyway. Lucas's expression darkens, and he looks less than amused. He's reminding me a lot of Ayad right now, and he's seriously going to need to lighten up if he's going to fit in with this group. If that's even possible. I'm still not sold on him being part of our team for the long term. I just don't know that I can trust him.

"Okay, so what are we doing here, boss?" Astra asks.

"Right. To business. Astra and I are going to hit the crime scene—if it even is a crime scene," I say. "Mo, I want you and Lucas to go down and liaise with DPD. Gather up whatever they have, then head for the hotel and get us checked in. After that, get us set up in one of their conference rooms. We'll run our command center from there."

"We're not going to work out of the Denver Field Office?" Lucas frowns. "Or down at the local PD station?"

"No," I reply. "I prefer working in a clean environment free of distractions. I don't particularly like being locked in a room and stared at like a zoo exhibit whenever somebody walks by."

Lucas frowns. "I understand, I just thought—"

"Agent Okamura, leave the logistics to me," I say, my voice cold.

"Right," Mo says brightly, obviously trying to defuse the tension in the room. "Let's head down to the police station, Agent Okamura."

"I don't mean to speak out of turn," Lucas says. "But I think I'd be of more use going to the crime scene with you and Agent Russo."

"I want you and Mo to liaise with local PD. We need to let them know we're in town and then get our command post set up," I reply.

Lucas frowns. "I understand, but I'd like—"

"Agent Okamura, this is my team, and I've given you an order," I say. "You and Agent Weissman will meet with local PD. Am I clear?"

I exchange a look with Mo and see that she understands what I'm doing and gives me a nod. I like that we can communicate without needing words. And that sort of silent communication is something that can only develop between people who trust each other. So, until I can trust Lucas, I intend to marginalize him. I don't want him looking over my shoulder. At least not until I know whether he's Ayad's flunky or not.

"Agent Okamura, we should go," Mo says.

Lucas glares at me, and I can see he knows exactly what I'm doing. I only wonder if he knows why. To his credit though, he bites off his next words instead of saying something I would make him regret almost instantly. Grudgingly, he turns away and walks with Mo over to the Bureau ride—a black GMC Yukon with smoked windows. I'd arranged to have two at the airfield when we arrived, knowing I'd be sending Lucas off to do the busy work well away from the crime scene Astra and I are headed for.

We watch as they mount up and head out. Once they're gone, I turn to Astra and find her smiling at me.

"You know he's not going to be thrilled with getting pushed to the sidelines all the time," she says. "The boy wants to be on the field."

"I'm not putting him in the game until I know that I can trust him. Until I know he's not just Ayad's lackey," I tell her. "And also not until I think he's ready."

"Oh, I know that," Astra replies. "I'm just saying, expect him to push back every single time you order him to do something he doesn't want to do. He strikes me as the persistent sort."

"Let him push," I say with a shrug. "I outrank him. And if he doesn't like it, he can find another sandbox to play in."

"Look at you flex those Supervisory Special Agent muscles," Astra says with a laugh. "It's kind of hot."

"Shut up," I reply, laughing along with her. "Let's go. We have a family to find."

"Talk about a house on a hill," Astra comments.

The gate at the bottom of the driveway is open, so I pull through and drive up the incline that leads to a small roundabout in front of the house. I pull to a stop, and we climb out to take a look around. The home itself is a two-story, red brick colonial with a steeply pitched roof the color of slate, white window frames, and dark shutters. A tall arch covers the porch, and the front door is recessed. Flowering bushes run along the front of the house beneath the windows, and the yard is tastefully landscaped. For being such a large house on a lofty perch, it somehow manages to avoid being ostentatious.

"Cars are still in the driveway," I note.

A black Escalade and a blue Chrysler Pacifica Hybrid are parked to the side of the roundabout. I notice a dark stain behind the minivan and surmise the Kellers had a third car.

"We'll need to look at cars registered to them," I say and point to the stain on the driveway. "Looks like they have a third vehicle."

"Nice catch."

I turn and look at the neighborhood spread out below. Whoever designed the house put it on a plateau well above the rest of the neighborhood but did a nice job of crafting a gentle grade down to the sidewalk below, so the drop-off isn't sharp or steep. Red brick columns and black wrought iron encircle the property, and there is a large tree about halfway down the slope with wide, leafy boughs. When it gets warm here, I bet it's nice to spread out under that tree and read a book or just doze for a little while.

"I think I can see my house from up here," Astra says, drawing a grin from me.

"Yeah, it does stand above the crowd, doesn't it?"

"Just a bit."

"This is a really nice house," I say.

"Yeah, it is," she replies. "I guess Keller wasn't doing too bad for himself. I mean, look around. The entire area is pretty nice."

It's an affluent neighborhood. Everywhere I look, I can see the trappings of wealth—Jaguars and Teslas in the driveways of homes that are downright palatial. Swimming pools, tennis courts, stables, and riding rings dot the backyards of the homes that I can see from this vantage point. Astra has a small smile curling her lips as she surveys the area.

"Making retirement plans already?" I ask.

She scoffs. "I'm a lowly civil servant. No way I could ever afford a place like this."

"That makes two of us," I reply. "Come on, let's go take a look and see what we see."

We head up the walkway that leads to the front door. I look through the window to the right of the door, and Astra peeks in through the one on the left.

"Looks deserted," I observe.

Astra pulls a small knife out of her pocket and slices through the yellow crime scene tape the cops put over the door for some reason. I can only imagine what the Kellers would have thought if they'd come home to find that on their door. Astra tries the knob and looks at me when it turns in her hand.

"Might as well," I nod. "We're not going to learn anything standing out here."

"That was my thought too."

She opens the door, and we step into a small foyer. Narrow tables of dark, polished oak flank the door and sit beneath the windows we'd been looking through. To our right is a staircase that leads up to the second floor, the banister of the same polished wood the tables and the floor is made from. To our left is a wide archway that leads into a formal sitting room, and in front of us is a round table made of white marble that accents the dark wood flooring and holds a vase of flowers that are dried up and withered.

Dead petals litter the tabletop, and most of the water in the vase has evaporated already, leaving a dry, white grime on the glass. It's the only sign of disarray anywhere in the immediate part of the house though. There is a light layer of dust on every surface, but I don't see any windows open, and the door was closed. That tells me the place hasn't been cleaned in a few days. Maybe a week tops.

"We'll need to check to see if the Kellers had a maid," I say.

"Can't imagine they don't in a place like this," Astra replies, then points to the flowers. "Though those flowers haven't been changed out in a while, which brings a few questions to mind for me."

"I don't think she's been around in a while," I reply. "Maybe she doesn't come weekly."

"Two kids in the house, she doesn't come weekly, and the place still looks this clean? Aside from the flowers, I mean. Other than that, this maid must be a wizard."

"Assuming there is a maid. There might not be. Mrs. Keller might be hands-on about everything around here," I offer.

"That's possible," Astra concedes.

We walk deeper into the house, passing through the sitting room then into a formal dining room. Near the back of the house, we find the kitchen, which is thoroughly modern, then step into the casual living room. With toys in a box in the corner, a stack of books on the coffee table, and reading glasses on an end table, this place looks a little more lived-in, though no less rigorously clean.

Astra opens one of the sliders that make up the back wall and steps out onto the deck. The sun sparkles dazzlingly off the water in the kidney-shaped pool and the octagonal jacuzzi. The image of sitting out in the hot water, watching the steam curl off the surface and rise into the darkened night sky with a glass of wine in my hand pops into my brain, and I feel a flash of envy. Throw in a little soft jazz, and I can't think of a better way to spend an evening.

As Astra pokes around outside, I head upstairs and search the bedrooms. I find what has to be Cole's room at one end of the second floor. His room is tidy—the bed is made, all the toys put away, and everything on the surface of his desk is in its place. The walls are plastered with Denver Broncos and Colorado Avalanche posters and pictures of his favorite players.

The room is a light blue, and there's a dark blue round rug on the floor that contrasts nicely with the walls. The sheets are crisp and a blue that matches the rug, and he's got a thick gray comforter. There are books on the shelves and a TV in the corner with whatever the latest game console is set up and a slew of games to go with it. Everything, including the long cords attached to the game system, is neatly rolled and stored.

I can't say I've ever seen a preteen's room this clean. There's not even so much as a smelly pile of laundry in a hamper in the corner. Maybe the family really does have a maid. I file the thought away for later as I close the door behind me.

Whereas Cole's room has masculine overtones, Lyssa's room, which is directly across the hall from her brother's, is the picture of femininity. The walls are a pastel yellow and littered with pictures and posters of various boy bands—Lyssa seems to be a big K-Pop fan. She's got a four-poster bed with a princess canopy over the top that's got white gauzy curtains that fall over the sides. At nine years old, she might be getting a little old for that. I wonder how long that canopy will remain.

Like her brother's room, she's got a desk in the corner where I assume she does her homework and a television in the other corner. She has her own game console and quite the array of games lined up on the shelf beneath the television. While Cole favored sports and first-person shooter games, Lyssa seems fond of adventure and puzzle games.

Like her brother's room, it's perfectly clean. The bed is made, the rug is freshly vacuumed, and all the items on her desk are perfectly neat. It almost seems more like a snapshot than a real child's room.

Not seeing anything of interest, I head down to the other end of the floor and step into the master suite. The first word that comes to mind is *cozy*. The walls and the bedding are all done in soft, soothing earth tones, and the entire vibe is mellow. There are two walk-in closets, and given that the one on the left is half-filled with shoes, I'm guessing that was a big selling point when the Kellers looked at the house.

I poke through both closets, something nagging in the back of my mind that I can't quite place just yet. Trying to avoid overthinking it, I wander into the bathroom and feel that flush of envy wash through me again. There's a tall standing shower and a large freestanding bathtub that looks like half an egg. It's wide, long, and looks comfortable. I'm already picturing taking long, decadent baths in that thing. The vanity is his and hers, with round mirrors standing over a matched pair of eggshell basins that look like smaller versions of the tub with sleek, modern water fixtures.

Each side of the vanity has its own medicine cabinet, so I take a moment to poke around in them and don't see anything of much value or interest. Neither of them seems to be on anything—unless they took it with them, of course. Three diamond-shaped light fixtures made of frosted glass and burnished steel are mounted on the wall in front of me—one on each side of the two mirrors and one in between.

"God, it must be nice to be rich," I mutter.

After rifling through the drawers and finding nothing, I step back out into the bedroom and fold my arms over my chest. That nagging in the back of my mind is getting more insistent, and I look around, hoping something I see will unlock it for me. Usually, when I get that feeling, it's because my unconscious mind saw something, some little detail that I didn't immediately pick up, and my brain is working to bring it to the forefront.

With my arms still folded over my chest, I turn around and look at the room again, trying to figure out what it is that I missed. The entire house just feels… empty. And not simply because it's currently devoid of people. It's more than that. The best way I can describe it is that it feels abandoned. It feels like the energy of the family that lived here is gone and isn't coming back. It feels like every trace of the Kellers evaporated like the water in the vase sitting on the table in the foyer.

"You find anything?" Astra asks as she steps into the room. "Because I've come up with absolutely nothing. I can't tell you if the Kellers left on their own or were taken."

I start to shake my head and open my mouth to reply when that nagging in the back of my brain finally unlocks what it's been wrestling with.

"They were taken," I say. "They didn't leave voluntarily."

"How do you know?"

Feeling more certain by the moment, I step into Mr. Keller's closet and pull his bags down off the shelf. Walking back into the room, I set them down.

"People who go on voluntary trips don't usually leave their luggage behind."

CHAPTER SEVEN

Rocky Mountain Inn & Suites Conference Room; Denver, CO

THE HOTEL ISN'T ANYTHING FANCY. BUT IT'S A LOT BETTER than some of the hotels Astra and I had to stay at when we had cases outside Seattle. The rooms are all plain, but nice. The best thing about the rooms is that they're crisp and clean. The housekeeping department is on point and keeps everything in their hotel tight and fresh—which I appreciate.

After we finished up at the Kellers' house, Astra and I came back to the hotel to freshen up. Mo and Lucas had done as I asked and got us checked in and set up our command post in one of the hotel's conference rooms. They were getting the computers set up when we came in, so I told Mo I wanted to freshen up. I got my room key then came upstairs and took a quick shower. Something about flying always makes me feel grimy. It's probably marinating in the recycled air inside the plane for the two-and-a-half-hour flight.

After my shower, I towel off then throw on a pair of jeans, a black turtleneck, and a pair of black Chuck Taylors. Dressed and ready, I grab my coat and head back downstairs. As I step off the elevator, my stomach rumbles, reminding me I haven't eaten since early this morning. I make a mental note to include protein bars and other snacks in my go-bag.

"Jesus, Blake. Was that your stomach, or are you hiding a werewolf in your pocket?" Astra asks as she falls into step beside me.

"Where did you come from?"

"I came down the stairs," she replies.

"We need to get some food," I say.

"And a drink."

"I could go for that," I nod. "Let's get things squared away with the command post, and then we'll go forage for some food."

"Deal," she says.

We find the conference room, and I hold the door open for her. I follow her inside and let the door close behind me. The walls are a soft shade of cream, and the carpet is a nauseatingly busy pattern designed to hide the stains. There's one long conference table that runs down the middle of the room with three plush office chairs on either side, one at the head, and one at the foot. A projector that's probably twenty years old sits on a rolling cart in the corner, across from a pull-down screen that's littered with scratches and scuffs. The thick layer of dust covering the entire unit tells me nobody's used the hotel's A/V equipment in a long time.

Mo is sitting on one side of the table with her laptop open in front of her and a couple of notebooks and pens to her right. Lucas is sitting on the other side of the table staring at his laptop screen and jotting down a couple of notes on a pad of paper next to him. They both look up as Astra and I walk in.

"We're all set up in here," Mo says. "Rick's got us all connected and wired in."

"Good work," I reply. "What's the word from the locals?"

"Not much more than what they told us before we arrived," she says. "They can't say whether they left voluntarily or were taken. What did you find at the scene?"

"No obvious signs of a break-in," Astra says.

"But I'm convinced they were taken," I add.

"Why's that?" Mo asks.

"Their luggage was still in their closets," I explain.

"That's it?" Lucas asks. "You're basing your theory that they were abducted on the fact that you found luggage in their closet?"

The haughty tone in his voice sends a bolt of irritation through me, and I have to bite back the scathing reply sitting on the tip of my tongue. I fold my hands behind my back and pace the length of the room behind Mo, taking a beat to compose myself. I don't want to bite Lucas's head off this early into our relationship, but he's going to have to learn to keep himself from sounding like such a condescending ass.

"We're only planning on being in Denver what, a few days?" I ask. "And we all packed a bag with a few changes of clothing, right?"

"Yeah," Lucas replies grudgingly.

"The Kellers have been gone at least a week," I say. "But their bags are still there."

Lucas shakes his head. "It still seems pretty thin," he presses. "I mean, they could have had a second set of bags."

"Yeah, it's possible. But it's unlikely," I reply. "It's also the only lead we have—"

"I wouldn't exactly call it a lead."

It feels like every muscle in my body is clenched up; I'm having a really difficult time keeping my temper in check. At this point, it seems like Lucas is just trying to be argumentative and contrary. I mean, he's not wrong. It is thin and not much of a lead. But it's the only thing we have, and it's enough of an anomaly that I'm willing to give it a little time to investigate and see if anything comes of it.

"Chief Ayad sent us down here for a reason. He believes there's a case to be made," I say. "I'm not willing to go back until we've looked into this deep enough to determine whether there's a case here or not. You're welcome to fly back to Seattle if you're not willing to do your job, Lucas. But you'd better fly coach."

Lucas turns back to his computer screen, a sour and sullen look on his face. I swear to God he looks like a petulant teenager. He doesn't argue further, but there's a big part of me that wants to tear into him anyway. You can only poke the bear with a stick so many times before it bites back. Lucas needs to learn his place in our team's food chain. Perhaps sensing my imminent Krakatoa-like eruption and wanting to head it off, Astra gives me a subtle shake of the head. She's right, so I swallow it down and turn to Mo instead.

"Can you get in touch with Rick and Nina? I want you to have them run down any and all vehicles registered to either Brad or Bridget Keller," I say. "And while you're at it, have them find any properties in either of their names as well. If this is a case of them just getting out of town for a little while, maybe they've got a place to go to."

"Will do," Mo nods, already typing up an email to both of them.

"Also, see if you can get the name of a maid, gardeners, or any other employees they might have," I add. "We're going to want to talk to them."

"Got it."

"For now, go ahead and knock off," I tell them. "Go get some food and get some sleep. We're going to hit the ground running in the morning."

"I just need to finish up a couple of things," Mo says. "You guys go on ahead."

Lucas closes his laptop and stands up. Without looking at us or speaking a single word, he turns and walks out of the conference room, only reinforcing the image of a sulking, petulant child. Irritation flashes through me, but I do my best to stifle it.

Letting out a long breath, I turn to Astra. "Drink?"

"Drink."

"I don't know," I say. "On paper, Lucas seems ideal. Solid track record in counterterrorism, high marks from all his superiors, no red flags to speak of."

"Maybe he just doesn't like you," Astra offers with a grin.

"What are you talking about? Everybody likes me."

Astra laughs. "Yeah, you believe that if it helps you sleep at night."

The waitress drops off our drinks and takes our order—steak and a baked potato with all the trimmings for me, salmon in a lemon and white wine sauce, rice pilaf, and veggies for Astra. After leaving the hotel, I looked up the best steakhouses around our immediate area. Astra suggested we head out for sushi and sake, but I vetoed that right away. Colorado's a landlocked state, and there's no way in hell I'm trusting sushi in a state that doesn't have a coastline. But I know Colorado has a lot of beef and a good reputation for doing steak well.

"I know he's eager to make his bones with us, but if he thinks pissing me off is the way to go about it, Lucas is going to have to learn a very painful lesson," I tell her.

"What did he do in counterterrorism?"

"He was an analyst."

"So, he wasn't a field agent?"

"No, but his supervisors all agreed he had the makings to be a good one."

"Why in the hell did Ayad stick a guy with no field experience and a tech straight out of the Academy in our unit?" Astra asks.

I shrug. "Got me. Maybe they're hoping we'll shape them into the sort of top-flight agents that we are."

"You know, I think you might be right. There should be more like us in the Bureau," Astra says with a laugh, then takes a drink of her martini.

"His instincts are good though," I say. "He knows what questions to ask. Seems to have a sharp, investigative mind. I think he could be a solid agent. He's just got an attitude problem and seems like he thinks he's better than everybody. Even me. And we both know that can't possibly be true."

"No, of course, it can't be true. Perish the thought."

Astra and I share a laugh, then I take a drink. The waitress arrives and drops off our meals, and I stare at the slab of meat on my plate and feel my mouth begin to water. It's an absolutely gorgeous cut of meat, and when I slice into it, I smile wide. It's cooked perfectly.

"I told you they do a mean steak out here," I comment.

"The side of beef is all yours, cavewoman," she replies.

We both take a few quiet moments to tuck into our meals, and I'm delighted to find it tastes every bit as good as it looks. They definitely do steak up right here in Colorado.

"He's right, though, you know," Astra says.

"About what?"

"The luggage was a good catch, but it's pretty flimsy."

"Yeah, I know," I admit, then take a sip of my drink. "But it's all we have. So, we've got no choice but to run with it."

Astra nods as she takes a bite of her salmon, a thoughtful expression on her face. She chews, then takes a drink to wash it down. She looks at me with that furrow in her brow she gets when she's been thinking of something and is trying to find the right way to approach it with me. That usually means I'm not going to like it. I can't believe I thought, even for a second, she was starting to pull her punches with me.

"Just rip the bandage off," I implore her. "Out with it."

"All right. I talked to Lucas for a bit on the way down here," she says. "I'm not saying I got to know his deep, intimate secrets or anything, but I got a good sense of him."

"All right. And?"

"I think maybe part of his attitude problem is that he knows you're marginalizing him," Astra says. "He seems like a guy who's eager to get into it and doesn't like being held back."

"I get that. But that also tells me he needs to learn a little patience," I reply.

"I don't disagree with that. I'm just saying it might not be a matter of arrogance or thinking he's better—though I don't doubt that's part of it. He carries a bit of a holier-than-thou vibe sometimes. But I think maybe he just wants to see some action. He wants to prove himself, and it was pretty obvious you were putting him on the sidelines and weren't going to give him that chance. That's all."

"He's been questioning my authority from the jump. He needs to learn his place," I say. "This is my team, and until he learns to follow orders, I can't trust him in the field. And until he proves I can, I'll keep sitting him on the bench."

Astra sets her fork down and looks at me. "I've never seen you like this before, Blake. You're so... strident. You're so intent on imposing your authority on him that you're coming off like you're insecure," she says. "What's going on with you?"

"I just don't like the way any of this went down. I don't like Ayad, and I resent him putting people I don't know or trust on my team," I say.

"So, it all comes down to your control issues again," she says.

"That's not it—"

"It is, though. Both Nina and Lucas seem solid. You said yourself that Lucas has great instincts and has a sharp investigative mind," she presses. "So, it seems to me that your biggest objection is that he wasn't your choice."

"He's also got no practical experience."

"Neither did Mo. But you took her under your wing, and look at her now. Aside from that whole vomiting episode when she saw her first corpse, she's great in the field," Astra says. "All of that, taken together, adds up to your real issue being that Lucas wasn't your choice. Which makes this all about your control issues."

"There's also the issue of him reporting back to Ayad that makes me leery of him."

"If he is. We have no proof of that," she replies evenly. "And so what if he does? Do we ever do anything that would cause an actual issue with OPR? Sure, we push the envelope at times. But so did Stone, and look where he is."

"Yeah, well, we're not Stone."

"No. We're not. But the point is that we push boundaries, but we've never crossed the line. You make sure we don't," she presses. "So, what are you afraid of him telling Ayad? If he actually is reporting to him behind your back?"

I sit back in my chair and drain the last of my martini, then look at my empty glass longingly. I wouldn't mind another one, but I know I need to be sharp tomorrow. This isn't the conversation I expected to have tonight. In truth, I expected that Astra would come down on my side on this issue. She's usually as protective of our unit as I am. I never anticipated getting pushback from her on this, and I'm not quite sure what to do with that.

"Astra Russo. Champion of the people," I say with a small laugh.

"The Bureau's changing. The world's changing," she tells me. "We're going to have to change with it or we'll end up like Winslow—fighting and alienating everybody we come across to protect our little fiefdom, rather than growing, evolving, and flourishing."

Her words are like a cold slap across the face. She says *we*, but I know she's saying *me*. If *I* don't learn to adapt, *I'll* end up like Winslow. Never in a million years would I have ever even considered the possibility that I would end up like him. He clings to notions of how things used to be.

He runs his good ol' boys club like these are still the days when men like him ruled the world and could do whatever they wanted—and often act with total impunity. She's not wrong about him desperately clinging to his little fiefdom. His little boys' club. And she's not wrong about Winslow fighting and alienating anybody who's not part of his circle.

But time and change caught up to him, and now look at him. He's been completely marginalized. The Bureau neutered him. And they did it because he clung to those notions in his head of how things should be—how they used to be. The idea that I might have a similar mindset and could be following in his footsteps is shocking. To say the least. It's also nauseating to think I could be that myopic and unable to adapt to the whirlwind of changes blowing through the Bureau these days.

This is not the conversation I expected to be having tonight. But something in the back of my mind tells me it's, perhaps, a conversation I needed.

CHAPTER EIGHT

Rocky Mountain Inn & Suites Conference Room; Denver, CO

I HAD A NEW SCREEN BROUGHT IN THIS MORNING. IT'S ALMOST more of a television, really, but it has a webcam, and Mo was able to hook it up wirelessly to a laptop. I'm sitting at the foot of the table with Astra to my left. Mo and Lucas are in their seats from yesterday—across from each other near the head of the table. I watch as the TV comes to life and the screen fills with Nina Alvarado's face. She gives us a big smile.

"Good morning, team," she beams. "How are you finding Colorado? I'm from Fort Collins, you know."

I should have known that. I'm sure it was in the personnel file I skimmed, but that detail didn't lodge into my brain.

"It's nice out here," I say. "Astra's considering retiring in your fair state."

Astra shoots me a grin as Nina laughs. "As long as you like the quiet and not much ever really happening, then it's a good place to retire."

"Sounds ideal to me," Astra says.

"Is Rick there?" I ask.

Nina shakes her head. "He's coming in late this morning. He texted me and said he needed to take his girlfriend to a doctor's appointment."

"All right, but make sure he's not pawning off all his work onto you, Nina," I say.

"He'll totally make you do everything while he naps," Astra adds. "Don't let him get away with that."

Nina laughs. "I'll make sure to put my foot down."

"Actually, you can put your foot up his—"

"Don't mind Astra. She thinks Rick is her kid brother," I say. "Anyway, were you able to track down the information I asked for yesterday?"

She nods, and her eyes shift as she looks at her second computer screen. "We did—and, yeah, Rick helped," she tells us. "In addition to the Escalade and the Pacifica, the Kellers own a blue 2021 Chevy Suburban. I'm sending the VIN number and license plate number to your emails now."

"Excellent," I say. "What about properties?"

"According to what I found, Mrs. Keller's parents passed on, and they left her a house in Hope," she says. "Since I'm sure none of you have ever heard of Hope, it's a small city on the edge of the Pike National Forest—kind of a little camping area more than a real town. People rent out cabins by the creeks. But the main town itself is super retro. There's a diner there with a really amazing peach pie."

"Peach pie, huh?" I ask.

She shrugs. "I guess being known for your peach pie beats being known for a ton of other horrible reasons like, you're the hometown of a notorious serial killer, domestic terrorist, or the guy who invented Twinkies."

"Hey, what's wrong with Twinkies?" Mo asks.

"Nothing, if you don't mind eating something packed with so many preservatives it can sit on a shelf for a thousand years and never go bad," she replies with a grin.

"Girl, if you don't enjoy Twinkies, you're dead inside," Mo tells her.

"Well, at least I'm not going to be dead and rotting inside from all the chemicals they pump into those little toxic death-cakes."

"Who hurt you?" Mo asks.

We all share a laugh, and I feel some of the tension I'm holding toward Nina dissipate. The fact that she's able to banter back and forth with us, giving as good as she takes, encourages me. It makes me feel a bit better about having her on the team. Lucas, on the other hand, sits in his chair, unmoving, unsmiling, and I think maybe even unblinking. He's just sitting there as still as a statue, reading something on his computer screen, the hostility radiating off him like heat from the sun. For a twenty-eight-year-old man, he has perfected the look of a surly teenager.

"All right, aside from the house in Hope, any other properties under either name?" I ask. "Apartments, condos, timeshares—anything?"

"Nothing," she replies. "I even searched for the children's names, just in case. That's all we got."

"Good thought to have, though. Nice work, Nina."

"Thanks, boss."

"Hey, Nina," I say as a thought strikes me. "That Suburban... they wouldn't happen to be equipped with OnStar or some other GPS device, would it?"

"GPS was disabled," she replies. "Sorry."

"Of course not. That would be too simple," I say. "Thanks for checking."

"You got it. You know where I'll be if you need me for anything."

The screen goes dark, and we all remain silent for a moment as we chew on the information at hand. Not that it's much more than what we had before, but at least it's something. There's a lot to do today, and I take a moment to figure out how to divide up

ELLE GRAY

the labor. When I come up with a plan, I get to my feet and pace the room behind my chair.

"All right, Mo, I want you and Lucas to go check out the house in Hope," I say. "I want to know if they're just down there for some family time away. If they are, we can put this to bed and go home."

"Copy that," Mo says.

"Where are we headed?" Astra asks.

"I want to talk to the guy who reported them missing," I tell her. "I want to see if he's got any insights about the Keller family. I don't know what it is, but I woke up this morning with a hinky feeling about all this. I just feel like something's up."

"You sure that hinky feeling wasn't one too many Cosmos last night?" Mo asks with a mischievous grin.

"I had one martini, not a Cosmo, thank you very much," I fire back. "I'm a lightweight, but I'm not *that* much of a lightweight. Give a girl some credit."

"Fair enough," Mo says with a laugh as she starts to pack her things.

"SSA Wilder?"

I turn to Lucas to find him staring at me evenly. I have a feeling I already know what he's going to ask before he even opens his mouth.

"Yes?" I ask.

"I'd like to come with you and Agent Russo to interview the neighbor who reported the Kellers missing," he says.

"No. You're Agent Weissman's partner," I say. "We work in teams of two. I need you to go with her, so I know somebody's watching her back."

"She's going to a house that's probably empty. And even if it's not, it's likely filled with people who are away on vacation. What's going to happen to her? She gets invited in for a piece of this world-famous peach pie?"

I grit my teeth and try to keep the anger and frustration that's bubbling up inside of me from boiling over.

"Astra, Mo, can we have the room, please?" I ask quietly.

Astra gives me a concerned look, but I shake my head. I need to make a point, but I don't want to humiliate him in front of the others. It's time Lucas learns some boundaries. Without a word, they both get up and walk out of the conference room, leaving the two of us alone with an oppressive tension filling the space between us.

Standing behind my chair, I clasp my hands behind my back and look at him for a long moment, saying nothing. He looks back at me, his expression smug. It's time I, as Astra said, flex my Supervisory Special Agent muscle and make sure Lucas knows his place in the pecking order in this unit—*my* unit.

"Agent Okamura, you do realize you're a subordinate on my team—do you not?" I ask. "Further, you do realize I am the leader of this team, and you are a junior agent, right?"

"Yes, but—"

"We need to get this straight, right here, right now, Agent Okamura. This is my team. When you are given an order, you are expected to follow that order without questioning me or trying to undermine my authority," I say, my voice hard and flat. "Do you understand this?"

"Yes, I understand, but—"

"I appreciate your enthusiasm. I do. But you are a junior agent without practical field experience. I'm easing you into this, and you will work at the pace I set for you," I continue. "The first 's' in my title is Supervisory, meaning I am your supervisor, Agent Okamura, which means part of my job is to put you in positions to succeed. Conversely, that means I must avoid putting you in positions where you will fail. And those are determinations I cannot make until I see your complete skill set."

"With all due respect, Supervisory Special Agent Wilder," he sneers, "how can you see my skill set without putting me in positions where I can show you?"

"This is your first field assignment, Lucas, and I understand that you want to prove yourself. I get it. I do. And if you want my honest opinion, I believe you will make an excellent field agent," I say, trying to adopt a more neutral tone. "But part of being a good field agent is knowing how to take orders. You need to add 'good team player' to your skill set. Until you show me you can do that, I will never think you are ready and will keep the training wheels on. Show me different, and we can talk about taking them off."

71

"My understanding was that your unit was less top-down like most of the others and more of a collaborative effort," he says.

"We're very collaborative. I welcome input when we're developing and refining our theories and profiles," I tell him. "But don't mistake collaboration for anarchy. This is still my unit, and I run it by my rules. I run it the way I see fit."

He sits back in his seat and runs a hand over his face, but his surly, sullen expression slowly fades. He's still frustrated, but I can see that my words have impacted him. That gives me hope he's not a lost cause after all. Maybe Astra is right and my initial assessment of him is off. Maybe he is more than he's shown me to this point. In my defense, it's hard to think otherwise based on first impressions.

I give him a minute to object, all but daring him to do so, but he doesn't. Instead, he remains quiet and seems to be thinking about my words, which I take to be a good sign. But there's still more he needs to learn, so school remains in session.

"Now, about you going with Mo to check out the house in Hope. You're making a lot of assumptions, Agent Okamura," I say. "And when you're out here in the field, assumptions can get you dead real fast."

"I don't understand," he replies.

"Suppose the Kellers, for whatever reason, don't want to be found. Suppose they went to Hope because they're in hiding—"

"We have nothing to indicate that's the case."

"We have nothing to indicate that's *not* the case either. And that's the point. We can't make assumptions," I prod him. "Suppose I let you come with me and Astra and let Mo go down there on her own. Further suppose the Kellers don't want to be found, and when Mo walks in, and maybe they mistake her for somebody else, flip out and shoot her."

"But why would they? Brad Keller has no criminal record. Neither does his wife," he says. "Why would two people with no criminal past, up and shoot a federal agent for no reason?"

I put my hands on the back of my chair and lean forward, pinning Lucas to his seat with my gaze. He shifts in his seat, obviously uncomfortable under my scrutiny.

"So, you're telling me that only people with criminal backgrounds commit violent crimes?" I ask. "You're telling me that only people with criminal backgrounds flip out and commit unthinkable, unimaginable crimes?"

He opens his mouth to reply, but seems to think better of it and closes it again without saying a word. It's probably the smartest thing he's done this morning. Of course, people with a history of violent crime are more likely to commit violent crimes. Of course, people with a history of violent crime would be more likely to shoot a federal agent. But normal, ordinary people without a criminal record can do the same thing too. It's not just career criminals out there murdering, raping, and robbing innocent people.

"That's why I say you're not ready, Lucas. That's why I'm holding you back right now," I tell him. "And that's why I want you out there watching Mo's back and why I want her watching yours. Regardless of how minimal the risk is, it's not zero."

He remains silent, but that surliness is gone from his expression. I'll take that as a win.

"Do we understand each other?" I ask.

It's somewhat grudging but he nods. "Yes ma'am. We understand each other."

"Good. Then I don't want to have this conversation again," I reply. I take a moment to take a breath before I continue. "Here's the deal, Lucas. On paper, I think you've got what it takes to be a stellar field agent. You're smart, you've got good instincts, and you have a knack for asking the right questions. But you need to learn to function as part of a team. And that includes following orders from your superior—even when you don't like the orders you're being given."

"Understood."

"It's my job to give you every chance to succeed and to bring out the best in you," I tell him. "And I plan to do that. I promise you this is nothing personal. It's not a vendetta or a grudge or a punishment. It's a matter of experience. A matter of time."

He opens his mouth again, but I raise a hand to stop him. "I already know what you're going to say: How can you get field experience if you're not allowed out in the field? I know. I've been there. I was chomping at the bit to get my first field assignment too. But I just need to know you can function within the structure of my team. If you can't, that's fine. If you don't like the way I run my team and want to transfer out, that's fine too. No hard feelings. I wish you nothing but the best. Just let me know now so I can start vetting your replacement."

"No. I want to be here," he replies. "I wanted to join your team for a reason. And that reason hasn't changed."

"Are you sure?"

He straightens up and looks me straight in the eyes. "One hundred percent."

I can tell he means it.

I tried to take Astra's advice and walk a neutral line, wanting to give Lucas a chance to prove himself while also maintaining clear boundaries. She was right about everything she said at dinner last night. It's all something I need to absorb and factor into my thinking, not to mention the way I operate.

But this is my team, and while I have no desire to be the sort of supervisor Winslow was, I still have to draw the line at certain behaviors. But I also need to be flexible enough to adapt to new personalities and give people like Lucas the chance to flourish and grow. I see that now.

"All right," I give him a smile. "Then let's go to work."

CHAPTER NINE

Malvern Residence; Denver, CO

"**W**ELL, IT SOUNDS LIKE YOU GOT THROUGH TO him," Astra comments with a smug smile on her face. "And it sounds like I got through to you."

"Yeah, yeah, yeah," I brush her off. "I decided there was a little bit of wisdom in your words. Emphasis on *a little bit*."

"Well, knock me over with a feather," she replies.

I pull up to the curb in front of the house owned by Pete and Sherry Malvern—the couple who reported the Kellers missing in the first place. They're about half a block down from the Keller house, and from this vantage point, the house almost looks like a feudal castle high above the homes of the peasants and serfs.

"That house looks even more imposing from down here," Astra says as we climb out of the SUV.

"I was just thinking that."

The Malvern home is a side-split, ranch-style home. In front of us sits what looks like a two- or three-car garage with windows indicating there are bedrooms above it. A short flight of stairs leads you from the driveway up to the front door just to our left. The living area of the home has large panes of glass looking into a living room and kitchen on the first floor and what looks to be a bonus room on the level half a flight of stairs up from that.

A short portico extends from the front door and is supported by a pair of white pillars set upon a stone base. The house itself is made of clapboard that's a light shade of blue—almost, but not quite, turquoise. The windows all have white trim, and it has a steeply inclined roof made of dark gray slate-colored tiles. The front yard is tastefully landscaped with bushes and trees positioned strategically to cut down on the open view through all the glass windows set into the front of the house.

"If you need more proof that it's all about status in this neighborhood," Astra says, waving at the cars in the driveway.

A late-model BMW SUV and a sporty Mercedes sit in the driveway, rather than in the garage they're parked in front of. Obviously, the Malverns want people to see what they're driving. But it seems the same can be said for most of the people in this neighborhood, given the expensive cars all over the place. Keeping up with the Joneses indeed.

We walk up the steps that lead us to the front door. I press the button for the doorbell, and we wait. A moment later, a woman's voice resonates out of the speaker in the doorbell camera security unit. Apparently, even in an affluent neighborhood like this that I'm sure gets regular police patrols, you just can't be too careful.

"Yes? Hello?" she says.

"Mrs. Sherry Malvern?" I ask.

"Yes, how can I help you?"

"Agents Wilder and Russo, ma'am. We're with the FBI," I say. "We'd like to ask you a few questions about a missing persons report you filed."

"Oh, it was my husband that filed that," she replies.

"All right, is your husband here, ma'am?" I ask.

"Yes. Yes, he is."

When she doesn't say anything further, I exchange a glance with Astra, and though it's a Herculean effort, manage to avoid rolling my eyes.

"May we speak with your husband, ma'am?"

"Can you hold your badges up to the camera, please?"

It's not an unreasonable request, so we pull out our creds and take turns holding them up to the camera. There's a long pause on the line, and I'm just about to speak when I hear the locks on the front door being disengaged before it opens. A woman in her mid-fifties is standing before us with a sheepish smile on her face.

Her hair is a near platinum shade of blonde—she obviously colors it to cover the grays—and it's pulled back into a bun. Her blue eyes are set behind a thick pair of black-framed glasses, and she's wearing a blue, floral print dress that reminds me of something out of an old *Leave it to Beaver* episode.

"I apologize for making you jump through all the hoops. You can just never be too sure these days," she says.

"It's no problem, ma'am," I reply. "It's always good to be vigilant. It's smart because you're right, you can never be too sure or safe these days."

"Please, come in."

She holds the door open for us, and we find ourselves in a small entryway. To our left through a large archway is the living room. To our right is the short staircase that leads to the bedrooms. Mrs. Malvern gestures to the archway, inviting us into the living room.

"Please, have a seat. I was just making some tea," she says. "Would you care for a cup?"

"No, we're fine, thank you, ma'am," I tell her. "We just need to speak with you and your husband if that would be all right."

She nods. "Of course. Let me just go wake him. Ever since he retired, this has become his nap time," she says with an apologetic shrug.

We sit down on the long, plush sofa as Mrs. Malvern heads through an archway at the rear of the living room which presumably leads into the kitchen and the back of the house. She passes another short staircase that leads up to the bonus room I noticed from the street. I would have thought Mr. Malvern would be napping up there, but judging by the sound of talking and canned laughter, there is another living room of some sort in the back of the house.

The interior of the house is a little cluttered—there are stacks of newspapers and magazines lying around, a few empty wine glasses on the tables, and a thick layer of dust over most everything. The disarray inside surprises me given how buttoned-up the exterior is.

"Guess it's the maid's week off," I whisper to Astra.

"Don't judge. I've seen your place."

"Shut up," I reply with a grin.

Mrs. Malvern steps back into the room with her husband shuffling behind her. He's got dark hair that's curly but thinning on top, dark eyes, and a stocky build. He's wearing a T-shirt that looks pretty stretched out, a pair of striped pajama bottoms, and black house slippers. He looks like a man just roused from sleep. Astra and I stand up as they enter and wait for them to sit down on the love seat across from us before we take our seats again.

"Good afternoon, Mr. Malvern," I start. "I'm Agent Wilder; this is Agent Russo."

"It's about time somebody took this seriously," he grumbles. "The Kellers still haven't come back. I'm really worried about them."

"We understand, sir. We just got the case ourselves, and I can assure you that we're going to do everything we can to figure this out," I tell him.

"Peter worries," Mrs. Malvern says. "I'm sure the Kellers are just out of town. They're young and still full of life. They're always on the go."

"They're nearing forty now, Shelly. Forty-year-old parents with two small kids who are still in school don't just up and go out of town," he snaps.

They snipe at each other like a couple who've been together a long time. But I hope that when I get to be forty, kids or not, I'm not the kind of person who doesn't do spontaneous things like go out of town. I can't imagine a life where all I do is come home, flop on the couch, and watch reality TV. If that's what my life is like when I turn forty, I hope somebody has the decency to put me out of my misery.

"All right, so what makes you think there's foul play, Mr. Malvern?" Astra asks.

"Their newspapers are stacking up. Mail too!," he replies. "And Brad would've told me if they were going out of town. He'd have asked me to keep an eye on his place."

Sherry shakes her head. "They've gone out of town without telling us before. I've tried to tell this one there's no foul play, but he won't listen. They're a young couple in love. They more than likely just went for a romantic weekend away."

"With two small kids in tow?" Pete cracks. "How romantic can that be?"

"They probably dropped the kids off with Bridget's sister. They only live over in Boulder," she counters.

"You're sure making a lot of assumptions," he says.

"So are you," she snaps back.

They're both making a lot of assumptions. The problem is that both of their theories could be right. But right now, I need to focus on getting them to talk to me—not each other.

"Mr. Malvern, do you know if the Kellers were having trouble with anybody?" I ask.

He shakes his head. "No, nobody in particular."

"You haven't noticed anybody unusual in the neighborhood lately?" Astra asks.

"No, I haven't noticed anybody," he replies.

"No neighborhood rivalries or anything like that?" I ask.

He shakes his head again. "No. Not that I'm aware of," he says. "We're a pretty tight-knit community here. Everybody gets along."

I notice a strange expression on his wife's face. Her lips are pursed, and she's looking down at her hands, her brow furrowed.

"Mrs. Malvern?" I ask. "Have you seen something?"

"Now that you mention it," she replies slowly. "I have seen a black van in the neighborhood I haven't seen before—a few times in the last couple of weeks."

"And you didn't mention this before?" Pete scolds her.

"I didn't think about it until now."

"That's great, Mrs. Malvern," Astra cuts in. "Did you happen to notice the people in the van? Did you see them?"

"No, I'm afraid I didn't see them," she sighs. "There are usually two people in the van, but I've never seen their faces. I'm sorry."

"Did you happen to get the license plate, Mrs. Malvern?"

She shakes her head again. "No, I'm sorry. I didn't think to get it."

"That's all right," I say. "Do you think you can get us the footage from your doorbell cam from the days you saw the van though? We might be able to pick something up that way."

"Great thinking!" she exclaims. "I'll make sure we get that to you."

"Perfect, thank you," I nod. "What about the Kellers themselves? Have they been acting strangely lately? Any change in personality that you've noticed?"

The Malverns exchange a look and some silent communication passes between them. I guess that, too, is something that develops between a couple that's been together a long time. He gives her a small shrug, and she turns to us.

"It wasn't anything big," she says. "But Bridget mentioned that she felt like she was being watched a couple of times when we were out. I didn't think much of it, to be honest. She's a pretty girl. I'm sure lots of men look at her."

"Did she say who she thought was watching her?" Astra asks.

Sherry shakes her head. "No, she didn't know. It was just something she mentioned in passing, but she didn't have any specifics."

"One last question," Astra chimes in. "Do you happen to know of any place they might go? Did they have a cabin or someplace they go to get away?"

"Well, they've got that place down in Hope," Mr. Malvern offers. "Bridget's parents left it to her when they died."

"Right. But do they have any other places that might be… off the grid?" Astra presses. "Any other apartments or condos they kept that they might not advertise?"

"No, I don't believe so," Mrs. Malvern replies.

"Secret, off-the-grid places? What do you think the Kellers are, a family of spies? Maybe they're in the mob?" Mr. Malvern says with a laugh.

"No, nothing like that," Astra says. "Just a place where the family might go when they want to get away for a weekend or something?"

He shakes his head again. "If they had a place like that, they never mentioned it to me."

"All right," I reply and glance at Astra to see if she has any other questions. She doesn't. "Thank you for your time, Mr. and Mrs. Malvern."

I get to my feet and pull a card out of my jacket pocket and hand it to Sherry.

"If you could email that doorbell footage to the email address on the card, I'd appreciate it," I tell her. "And if you think of anything else, please don't hesitate to give us a call."

"I will," she says.

"Please find them," Pete says. "They're good people. A good family."

"We'll do everything in our power to track them down," Astra tells them.

"Thank you for your time," I add.

We leave the Malverns, feeling no closer to finding their neighbors than before.

CHAPTER TEN

Mile High Design Group; Denver, CO

BEFORE HEADING BACK TO THE HOTEL, I WANTED TO MAKE one last stop. I wanted to see where Brad Keller works. We pull into a lot in a section of downtown Denver that's filled with boutique shops and local restaurants. The only big corporate entity with a presence in the area looks to be Starbucks. The area is clean and well-kept. All the buildings have fresh paint, the street is lined with trees that are neatly trimmed, and there isn't a speck of trash to be seen anywhere.

After parking and getting out of the car, we walk down the block to a building set between a vinyl record shop and a Thai-

Mexican fusion restaurant. I'm not convinced those two cuisines go together, but the aromas filling the air as we walk by make me want to give it a shot and see what it's like.

"I think we should grab some lunch at that place when we're done here," I offer.

"You must be reading my mind," Astra says.

The front of the building is frosted glass and dark brick. The only signage indicating what the building houses is the name of Keller's company on the two glass front doors. I hold the door open for Astra and we step into a dimly lit lobby with a floor made of black stone tile that has silver veins running through it. Four chairs line each side of the small room, and a chest-high desk stands across from us.

The woman behind the desk is young, probably a college student. Her long, extremely straight brown hair is parted perfectly down the middle, and she has sparkling green eyes and the flawless skin of youth.

"Good afternoon, welcome to the Mile High Design Group," she greets us. "How can I help you today?"

"Hi, we're here to see Brad Keller," I tell her.

"Oh, I'm sorry. Mr. Keller isn't in today," she replies. "Did you have an appointment?"

Astra and I badge her, and I shake my head. "No, we didn't have an appointment," I say. "I'm SSA Wilder, this is Special Agent Russo."

Her eyes widen and an expression of fear crosses her face. She licks her lips and nervously shifts on her seat as she eyes our credentials.

"Uh, is there a problem?" she asks.

"We're not entirely sure just yet," Astra tells her. "Can you tell me the last time Mr. Keller was in the office?"

"Oh. I guess it's been a little more than a week now," she replies. "But it's not unusual for him to be out of the office for a week at a time. He travels quite a lot."

"I see," I reply. "Well, can you tell us who runs the office in Mr. Keller's absence?"

"That would be Mr. Waters," she tells us. "He's the General Manager and one of the firm's main architects as well."

"Great. Is he in?" I ask.

"He is," she nods. "Let me see if he's available."

"Please."

She picks up the phone and taps a couple of buttons then turns away. She speaks in a low tone, doing her best to keep us from hearing what she's saying. After a minute, the woman turns back to us as she hangs up the phone.

"Mr. Waters will see you," she tells us. "Go through that door, and behind all the cubicles is a row of offices. His office is the second from the end. He's expecting you."

"Terrific. Thank you," I say.

Astra holds the door open for me, and we walk through a room that's got a dozen large cubicles, each of them equipped with a drafting table, a regular desk, and an oversized computer monitor. There are eight men and four women working in the cubicles, and each of them looks up as we pass by, curiosity painted on their faces.

We follow her directions and find our way to Waters's office. The door is open, and we see that he's on the phone; but he waves us in and points to the pair of chairs in front of his desk, so we walk in and take a seat. Waters's office is a testament to efficiency. There doesn't seem to be a thing in his office that doesn't serve some practical purpose—save for two shelves on a bookcase on the wall to our right. On those two shelves are pictures of what I assume are his family—a beautiful wife and three kids—and various awards.

Waters's diplomas from Carnegie Mellon and award plaques hang on the wall behind him. His desk is a large slab of some dark, polished wood set on four industrial steel legs. Like everything else, the top of his desk is clean and efficient. All that sits on it is his laptop, a phone, a cup of pens, and a few files, all neatly stacked and color-coded. Against the wall to our right is a high-tech drafting table. It's computerized and looks like he does his designs virtually rather than with old-fashioned pencil, paper, T-squares, and drafting tools.

"Listen, Tom, I'll need to call you back on this," he says into the phone. "I have to talk to a few people and see if it is even remotely viable."

He pauses and listens to Tom. Waters reminds me a lot of that actor, Andre Braugher. He's tall and lean with a crisp, deep voice and a very precise, formal way of speaking. His black hair is cropped extremely close and is flecked with gray, his skin is dark, and his dark eyes have an intensity about them. He looks like a man who doesn't miss much. Waters is wearing a white shirt that's been starched to within an inch of its life with an electric blue tie beneath that stiff, white collar, and a pair of red suspenders. A charcoal gray jacket that matches his slacks hangs on the back of his chair, completing his smart ensemble.

"Yes, I will reach out to you soon, Tom," Waters insists. "And don't worry. We will figure this out one way or another. You have my word. All right. Thank you."

Waters hangs up the phone then leans forward, folding his hands on top of his desk. He gives us a small smile.

"Apologies," he says. "Clients can be a little demanding at times."

"No need to apologize," I tell him. "You're running a busy and successful company. We appreciate you taking a little time for us."

"So, Madison says you are with the FBI?"

"That's right," I say. "Agents Wilder and Russo."

"What can I do for you, agents?"

"We're looking for Mr. Keller," I tell him.

"Oh my. Has he done something wrong?" Waters asks.

"No, nothing like that," Astra says. "He was reported as a missing person, so we're following up to see if we can find him and put this to rest."

Waters frowns. "Come to think of it… I don't think I've seen him in a week or so," he says. "But it's not unusual for Brad to be out of the office. He comes and goes. He is usually out at a job site or attending conferences. He has big plans for aggressive expansion and making us more of a national brand."

"And he leaves the running of the company to you?" I ask.

Waters nods. "He does. I wear a lot of hats around here, but the arrangement works well for both of us. I enjoy what I do. I also enjoy having a hand in shaping the future of the company. Plus, the pay and benefits are terrific."

I point to Waters's diploma. "Where did Mr. Keller go to school?"

"Oh, Brad went to Notre Dame. It has one of the leading architectural programs in the country. It's a step above even Carnegie Mellon. A small step," he tells us with a smile. "Don't tell Brad I said that though. I would never hear the end of it."

"So, Mr. Keller didn't tell you he was going to be out of town this week?" Astra asks.

Waters shakes his head. "No, I am afraid he did not."

"Does he do that often?" I ask. "Take off without any notice?"

A thoughtful expression crosses Waters's face. "It is unusual, but hardly unprecedented. This would not be the first time Brad disappeared only to reappear a couple of weeks later. When that has happened in the past, it has usually been because he took his family on a surprise trip. I would imagine he'll stroll back in next week sometime with tales of their trip to St. Kitts or the like. The last time he vanished for a couple of weeks, he'd whisked his family away to Paris just so he could take his kids to Disneyland." He gazes off and gives a slight smile as if reliving the memory. "I asked him what was wrong with the domestic parks, and he just said they had already been to those and wanted a new experience."

I can't say what it is, but something is striking me funny about all of this. Not that I think Waters is lying. I believe the man. I believe every word he just told us is true—and that he believes every word he just said too. But there's something about Keller that's hitting me funny. As I said, I don't know what it is exactly, but something doesn't smell right to me. Maybe it's a quirk in the man's personality that lets him take off whenever the urge strikes him. Or maybe he's just rich and eccentric. Something about all of this just doesn't pass the smell test with me though. Something's off.

I glance at Astra and see that her brow is furrowed, too, telling me she's on the same page as me. Or is at least in the same chapter that I am.

"Mr. Waters, other than the house in Hope and the one here in Denver, do you know if the Kellers had any other properties they might go to if they wanted to lay low?" Astra asks.

He frowns as he considers the question but then shakes his head. "No, not that I know of. As far as I know, those are their only two properties. The one in Hope is going to waste though. I have tried to get him to rent that out or make it an Airbnb or something. Seems like a missed investment opportunity, if you ask me."

"Mr. Waters, I wonder if you'd let us take a look at Mr. Keller's office?" I ask.

"Oh, well, I'm not sure," he replies, a look of worry crossing his face. "Do you need a warrant for that?"

Technically, yes, we do need a warrant. But not if we're given permission by the general manager of the company.

"We're not investigating Mr. Keller, sir. We're investigating the possibility that he is the victim of a crime. There is a possibility he's been abducted," I reassure him. "We just want to see if there's anything in there that might point us to the truth of the matter. He may be in St. Kitts, as you said. But we stopped by the home, and what we found leads us to believe there is a chance the family was taken. And if that's the case, we want to find them. Chances are there's nothing in his office that will help us. But it's up to us to turn over every stone and do our due diligence. I'm sure you understand that."

Waters nods. "Of course. Yes, of course," he says, his expression stricken. "And if Brad and his family were taken, of course, I want to help. I just cannot believe somebody would have ever harmed the Kellers. They're good people."

"So, you're not aware of any specific threats made against him?" Astra asks. "No problems he's had with anybody recently? We were told Mrs. Keller felt like she was being watched, and there was an unusual vehicle in their neighborhood. You haven't heard anything about this, have you, Mr. Waters?"

"No, nothing like that. At least, Brad never mentioned problems with anybody. Nor did he mention that Bridget felt like she was being watched. Dear God."

"We don't know anything for certain yet, Mr. Waters. But it's vital we cover all the bases, and as I said, turn over every stone."

"Yes, yes, of course," he nods. "Brad's office is upstairs."

"Upstairs?"

He nods. "Yes, we both keep offices up there. I like having one down here on the ground floor with our team, though, so I keep this one as well," he explains. "But Brad prefers keeping his office upstairs. The stairway is at the end of the row here. Please, take your time, and if something has happened to the family, I beg you to find them. They are good people, agents."

"We're doing everything we can, Mr. Waters," I say. "And thank you."

Astra and I get to our feet and turn to go. Waters looks ashen and genuinely heartsick to have learned that something may have happened to his friend and boss. If something did happen to Brad Keller and his family—and I'm starting to think that it did—I'm fairly confident in saying that Daniel Waters didn't have anything to do with it. Not only did I get the feeling of genuine affection for Brad Keller, but I also just don't think Waters is that good of an actor.

We quietly make our way to the staircase, then ascend to the second floor and find ourselves in one long hallway that bisects the floor. There are two doors on the right—one that leads to a supply closet and the second opening into Waters's upstairs office. On our left is the door that leads into Mr. Keller's office, so we let ourselves in.

"Nice place," Astra comments.

The office is done in a light oak that's polished to a high glossy shine. Three large plate glass windows are set into the wall behind Keller's desk, which looks a lot like Mr. Waters's. The office is big enough to have a sitting area complete with a sofa and two plush wingbacks set across an oval-shaped coffee table at the far end of the room. A large area rug sits beneath the furniture, and there is a small counter that holds a coffee maker and a toaster oven. An apartment-sized refrigerator is set into the counter below it. Near the sitting area is a sideboard that holds an array of crystal bottles that hold different liquors and matching glasses.

To the right of the desk is Mr. Keller's drafting table. Like Waters's, it's high-tech and modern. It's powered down, though, so I can't see what he's working on. A set of three bookshelves stand against the wall to our left and hold an array of books but quite a few more personal knick-knacks than Waters has in his office. There are pictures of his family in silver frames and some personal mementos.

We take a couple of minutes and poke around the office. We aren't looking for anything in particular, we're just hoping we stumble across something that will give us a clue. Unfortunately, my first sweep of the place reveals nothing. I keep coming back to the bookshelves, though, and find myself looking at the photos in the frames. After that, my eyes are drawn to the pictures on the walls—they're all artistic black and white photos of buildings in various states of construction in and around Denver. I assume they're projects Keller was involved in.

After a few minutes of looking at all the photos and studying his mementos, I realize what it is that's bothering me.

"Keller doesn't have his diploma hanging up, nor does he have any awards on his shelves," I say.

Astra joins me in front of the bookcases and shrugs. "Not everybody feels the need to have a vanity wall."

"But if he meets clients in here—and judging by the layout and amenities, I have to believe he does—he would want them to see that he comes from a prestigious program and has accolades for his work by the bushel. It would make a prospective client feel better about putting their money into his hands."

"Maybe. Or maybe he prefers to let his work speak for itself," she offers. "It's like the rich people who go out of their way to downplay displays of their wealth. They let their reputation speak for themselves."

"It's possible. But think about all the executives and business professionals you and I have dealt with," I say. "How many of them didn't have a vanity wall? How many of them downplayed their successes and achievements?"

Astra takes a moment in quiet thought. "Yeah, you're not wrong," she says. "But there are always exceptions to the rules. Maybe Keller is one."

"It's very possible. But just from a business psychology standpoint, displays of achievement and success trigger an almost subconscious sense of reassurance and belief in clients," I press. "When they see a business executive that's highly decorated, it subconsciously makes them feel more at ease. It makes them believe their reputation is earned. Displaying awards and accolades has a very sound psychological basis. It's one reason you see these guys have massive vanity walls—it's psychological reassurance for their clients but also for themselves."

Astra thinks about it for a couple of seconds, her lips pursed and her brow furrowed. I can see she's trying to follow my train of thought, but her expression tells me she can't quite get there. Not yet. The truth is, I'm not there yet either. I'm not sure what it means—if anything. But the absence of his awards and diplomas just stands out to me. It's then I feel that nagging in the back of my mind again and know that my brain is already trying to work out the knots that will allow me to see the bigger picture.

"All right, so, what does it mean?" Astra asks.

"I'm not sure yet," I admit. "But it's an anomaly that's bothering me. And after listening to Waters, I'm convinced there's more to Mr. Keller than meets the eye. I have nothing tangible to support my thoughts, but something about Keller and this whole situation is just—off."

Astra nods. "The same thought crossed my mind, but I thought it was simply paranoia or wanting to see something that wasn't there, so I brushed it aside," she tells me. "But yeah, I got the feeling there was something more there. I don't get the feeling that Waters is trying to cover anything up, but there was just something in his story that was pinging my BS meter. Hard."

"That makes two of us."

"So, what now?"

I shake my head as I look around the office again. It might just be a case of wanting a thing so bad I trick myself into believing it, but I just have a feeling there's something here to be found. What and where it is, I can't say. But that whisper of intuition in my ear is telling me I need to look harder because there's something here.

"Let's sweep the office again," I state. "Look close. Look hard. I just feel like we're missing something in here."

"Okay, what am I looking for?"

I frown. "Not sure. But look for hidden nooks, things that don't seem like they belong. Anything that stands out."

Astra looks skeptical but she wanders off to the other side of the office and starts with the sideboard. Because my mind kept bringing me back to the bookcases, I start with those. I look behind all the books and picture frames, picking things up and turning them over, searching for a key, a code—something—that will put me on the right track. I spend at least twenty minutes searching the shelves but come up empty.

Frustrated, I'm just about to give up and search elsewhere when my eyes fall on something in the base of the bookcase. The shelves are built on what looks like a solid base of hardwood that stands about a foot high and is intricately carved and decorative. It's a beautiful piece that I honestly wouldn't mind having in my home. It takes me a minute to understand what it is that drew my attention in the first place.

"You're kidding me," I mutter to myself.

"You find something?" Astra calls.

"Maybe."

I squat down and run my hands over the surface of the wooden base and feel the electric thrill of discovery rush through me. Dropping to my knees, I lean forward and stare at the wooden base even closer. A smile stretches my lips when I see what the subconscious part of my brain has been trying to show me.

"What is it?" Astra asks.

I slide my hand over the wood and get confirmation of my theory. I can feel the outline—the separation of the wood. There's a compartment built into the base of the bookcases that's so subtle, anybody would miss it at a glance. You need to be searching for it to know it's there. But knowing it's there and accessing it are two different things. I don't see any obvious latches. There are no keyholes. There's no obvious way to open it.

Gnawing on my bottom lip, I think about it for a moment, then lay my palm flat against the panel and press down. I feel a flush of triumph when there's a slight give in the wood, and when I pull my hand away, there's a click, and the panel springs up revealing the hollow. Astra draws in a sharp breath when I reach in and start pulling everything out of the secret compartment. I take a moment to examine the contents before I lay it all out on the base. I stand up, and we both look at the contents I pulled out of the hollow for a moment before I turn to her with a grin on my face.

"Tell me, what does an architect need with four passports in other names, a hundred grand in cash, and a Sig Sauer nine-millimeter?"

CHAPTER ELEVEN

Rocky Mountain Inn & Suites Conference Room; Denver, CO

"WHAT DID YOU GUYS FIND DOWN IN HOPE?" I ASK.

"Nothing," Lucas tells us. "House was empty. They have a caretaker who comes in once a month to keep things fresh, but they haven't been to the house in Hope for a while."

Lucas's tone is slightly miffed. It's as if he's subliminally saying, "I told you so," but I can tell he's trying to adopt a more neutral, less aggressive tone with me. He's trying to learn to be a good teammate, which I appreciate. That's progress.

"It's been at least a year," Mo adds. "Mrs. Flood—she's the caretaker—does the upkeep. They'll call her when they're coming down so she can give it a quick sprucing, but she says she hasn't heard from them in a year or so. Checks arrive every month like clockwork though."

"All right, so they don't get to Hope often," I muse. "Not surprising. If anybody was surveilling them, they'd know about that property. Makes sense they wouldn't go there. They'd have someplace else."

"Are we sure they went to ground somewhere?" Mo asks. "Has something happened to change our minds about them taking a little unscheduled family vacay?"

Astra and I exchange a glance, and I open the box we took from Keller's firm. For obvious reasons, we didn't share what we were taking with Mr. Waters. He was disturbed enough by the fact that we were hauling a box of evidence out of the firm as it was.

"Nothing concrete," I say. "But we did find some things that opened up a whole new avenue of investigation."

"Not to mention about ten thousand new and interesting questions," Astra adds.

"Oh, show and tell time," Mo chirps. "Let's see what you brought in."

With a small laugh, I pull everything we found in Keller's secret compartment out of the box and lay it on the table in our makeshift command post. Astra and I bagged everything as evidence before we left his architectural firm just to be safe. Evidence of what, I'm not sure yet. But the fact that Keller has four different identities, I think, is more than a little intriguing.

"Whoa," Mo gasps. "Didn't see that coming. Four passports?"

She picks up the first bag with the Drake Weathers passport in it and examines it closely, turning it over and looking at it from every angle. I watch as she scrutinizes the others. Coming from white-collar crimes, I know Mo has some experience with forgeries, so her input will be invaluable.

"This is high-quality work," she says. "Whoever made these passports knew what they were doing. Had the right equipment and know-how too."

"Any possible way to track down the forger based on those passports?" Astra asks.

She shakes her head. "Unfortunately, no. A lot of newbie forgers like to leave a signature so they can claim ownership of the work. It's usually subtle, but anybody worth their salt can pick it out. It's a total rookie move," she says. "The experienced forgers don't need to leave their mark because people in the know already know who they are. And based on what I'm seeing here, a very experienced forger made these. I mean, these are flawless."

"Well, that sucks," Astra groans. "Why can't life ever be simple for us?"

"The gods conspire to make sure we earn our paychecks," Mo says with a chuckle.

Lucas had quietly picked up the evidence bags and is examining the passports as well, perhaps hoping to pick up a flaw that Mo had overlooked. He's desperate to prove himself to me, so I take him off the bench. But his disappointed frown tells me he's not finding anything either.

"I don't know why Keller has the passports, the cash, and the gun," I say. "But I think this tells us he's not just an architect."

"If he's an architect at all," Astra points out.

"So, what are we thinking?" Lucas asks as he sets the last passport down. "Is Keller into drugs? Running guns? Maybe human trafficking? It would make sense for him to have a cache of money and documents if he ever needed to bolt. I saw it a lot in counterterrorism."

"All possibilities, but right now, we just don't know. We are going to have to explore every possibility though," I say. "I think the only thing we can safely say at this point is that Brad Keller is not who we thought he was. Who and what he is, we don't know yet."

"All right, so what's our next move?" Mo asks.

"Can you get Rick and Nina up on screen for me?

"On it."

She sits down in front of her computer and starts tapping keys. A moment later, the screen at the head of the table flashes to life and gives us a view of Rick and Nina.

"Boss, how goes it out yonder?" Rick asks.

"The plot is thickening," I tell him.

"Oh, so the family didn't just take off for Disney World after all?"

"Unclear at this point—we need more information."

"Then you've come to the right place. Between me and Nina, there's no scrap of information we can't find," Rick says. "I mean, I can say the same if I were on my own, but it's nice having somebody to split the labor with."

Nina laughs. "He'd be lost without me."

"Be prepared, he's probably going to be lost with you," Astra says.

Nina seems to be fitting right in with our motley crew. Now that she's gotten her feet wet, she seems like she has the right sort of personality and temperament I want in my team. Lucas is sitting in his chair stiff and silent, as big of a question mark now as he ever was. But he does seem to be making an effort. He's maybe not trying to fit in necessarily, but I can see that he's trying to be a good agent and member of the team. I honestly don't know if he's going to fit. Not unless he figures out how to loosen up a bit.

"All right, what is it you need?" Rick says.

"We need you guys to do a full workup on Brad and Bridget," I say. "I want socials, financials, phone records—I want everything you can dig up on them. No piece of information is too small or insignificant at this point. Cast the widest net possible. I want you guys deeper into these two than their proctologist."

"There's a pleasant image," Astra groans, drawing a laugh from Mo.

I catch Lucas's eye and can tell he doesn't approve of the banter. The man desperately needs to loosen up. I just don't know if he has the ability. It makes me understand why he was stuck as an analyst with counterterrorism for so long. He was able to work on his own and didn't have to worry about interpersonal dynamics. And so far, he just doesn't seem to have the temperament for a team setting.

"Also, I need you to dig up whatever you can on four more names," I say and motion to Astra, who picks up the bags with the forged passports.

"Drake Weathers, Thomas Cooper, Charlie Mullins, and August North," Astra says.

On the screen, Rick frowns. "Boss, we may have a problem."

"What is it?"

"Well…"

His voice trails off, and he exchanges a look with Nina. Whatever it is he has to say, Rick knows I'm not going to be thrilled with it.

"Just spit it out," I say.

"We… uh… well, Section Chief Ayad was in here yesterday, and he went over the… rules," Rick tells me. "He wanted to make sure we knew what we could and couldn't do. Said there were lines we couldn't cross, or we could face prosecution ourselves."

I give Astra a look. She smirks and looks away, not needing me to say I told her so about Ayad's interference, but I did tell her so. What I don't know or understand is why Ayad would intimidate my analysts and put the fear of prosecution into them for simply doing their jobs. What is the purpose of him mucking up my investigation? What does he get out of it? Is he trying to make me look bad? Is he trying to tarnish my reputation by undermining me? Is he trying to make me look ineffective?

On the screen, Nina clears her throat and looks at me. "Ayad wants to make sure we understand that we need warrants to access personal information like financial and phone records," she says. "He told us to remind you of that and said if you have a problem with it, you can contact him."

"I'm sorry, boss," Rick says.

"That's all right. It's not your fault," I reassure him. "I don't want to jam you guys up."

I blow out a frustrated breath and start to pace as I work the problem over in my mind. We need that information, but we don't have nearly enough for a warrant. No judge would ever sign off on one. I mean, technically speaking, Ayad's not wrong to demand we have a warrant for the sort of deep information dives we do. But it's one of those legal niceties we've always looked the other way about.

"Damn Boy Scouts," I grumble.

"Chief Ayad is simply doing things by the book, SSA Wilder," Lucas reminds me. "The Fourth Amendment protects citizens against illegal search and—"

"Yes, thank you for the lesson in Constitutional law, Agent Okamura," I cut him off.

He falls silent and looks away as I start to pace again. Ayad is cramping my style. Before despair can take over though, the solution pops into my mind. I don't want to say anything in front of Lucas, though, so I bite my tongue then turn back to the camera mounted on top of the monitor.

"All right, dig up what you can that's in the public domain," I tell them. "Socials—hell, I don't know. Anything you can find, I want it. Also, work up the names Astra gave you as well. I doubt it'll be much since they're forged passports, but maybe we'll get lucky."

"We're on it," Rick says. "We'll find whatever we can."

Before I sign off, a thought occurs to me. "Oh, hey, this might be a wild goose chase—"

"We specialize in wild goose chases," Nina replies.

"That's a good thing because this one might be a doozy."

"Lay it on us," Rick says.

"I need you to get some school records from Notre Dame," I say. "I want to know about Brad Keller's time there. Find whatever you can."

"Don't we need a warrant for school records?" Lucas asks.

"Not if Rick can charm the registrar into giving them up," I say.

"I'll do it," Nina says. "Rick runs at a charm deficit most of the time."

"I like her," Astra says with a laugh. "She's a smart cookie, that one."

"Well, that wasn't very nice. You wound me so, madame," Rick says.

"Not nice but not untrue," Nina fires back. "I'll get them for you, boss."

"Great, thanks, guys," I smile. "Be in touch as soon as you can. I feel like we're up against it here."

"You got it," Nina says. "We'll talk soon."

The screen goes dark, and Astra looks at me. I can tell she knows what I'm going to do, but she's playing it cool.

"What should we do?" Lucas asks.

"Go get something to eat and get some rest," I reply. "I need to think about our next steps. Hopefully, Rick and Nina come back with something useful for us. If you guys need me, I'll be in my room."

After a hot shower and some room service, I stand at the window of my room looking out at the darkness beyond the glass contemplating my next move. If I do what I'm thinking about doing, it's going to put me on a collision course with Ayad since I'll be sidestepping him and gathering intel without a warrant. He's going to have questions I won't want to give him the answers to. But he's handcuffing me with his Boy Scout attitude.

If I don't do this, though, we're not going to be able to get a handle on what's going on down here. We're not going to know who Brad Keller is or what he's up to. And we're never going to figure out if he's been taken—and if he has been taken, by whom—or if he's simply taken his family and consciously disappeared. That, of course, would lead to a host of other questions we'd have no way of answering. But that's a bridge to cross when we come to it. At the moment, there's only one question I need to answer for myself—defy Ayad or not.

"Screw it," I mutter.

I grab my cellphone and punch in the number then press the phone to my ear. It rings twice before he answers the call.

"Blake Wilder, as I live and breathe," he greets me.

"Hey, Brody. How are you?"

"Humbled. It's not often I receive a phone call from a superstar G-man."

"G-woman, thank you very much."

"Oh, apologies for being an insensitive sexist pig," he says.

"That's all right. I really should know better than to expect otherwise of you."

"There's that trademark wit I love so much."

We share a laugh. I've always liked Brody, and it's good to hear his voice. The job keeps me jumping, and I don't get to see the boys as often as I'd like. It's something I'd like to change because they're both fun to hang out with.

"How's Marcy?"

"Better and better every day, thanks for asking."

"Going to make an honest woman of her anytime soon?"

"Not if I can help it."

"So much for not being an insensitive, sexist pig."

He chuckles. "We don't need a piece of paper to declare our love for one another."

"You just don't want to give her half your stuff when she eventually figures out that she's too good for you," I fire back.

"That too," he chirps. "So, what can I do for you, Blake? I assume you need my help with something since you never call unless you do."

"I know. I'm awful," I say, feeling a stab of guilt. "I'm sorry, Brody."

"I'm giving you a hard time. I know you're a busy woman," he says. "I'm always happy to help you with anything. You know that."

"I appreciate that, Brody. More than you know."

"So, tell Uncle Brody what he can help you with, Blake."

"Yeah, the whole Uncle Brody thing is kind of creepy, so like, don't ever say that to me again," I tell him with a laugh.

"Fair enough," he says lightly. "So, tell me what's going on."

I tell him what's going on out here, what's happening back in Seattle with Ayad and Stone, and what I need from him. And when I'm finished with my story, he whistles low.

"Wow. You have a lot going on and a lot on your plate," he says.

"You can say that again."

"Wow. You have a lot going on and a lot on your plate."

There's a pause on the line then I burst out laughing and slap my forehead. "Yeah, I walked right into that one."

"Yes, you did. I'm shocked by that."

"So, do you think you can work your magic for me?"

"Of course, I can," he says. "But are you willing to take the heat when this guy Ayad is reading you the riot act for it?"

"I am. It's the only way we're going to figure out what's going on down here."

"Good enough for me," he shrugs. "I'll start digging and touch base with you as soon as I have something for you."

"I appreciate you, Brody."

"Always happy to help."

"Talk to you soon."

"Yes ma'am, you will."

I disconnect the call and drop my phone onto the table next to the window. I stare out into the dark. This is probably going to open up a big, fat can of worms. But if it helps us solve this case and find Keller and his family, the heat I'm going to take from Ayad will be well worth it.

It's probably going to be a different story if it doesn't help us solve the case and Ayad finds out what I've done.

CHAPTER TWELVE

Rocky Mountain Inn & Suites, Room 312; Denver, CO

"WELL, THAT WAS FAST," I SAY. "DID YOU PULL AN all-nighter?"

"Nah. Only half the night," Brody replies.

"I didn't mean for you to burn the midnight oil on my behalf."

"I was up anyway," he says. "I'm never able to sleep when Marcy's out chasing down a lead for a story. I worry."

"Marcy is a very capable woman," I remind him. "But that's sweet. I didn't know you had that in you."

He laughs. "Ouch. Be nice."

"Hey, I gotta be me."

Holding the phone to my ear with one hand, I use my other to keep running the brush through my hair. Brody caught me just as I was getting out of the shower.

"Did Marcy get her story?" I ask.

"She did. She came home wired and spent the rest of the night working on her piece," he says. "That girl has more energy than the damn Energizer bunny."

"The girl knows how to hustle. She's never not working," I say. "I like that about her."

"I wish she'd take a break," he replies. "She's got such a strong work ethic she makes the rest of us look bad."

"Or maybe you just really are that bad."

"Yeah, that's a possibility," he agrees with a laugh. "Anyway, I dug into your boy last night. His life story was about as scintillating as reading the tax code."

"That bad, huh?"

"Worse," he replies. "The man is the living definition of a straight arrow. He's a self-made man. Graduated from Notre Dame cum laude with a degree in architecture, then built his firm from the ground up and turned it into a powerhouse. He's charitable, is president of his kids' PTA, philanthropic, and pays his taxes on time every year. There isn't a single thing I can figure out from this guy's personal records, and he is the squeakiest clean person I think I've ever seen. Not a blemish anywhere to be seen. Wouldn't be surprised if this guy has perfect skin, perfect teeth, and the perfect body fat to muscle ratio."

I set my brush down and lean back in the chair, absorbing everything Brody just said. There's a long pause on the line, and in that silence, I realize that Brody is holding back on me. There's a punchline to this, and he's stringing it out like a master storyteller.

"What is it you're not saying?" I ask.

"You are a keen observer, Supervisory Special Agent Wilder," he says. "You're supremely intuitive. It's impressive."

I laugh. "That's why I make the big bucks," I say. "So, lay it out for me."

"Well, this guy just struck me as too clean, you know?" he asks. "I mean, who is as perfect as this guy seems on paper?"

"So, I'm guessing you went digging to see what isn't on paper."

"Again, your intuitiveness is amazing. Yes, that is correct," he replies. "The first question I had was, how in the hell did he get the money to start his firm after he graduated? He came from a single-parent home, and his mother wasn't exactly flush."

"So? How'd he get the money?"

"Unclear at this point. I have no way to track that," he says. "But he came into enough to start a sweet little shop in the Highlands neighborhood."

"Yeah, we were there. Swanky joint," I tell him. "Ultra-modern place. Took some money to put that place together."

"It all went up right after he graduated from Notre Dame," he says. "Before he hit the big time."

"So, where did he get the cash to set up shop?"

"Excellent question," he says. "But I dug a little deeper and started poking around the architectural program at Notre Dame. On paper, it all looks legit."

"There's that phrase again—on paper."

He laughs softly. "There's that intuitiveness again," he says. "Because I am such a talented sleuth, I found a picture of the architectural program's participants the year he graduated. Keller wasn't in it."

I frown. "Maybe he was absent the day they shot the photo."

"That's what I thought too. That led me to more photos from the School of Architecture's program. They've got a website and their archives go back years and years," he tells me. "Keller isn't in any of their class photos. He's not in any of the candid shots from the program—nothing. Not a single one. He's nowhere to be seen. Keller has no footprint other than what's on the official papers. What are the odds that he spends four years in the program and he's not even in the background of any photo? Not one?"

It strains credulity to think that Keller isn't in any single photo from the program. But that's not conclusive. Though it seems unlikely, it's entirely possible that somehow, Keller managed to avoid the camera during his time in the program. It does raise more questions though. Plenty more.

"Here's something else for you to chew on," he says. "Keller has a sterling reputation as a leading and innovative architect, right? His firm is one of the most prestigious in all of Colorado?"

"Yeah, that's right."

"Then why is Keller not credited with any designs?"

It takes my brain a second to process what he just said. "What?"

"I've searched the records, and there is not one building or home in Denver that Keller is credited with designing," he explains. "The firm's reputation was built on the designs of some guy named Waters. Daniel Waters."

"Yeah, we spoke with him," I say. "He's the firm's general manager and lead architect."

"He's also the reason the firm has the reputation it does," he says. "As near as I can tell, the only thing Keller has to do with his firm's success is that he owns the building it's housed in. He's got a talented team around him that's doing all the heavy lifting."

I sit back in my chair feeling like I've just taken a series of body blows. My head is spinning, and I feel breathless. I don't know what to make of anything Brody's telling me. Brad Keller is a construction. A façade. The man is a cardboard cutout. But I can't see who or what is lurking behind that cutout. Not yet. I can't help but feel that we're on the verge of something big though. Something really big. But right now, it's all just a bunch of disparate puzzle pieces that form one larger picture. A picture that I can't make out.

"This makes absolutely no sense," I mutter.

"I think it will when I finish telling you what I found," he says. "I wanted to finish it all off with a big flourish."

"Of course, you did," I reply. "Brody Singer, ever the showman."

"You know it," he says. "So, allow me to put a big, red bow on this for you."

"Please do."

"Brad Keller is a wholesome family man who probably sits around the dinner table with his wife, eating some bland spaghetti dinner while talking about their day. After that, they probably watch a few sitcoms, the news, then go to bed at a reasonable hour," he says. "He leads a productive, but uneventful and unexciting life."

"This is quite the setup. You've been thinking about this one, haven't you?"

"Indeed, I have," he confirms. "But then I ran the four names you gave me—the ones from the forged passports—and that painted a much different picture."

"This is getting intriguing."

"Indeed, it is," he replies. "All four of those identities have paper trails. They've got credit histories, bank accounts—the works. And at first glance, they're all solid. But if you dig deep enough, you see those histories only go back fifteen years—right around the time Keller graduated and started his firm. Before that, there's nothing on any of the four. These identities would pass a cursory check. It would take some extreme scrutiny to see these IDs for what they are—cover identities."

A picture is starting to form in my mind. It's still fuzzy and unclear, but it's starting to come together. I just don't know if the picture I'm starting to see is the right one. I don't feel like I have enough information to know exactly which way this case is going to break. Is Keller a victim, or is he something else? Something worse?

"And get this—all four of those identities have traveled extensively to the Middle East," Brody continues. "Syria, Jordan, Saudi Arabia, Iraq, Yemen, Oman—those four names have been everywhere over there."

It feels like a bowling ball just dropped into my gut. I run a hand through my hair and take a moment to process it all. And it's a lot to take in. I don't want to jump to conclusions or make any assumptions, but this is starting to look bad. The picture it's forming about Brad Keller is not flattering. The scales are starting to tilt away from him being a victim and toward being something worse. The only thing that's clear in this murky soup is that Brad Keller is not who we all thought he was.

"Kind of breathtaking, isn't it?" Brody asks.

"I don't even know where to start with all this. This is a lot," I say. "Breathtaking is certainly one word for it. This information changes everything."

"Well, to be fair, the little stash of passports you found is what changed everything," he replies. "I just added some important context."

"You are a genius, Brody. I can't thank you enough for digging up this treasure trove," I tell him. "I need to go brief my team, but I owe you one."

"I think it's more than one at this point, but I'll let it slide."

I laugh. "You know I'm good for it," I reply. "Thank you, Brody. Seriously."

"Anytime, Blake. And call me if you need anything else. My phone is always on for you," he says. "Now go do some good."

"I'll do that. Thanks again, Brody."

I disconnect the call and finish getting ready. I'm heading for the door when I pause and take a moment to think about my next steps. Knowing I need to tread lightly, I pull out my phone and key in a text, reading it over once and giving myself a chance to take a different route.

I hit send.

CHAPTER THIRTEEN

Javaland; Denver, CO

"WHY ARE WE MEETING HERE AND NOT IN THE conference room?" Astra asks.

We're sitting at a table in the corner of the small coffee house half a block away from the hotel. The interior is bright and cheery, looking more like an ice cream parlor than a coffee house to me. But the air is thick with the aroma of coffee and freshly baked pastries—both of which I need right now. Nothing like caffeine and sugar to kick off your morning right.

"And where's Lucas?" Mo adds.

I purse my lips and look away. I have a feeling Astra and Mo aren't going to like what I did, but I have no desire to deal with Lucas and his attitude right now. Things are in motion, and I want to build on that momentum.

"I have him working on a few things back in the conference room," I tell them.

Astra and Mo exchange a glance then turn to me. I can see the disapproval on their faces. They know exactly what I did to Lucas.

"Look, I don't want to have to answer questions about where I got the information I'm about to share," I admit. "There are a lot of moving parts right now and we don't have the time to play by the rules Ayad wants us to play by."

"But what does that have to do with Lucas?" Mo asks.

"Because I'm not entirely convinced that he's not Ayad's eyes and ears inside our unit," I tell her. "And until I am, I don't intend to give him anything he can run back to Ayad with."

"You could have asked me."

We turn as one to find Lucas standing there with a cup in hand, his jaw clenched tight. There's a crowd in the coffee house with clusters of people all around us, so I never even saw him come in. How he spotted us, I have no clue. It makes me think he followed me out of the hotel over here to Javaland—a thought that makes me dislike him even more. I don't like being spied on by members of my own team.

"I thought I gave you some tasks to complete, Agent Okamura."

"Yes, you did leave me with some meaningless busywork," he says. "I wanted to get some coffee before I started, and lo and behold, here you are. Having a meeting. Without me."

"We're getting some coffee," I say.

"No, you're freezing me out. I'm not a moron, SSA Wilder," he growls. "You've been freezing me out since I got here, and I'm here to tell you that I do not appreciate it. Like it or not, I am part of your unit, and as such, I deserve to be included in decisions."

"Lucas, you question every decision I make," I reply. "As I told you before, until you learn to follow orders, I will keep your training wheels on."

"With all due respect—"

"Astra, Mo," I say, my voice low and tight. "Can we have the table for a moment?"

They get up, both with uneasy looks on their faces, the air around us is thick with tension. When they step off to the side of the coffee house, I gesture to a vacant chair.

"Sit down," I tell him.

He does, but the hard edge of anger still strains his face. We stare at each other silently for a long moment, the tension between us swelling.

"If you think I'm Chief Ayad's mole in your unit, you're sorely mistaken," he starts. "But is that why you've been freezing me out of this investigation? Because if it is, I have to tell you that you are making a huge mistake."

"And why is that? Going to run back and tell Ayad?"

"No, because I'm a damn good agent," he snaps. "And because I can help this unit."

He scoffs and shakes his head, disgust painted on his features. "Why are you so hung up on this? Why are you so certain Ayad has a mole in your unit? Why are you so obsessed with this idea? Do you really think you're that important?"

Lucas doesn't know what I've gone through nor the enemies I've made. He doesn't know the Thirteen planted a man in my life for the sole purpose of watching me, nor lengths they've gone to undermine me, nor the fact that they've tried to murder me on numerous occasions. If anybody's earned the right to be a little paranoid, it's me.

"It's not that I think I'm all that important. I just don't like the way this entire thing went down. It's nothing against you personally, but I don't know you, Lucas, and I don't trust people I don't know," I tell him bluntly. "And out here in the field, you have to trust the people at your back. Until I get a better sense of who you are and your capabilities, I will utilize you as I see fit. This is my team, and if you have a problem with how I'm running it, file a beef with OPR."

"Right. And brand myself a snitch," he rolls his eyes. "That's a great solution."

I shrug. "It is what it is."

He glares hard at me. "I don't know about anything that went down before I transferred in. I had nothing to do with any of that," he says. "I didn't even know Chief Ayad before the day he introduced me to your unit. I'd never even met the man."

"No? Because the two of you seem to share a notion that everything in the world—and in the job we do—is black and white," I say. "Neither of you seems to grasp the reality that there are shades of gray in everything. *Especially* in doing what we do."

He opens his mouth to reply, but no words come out. Instead, he sits back in his chair and taps the plastic lid on his coffee cup; he seems to be thinking about what I said for a change. I can still see the reticence in his eyes though. Lucas clears his throat and sits up again.

"It's not that I see the world in black and white. I see it in terms of right and wrong," he says. "I believe that doing what we do requires us to hold ourselves to a higher standard."

"Sometimes, to protect people, we have to bend the rules, Lucas. To be an effective field agent, you have to not only understand it, you have to be all right with it too."

He swallows hard and looks away. I can see him grappling with the idea of bending the rules; I can see it's not sitting well with him. He's as much of a Boy Scout as Ayad.

"Tell me something, Lucas. How does somebody with no field experience get transferred into a unit like mine as a first field assignment?"

"Because my old Section Chief thought I would be good in the field. But there were no slots open in counterterrorism," he tells me. "Chief Dunning is friends with ADIC Stone. He asked if there was an open slot in the field, and Stone assigned me to your unit. That's how I ended up with your team. Not because I'm some secret double agent."

I sit back in my seat and take a drink of my coffee as I process what he told me. It could all be crap, of course. It could be nothing more than a convenient cover story. But as I look him in the eye and listen to his words, I can't not hear the ring of sincerity in his voice. But I've been wrong before.

"You tell me you're sidelining me because you can't trust me," Lucas says. "But at the same time, you're not allowing me to prove that you can. You're putting me in a no-win situation, SSA Wilder."

As I look at Lucas and ponder his words, I realize he's right. I'm putting him in a no-win situation. That realization brings me to a fork in the road, and I have two choices: I can either keep marginalizing him, or I can trust him. At least, start *trying* to trust him anyway. But if I'm being honest with myself, I have to admit that I might be seeing Lucas through the lens of dislike I have for Ayad.

It's then I hear Astra, Rosie, and Pax's voices all echoing through my mind. Not everything in the world revolves around me, and I might be letting my paranoia taint the way I see everything. It certainly could be tainting the way I see Lucas—to some extent anyway. I mean, I don't know him, and I will never trust somebody I don't know. But he is part of my team, and I can't keep crucifying him for Ayad's sins... nor should I be assuming he's part of some conspiracy against me.

My mind is warring with my instinct inside my head. Every instinct inside of me is telling me to keep marginalizing him. It's telling me I don't know him, and he could still very well be a mole for Ayad. The rest of me is screaming that I'm not being fair, that I'm not giving him a chance, and that I'm letting my own fears and paranoias taint the way I see him. It's making me see him as a bad person when I know I don't know him well enough to be able to judge him.

I gnaw on my lower lip, then look over to where Astra and Mo are standing. They're looking back at me, curiosity etched into their features. Blowing out a long breath, I wave them back to the table. What I'm about to tell them all isn't such an egregiously horrible thing that I'll get fired or prosecuted—not that I'd ever do anything that bad. But I'm going to have to give Lucas the chance to prove himself. If he screws me, he screws me. At least then I'll know.

"So, have we kissed and made up?" Astra asks.

Lucas and I exchange a look. Kissed and made up might be a bridge too far. I'd characterize what we've come to as a truce. An uneasy truce, but a truce, nonetheless.

"We're going to move forward," I tell her. "As a team."

Lucas gives me a small nod and the tension that filled the air around us starts to dissipate. I think the tension will exist until we find some level of comfort with each other. But it's a start. It's time I step up and be a leader. And regarding Lucas, I realize I'm projecting my issues onto him and not being a very good one.

"As a team," Lucas echoes.

"Good. Glad to hear you two are going to stop being children and work together," Mo adds with a mischievous grin, drawing an uneasy laugh from the rest of us.

"Anyway, so, what do you have, Blake?" Astra asks.

"A lot, actually," I say. "Everything we know about Brad Keller, we need to toss out the window. He is not who we thought."

After prefacing it all, I tell them everything Brody dug up for me. They all sit in rapt attention, listening to my story, disbelief coloring all their faces. And when I'm done, silence descends over the table. The three of them look off, processing everything I just dumped on them as they quietly sip their coffee.

Lucas finally turns to me. "And where did you come by this information?" he presses. "I assume you didn't have a warrant—"

"I'm a resourceful woman," I tell him. "Let's leave it at that."

"I can't," he counters. "Not if there's a chance this comes back and bites us all."

"It won't. This is all background information. It's a guidepost we'll use to find the next directional point. Then we'll use that to find the next," I say.

"Yeah, but—"

"Lucas, this is one of those shades of gray I mentioned. I got the information from a confidential source. Leave it at that."

He looks ready to protest again, but both Mo and Astra flash him a dangerous look that makes him back down. I can tell he's not settled about it though. This was my attempt to see if I can trust him. If he goes running back to Ayad with this, I'll know I can't trust him as far as I can throw him, and that will be that. But I will literally die—or let myself be fired—before I give up Brody as my source. He's not part of the Bureau, and they will prosecute him. I'm not going to let that happen.

"So, what are we thinking about all of this?" Mo asks. "I mean—"

"Terror cells operate this way," Lucas offers. "Their operatives build lives here. They establish themselves. And if Keller is using his false identities to travel to terrorism hot spots, I'd say it lends credence to the idea that he's part of a terror cell. He's a sleeper agent."

Mo and Astra nod in agreement. That was my original thought as well. But the more I thought about it, the more my thinking shifted and clarified the picture in my mind.

"It's not a bad theory. But neither Keller nor any of his aliases have any obvious connections to known terror groups," I say.

"But that's what would make him such an effective sleeper agent," Lucas notes. "The most effective are the cleanest—the ones without those obvious connections."

"And it could be that you're right. It was my initial thought too," I nod.

"But you've reconsidered that," Astra observes. "What are you thinking, Blake?"

"I think he's CIA," I say. "I think we're chasing a spook."

CHAPTER FOURTEEN

A FTER GRABBING MORE COFFEE TO GO, WE VENTURED back to our makeshift command center and got ourselves set up in there. I didn't want anybody in Javaland overhearing us, and we obviously have a lot to hash out before we can even begin thinking about our next moves.

"A CIA operative," Astra muses. "I'm having a hard time coming around to that. I mean, we have no links to the Agency, for one."

"And a deep cover operative wouldn't," I reply, "to avoid blowback and reprisal against their families, and to help insulate the government and the Agency, NOCs aren't officially employed by the CIA—"

"I'm sorry, NOCs?" Mo asks. "What's that?"

"Nonofficial cover operatives," Lucas explains. "They're CIA officers with no official ties to the Agency."

"Spies," I tell her. "These are the guys who don't have official covers and postings in diplomatic offices, consulates, and the like. These are the guys who go deep undercover to, among other things, infiltrate terror organizations, cartels, hate groups... things like that."

The three of them fall silent as they ponder what I said. I can see the skepticism on their faces. The easy theory is that Keller belongs to a terror cell. It lines up with what we have—from a certain perspective anyway. But turn the evidence we have on its side and look at it from a different angle, and it lines up with what I'm thinking. I just need to give them a little nudge to help get them there.

"How else do you explain Keller's lack of presence in the architectural program?" I ask. "In four years, not one photo? Then there's the fact that his name doesn't appear on any of the designs on any building in Denver—or in the entire state of Colorado for that matter. How do you guys explain that?"

Mo, Astra, and Lucas all exchange glances, each of them looking like they're trying to find an explanation. Trying to find an answer to my questions. They all look at each other as if they're waiting for somebody to speak, but none of them do. None of them can. I know it's just a theory though. And it could just as easily be that they're right and Keller has ties to a terror group. But this just doesn't feel like terror to me. It's something else.

"I find it more plausible that the Agency identified Keller early on. They recruited him, helped him get his degree, helped him start his firm to establish his cover, and he's been working for them this whole time," I say. "It explains the passports, the multiple IDs, the fact that he's rarely at work—it explains everything."

"All right, so, let's assume that's all true," Astra says. "Why is he running? And why leave his passports and everything else behind?"

I shake my head. "I've got to think his cover was blown. That his alternate IDs were compromised. Something must have happened that spooked him and set him running."

"What do you think it was that spooked him?" Lucas asks.

"Not sure. But if he was doing his work in the Middle East and was rolling up terror groups, I'm sure he had no shortage of enemies," I shrug. "Maybe somebody got wind of who he really was and sent somebody to take him out. I think in his place if I heard there was a kill squad coming for me and mine, I'd grab my family and bolt too."

"That's a whole lot of assumption and supposition," Lucas says.

"It is," I admit. "But if you've got a better theory, I'm all ears."

Lucas looks down at the table, his lips pursed, his brow furrowed. He doesn't have a better theory. He isn't wrong though. I am assuming and supposing a lot and forcing some facts into holes they don't necessarily fit in to as a means of explaining my theory. But it's all we have right now, and aside from that, it does make a certain amount of sense.

"All right," Mo says. "How do we go about proving your theory?"

"Well, the straight line is to get ahold of somebody at the Agency."

"Yeah, good luck with that," Astra says. "They're so secretive, they'll tell you the color of the sky is classified."

"She's not wrong about that," Lucas adds.

"Who's the Bureau liaison with the Agency?"

"Monica Hinds, I think," Astra says. "She's good. Straight shooter."

"All right, that's good. I know her a little bit. She's good. Make sure you allude to the fact that we have the identity of one of their NOCs but don't spell it outright. Not over an unsecured line," I say.

"I'm on it," she says.

"Mo, Lucas, I want you guys to keep digging on Keller. Find anything you can that can either prove or disprove my theory. Nothing's too small."

"You got it," Mo says, and Lucas nods.

"Good," I say and feel a sense of foreboding descend over me. "I have to call and update Ayad on what's going on out here."

"Do you want us to stick around for moral support?" Mo asks.

"Nah. I'm good. Thanks though."

The three of them get up and head out, leaving me the room. I take a few minutes to steel myself before logging into my laptop and sending a video conference call to Ayad. I'm hoping he'll be too busy to take my call—a hope that's dashed almost instantly when the screen flashes and fills with his face.

"SSA Wilder," he says. "I was expecting an update yesterday."

"I didn't have anything to update you on yesterday, sir," I reply. "Seemed like it would have been a waste of time."

"It would have been following standard protocol."

"So... you want me to call you simply to tell you I have absolutely nothing to tell you?"

He frowns and looks down for a moment. Probably because he's annoyed, but I want to believe it's because he realizes how stupid following that particular protocol is. Ayad clears his throat then raises his gaze to the camera again.

"Fine. Report," he commands.

I give him a heavily redacted rundown of where we're at with the investigation and the current theories in place, plus an inventory of the evidence we've collected. He looks unimpressed as he listens to my account. By the time I'm done, he looks positively bored. Judging by his expression, I'm surprised he didn't fall asleep in the middle of my report.

"Is that all you have?" he asks.

"I think we're doing pretty well for having only been in town a couple of days."

"From where I stand, it looks like you have nothing," he says. "Nothing substantiated or tangible anyway."

"That's why they're called theories, Chief Ayad. And again, we haven't been in town very long. My team's progress is—"

"Yes, yes, yes," he cuts me off with a wave of his hand. "What I would like to know is where you obtained the information you used to formulate these theories. Especially when I instructed your techs that warrants would be required to access private information."

"Sir, the information we've obtained to formulate our theories is from the public domain," I say. "Everything is legit."

The information Brody found that we're basing most of these theories on was public. More or less. As far as I'm concerned, Ayad doesn't need to know about the non-public domain information Brody dug up. It hasn't come in particularly useful at this point anyway, so there's no reason to tell him and get his panties in a twist. Ayad is staring at me through the video screen with open skepticism that's bordering on contempt on his face.

"Where did you get the information, SSA Wilder?"

"From the public domain, sir."

"Don't play word games with me. I've seen what your techs are working on," he sneers. "And you've gotten a lot farther along than they have. And, oh yeah, they haven't reported any of their findings to you yet. Don't bother lying, I checked already."

"Chief Ayad, is there some particular reason you're keeping such close tabs on me and the status of my investigation?"

"Because supervising agents under my command is my job. That includes staying abreast of current investigations," he says. "Now, I ask you once again, how did you come by the information you're using to base your theories on?"

"I came by it because I'm very good at my job, Chief Ayad," I snap. "Is there some reason you seem more interested in looking at what I'm doing than you are in saving the lives of Brad Keller and his family?"

He sighs and looks perturbed. "Fine. So, your theory is that Keller is a CIA operative—"

"A CIA NOC to be specific," I interrupt. "It's a small but necessary distinction."

"Fine. So, your theory is that Mr. Keller is a CIA NOC and that he and his family are on the run from a kill squad from another country? Do I have that right?"

"Yes. That's what I'm saying," I tell him. "And that's where we're at right now. We're working to confirm all this, of course, but we can use some help."

"What is it you need, SSA Wilder?"

"We need to talk to somebody in the Agency who can tell us about Keller," I tell him. "I have Astra reaching out to the Bureau's

CIA liaison, but frankly, I'm skeptical about the information we'll get from her... if she even tells us anything."

"I very much doubt I'll fare any better than Agent Russo," he says. "I'm sure you know the Agency is very secretive. That goes double for their NOCs."

"Chief Ayad, we need you to try. We need to find Keller and his family," I tell him. "He's got two small children, sir. Cole is eleven and Lyssa is nine. No matter what Keller may or may not have done, neither one of those kids deserves this."

He frowns again, his expression darkening. "Fine. I will try to get something from the Agency. But I wouldn't hold my breath."

"Don't worry, I won't."

"Is there anything else, SSA Wilder?"

I shake my head. "That concludes my portion of the show and tell hour."

He doesn't even crack a smile. The man is a humorless drone.

"Very well. I'll expect to hear from you again very soon," he says.

"Sure thing, boss," I say, the sarcasm dripping off my tongue.

He disconnects the call, and the screen goes dark.

"Nice talking to you too," I mutter.

CHAPTER FIFTEEN

Rocky Mountain Inn & Suites Conference Room; Denver, CO

"STONEWALLED," ASTRA GROANS THE NEXT MORNING. "I talked to Monica last night, and she would neither confirm nor deny anything. Totally stonewalled me and talked in circles. Refused to give me a single nugget of information. She was totally sweet about it, of course. She's one of the few people I know who can tell you to go screw yourself and make it seem kind."

"I thought you said she was a straight shooter," Lucas says.

"She normally is. The only time she's ever given me the runaround has been when there's highly sensitive information involved," Astra replies. "And most of the time, I understand it. National security or whatever. But this? When it's potentially one of their guys on the hook and we're trying to save his butt? It doesn't make sense to me."

"Which tells us that we're on the right track as far as Keller being an Agency man," I point out. "She confirmed it by refusing to confirm it."

"All right, so what do we do with that?" Astra asks. "I mean, it's not like she gave us anything to run with."

"It means we have nothing more than we did last night," Lucas adds.

Though he's coming off as a Negative Nancy at the moment, Lucas's attitude seems to be vastly improved over yesterday. He seems far more engaged and animated, which is a plus. I've never thought he was a stupid man, but he's really surprised me. Having him plugged into the situation and working with us can only benefit the investigation. And given that I didn't have Ayad crawling up my backside and reading me the riot act last night means Lucas didn't tell the man anything about the information Brody funneled to me. It gives me a flicker of hope that he can be trusted after all.

"Let's rattle Monica's cage a little harder," I say.

"What good is that going to do?" Lucas asks.

"The harder we rattle it, the better the chance it shakes something loose," I tell him. "If the Agency knows we're pressing hard on this case—and have the identity of one of their NOCs—there's a good chance we might get something out of it."

"Didn't Astra already do that last night?" Mo asks.

"One phone call they can ignore," I say. "Multiple calls they can't. Or rather, they won't. If they know we're actively and aggressively pursuing a case that involves one of their NOCs, I guarantee they're going to blink first. The Agency is one of the most paranoid organizations on the face of the earth. They literally kill to protect their secrets."

"Allegedly," Astra corrects with a wry smile.

"Bring her up on a video conference call," I say.

"On it," Mo says and types away at her keyboard.

A moment later, the monitor flashes, and the "call in progress," icon appears along with the irritating sound of the electronic "ring." It takes a minute, but the call is answered, and we find ourselves staring at the face of Monica Hinds, the CIA's liaison to the FBI. She's a pretty woman with smooth, olive-colored skin, dark eyes, and long, dark hair. Her face is smooth and unlined, and she's got the solid, sturdy look of the former college athlete she used to be.

"Blake," she greets me. "How are you?"

"Hanging in there, Monica. How are you doing?"

"Not too bad, thanks," she replies. "I can guess why you're calling, and like I told Astra last night, and your Section Chief Ayad this morning, we don't have any comment, nor any confirmation about the man you're looking into. I'm sorry, but I can't help you."

"Come on, Monica. One of your guys is in trouble," I tell her. "We're trying to keep him and his family from being slaughtered. Surely, somebody there cares that two small children are literally under the gun here?"

"Blake, I wish there was something I could do that would help. But as I told Astra and Chief Ayad, so far as I know, Brad Keller is not employed by the Agency. I'm sorry, but there's nothing I can do," she says.

"All right. I understand," I reply. "But we're going to keep looking into this. We're going to find Brad Keller and his family, and I'm sure when we do, he's going to have an interesting story to tell."

"I really hope you find him, Blake," she says. "I hope everybody you're looking for is safe. I hate to think that two kids are in danger."

My eyes meet Monica's, and even through the video screen, I can see the anger and frustration in her eyes. It feels like she wants to tell me what she knows but can't—nor would I press her too hard on the issue. This call is just a way to get the ball rolling, and I think Monica knows that.

"All right, Monica," I say. "Thanks for talking. If anything changes from the Agency's standpoint, give me a call."

"I'll do that. Be safe out there," she says and signs off.

The screen goes dark, and silence descends over the room. Mo, Astra, and Lucas all turn to look at me with curious expressions on their faces.

"And so, that accomplished what, exactly?" Lucas asks.

"Outwardly, nothing," I tell him. "But Monica is required to report our call to her supervisors. I hope that now that we've logged two—technically three if you count Ayad—about their NOC, somebody will reach out. I doubt I'll get the full story from whoever that is, but it might help us move this thing down the road a bit."

"But this is still a theory, right?" Lucas asks. "I mean, we have no proof Keller works for the CIA. No tangible connection between the two."

"No, but that's by design. NOCs have no tangible connection, precisely so the Agency and the US government can deny all knowledge of who this person is or what they're doing in other countries," I tell them.

"Right, I get that," Lucas presses. "But what I mean is that it's entirely possible Keller doesn't work for the Agency. I mean, with what we have in hand, he could work for a cartel or a terror organization."

"That's true. You're not wrong. I'm playing a hunch right now. But I'm also playing the percentages. The number of clean-cut white men who are involved with cartels and terror groups is exceedingly small. A white guy is more likely to be involved with a cartel—perhaps as a money laundering front," I tell them. "But neither Keller nor any of his aliases own any cash businesses that would make money laundering more feasible. He also has no known connections to any extremist, nationalist, or terrorist group. A man like Keller would stand out in either of those two worlds—cartel or terror—and have people talking. But I haven't seen or heard any chatter about a white guy in either group recently."

"So, this whole Agency angle is just a guess?" Lucas asks.

"An educated guess—but yes, a guess," I reply. "If it doesn't fit, we'll circle back to something else. That's the way this job works, Lucas. We try on different theories. Some work. Some don't. But when one doesn't pan out, we pivot and go another way."

"That's not the way we did things in counterterrorism," he says.

There's that crappy, I-know-more-than-you attitude again. The man just cannot seem to keep from opening his mouth and shoving his foot into it for long stretches of time. I glare hard at him. So much for both of us getting off to a fresh start together and sharing a bit of goodwill and camaraderie between us.

"Well, this isn't counterterrorism. If you prefer the way they do things there, you can go back to being an analyst," I snap. "If you're going to work in my unit, you will have to think fast, move fast, be flexible, and learn to adapt on the fly. Investigations are not a straight line from point A to point B. There are a hell of a lot of side roads, false paths, and dead ends on the way to solving a case. If you can't deal with that, there's the door."

He holds his hands up in surrender. "I apologize," he says. "I didn't mean… I just meant… I'm having to get used to doing things this way. Your way."

"This isn't counterterrorism, Lucas. It will never be counterterrorism. Their methods of investigation are different from ours," I tell him. "So, this is your fork in the road. You can either get on board with this unit and the way we do things, or you can go back to your desk in counterterrorism and analyze data for them. Either way, I don't care right now."

Without waiting for him to respond, I turn and storm out of the room, banging the door open and making sure it slams behind me to drive my point home. I'm sick of Lucas comparing his old unit to mine. And I don't think that's being too sensitive or thin-skinned. Comparing the two is pointless, and there is no reason for it other than to imply to me that counterterrorism is somehow superior to my unit.

Well, if he thinks it is, he's welcome to go back. I don't care. I'm just sick of listening to him run his mouth about it because the anger he stirs in me is a distraction. And right now, I need all my focus to catch a spy—somebody very well trained to avoid getting caught.

Good thing I've always enjoyed a challenge.

CHAPTER SIXTEEN

Rocky Mountain Inn & Suites, Room 312; Denver, CO

W ITH LIGHTS OFF AND MY PHONE IN HAND, I PACE back and forth in front of the window, looking out at the darkness outside. After my latest mini-blowout with Lucas, I spent the balance of the afternoon in a foul mood. I parked it at the table in my room and tried to do some research. What I was really doing, though, was waiting for a phone call from somebody at the Agency.

I'd been so sure that repeated phone calls about one of their NOCs would result in somebody getting antsy enough to reach out to me. But here we are, some eight hours after the third phone call they received about Brad Keller, and it's been nothing but radio silence. The Agency either has an excellent poker face, they don't care what we're out here doing, or they don't care about their man Keller and his family being in the wind and possibly on the run from a foreign kill squad.

If that's the case, the Agency is even more cold-blooded than I gave them credit for. I mean, I get the whole non-official cover thing. I get that if Keller were to get caught overseas playing his spy games, the Agency and the government can—and will—sever all ties and disavow any knowledge of him or his activities. That's the risk NOCs take. But the idea that an Agency employee, at home, living his life with his family, could be attacked by a foreign adversary, and the CIA does nothing to help, is mind-boggling.

The Agency can't operate on domestic soil. That's the Bureau's legal purview, and we are the only ones who can investigate Keller's disappearance. If a foreign kill squad arrived on US soil to assassinate him, I think Keller's career as a spy is probably over. And in that light, I'd think if they value an operative like Keller and he's on the run, they'd fall all over themselves trying to help us help them—or rather, help Keller and his family. That the Agency can just turn its back on Keller, his wife, and their children, is not only repugnant to me, but it should also be considered criminal.

I know the others have their doubts about whether Keller is an Agency man or not. But I'm positive that he is and believe that he's literally risked life and limb in service to this country. He's put himself in harm's way to do a job that makes our country safer and more secure. The fact that they've refused to give anything up and haven't even used back channels to feed me something we can use to find him is just horrifying to me. It shows me that we are all nothing more than pawns on the chessboards of this country's power brokers.

So, the question I find myself asking now is—what am I going to do about it?

The Agency isn't inclined to cooperate, which leaves me in a bit of a quandary. I'm positive something bad has happened to this family, and yet I can't prove anything. I can't even prove Keller is anything but an architect, the evidence we have in hand be damned. Given what we have, I know the narrative can be shaped to look like anything they want. They can paint any picture of the man they desire.

With false passports, and I'm sure plenty of money in offshore accounts I don't have access to, they can make Keller look like a cartel man. Or maybe somebody connected to a terror cell. They can make him look like a human trafficker if they want. Taken out of context, the evidence we have in hand can be twisted and turned so that Keller looks like the evilest man on the planet by the powers that be.

And I have to wonder if those conversations are being had in some shadowy back room out in Langley. I've got to think that one of their NOCs going off the grid as Keller did has to make those power brokers nervous as hell. The secrets he has in his head, the things he knows and could expose, would likely make a lot of people at the top of the food chain look bad. Which makes me think they may strike first—before he can tell his story. If they can dirty him up before he gets his story out, they'll damage his credibility. All that makes me wonder if that's why they're stonewalling me.

"I'm not going to let them do that," I mutter.

I punch in the number then press the phone to my ear, continuing to pace back and forth. The call goes through, and it's answered on the second ring.

"Stone," he says.

"ADIC Stone, it's Blake Wilder."

"SSA Wilder, it's good to hear from you," he says. "How are things going in Colorado?"

"To be honest, we've hit a roadblock, sir," I reply. "Do you happen to have a few minutes to talk? We could use a little help here."

"Of course, I've got time," he replies. "You've hit a roadblock, huh? Well, you better go ahead and fill me in on what's going on."

So, I do. I tell Stone everything we've found so far, pitch my theory, then share the other theories we've been discussing. Through it all, he's silent, and just listens to me. As I talk, though, I can hear the clink of ice cubes in a tumbler. And when I'm finished with my story, there's a long silence on the other end of the line.

"That's quite a tale, Blake."

"Yes, it is, sir," I say. "But we're at a standstill until we can get the Agency to play ball with us. And so far, they've been... reluctant."

He laughs softly. "As I'm sure you know, the Agency doesn't much like the idea of other people playing in their sandbox."

"Yes, sir. I'm well aware of that," I say. "I would have thought that after three calls about their man, somebody would have reached out."

"Yeah, that's not really their thing," he replies. "But you're also making a pretty big leap in assuming Keller is their man."

"I don't think it's that big of a leap, to be honest, sir. This just feels like the Agency," I say. "The architectural firm is an elaborate front. I believe they recruited Keller back in college. It's why he doesn't appear in any of the programs' archived photos."

"Again, that's a leap."

"A small one perhaps. But I don't think it's nearly as wild as you seem to believe," I say. "Everything we've uncovered so far seems to fit with a CIA deep-cover agent."

"I don't disagree. But getting the Agency to cooperate is a tough sell," he says with a rumbling chuckle. "Hell, getting them to admit Keller is one of theirs might take an act of God Almighty."

"I understand, sir. But if there is a foreign kill team on US soil, and they're coming after an American citizen—Agency-connected or not—it's our duty to run this down."

"Do we have any evidence to support the idea there's a foreign kill team here in the States?" he asks.

I gnaw on my bottom lip. "No. Not yet. But that's why it's so important that somebody in the Agency cooperate with us. We need to see what he's worked on. We need to find out who he's pissed off enough that they'd come for his whole family," I urge him. "If we can find out where he's been and what he's done, we can narrow down our suspect pool which, based on what we've discovered so far, includes pretty much the entire Middle East."

There's a long pause on the line, and in the silence, I hear the ice cubes clinking against the glass again. I pace when I'm thinking. ADIC Stone drinks to get his brain working. The silence feels heavy, though, and the longer it continues, the more I start to think he's going to turn down my request for help.

"I appreciate your drive and your passion, Blake. I do—"

I let out a quiet breath of frustration. I know I'm right about this, and I know I need to do something to get him thinking less like a politician whose only goal is to cover their ass and more like the legendary agent he used to be.

"Sir, you built your career on taking leaps of faith. You built your legend on following your gut and going where your instincts led you," I cut him off. "I'm telling you that I'm right about this, sir. Brad Keller is a CIA NOC, and there is a kill team on US soil looking for him. Foreign nationals are trying to murder a US citizen and his entire family. I know I don't have the evidence to support it all just yet, but I will get there. I give you my word I will. That's how much I believe in this theory. This is how much I believe that I'm right."

There's another pause on the line and Stone seems to be considering my words. This time, there's no ice clinking in his glass, and there's a heavier, more sober feeling in the silence.

"All right," he says. "What is it you need me to do?"

"All I need you to do, sir, is make a phone call for me."

The shrill bleating of my phone yanks me out of sleep, and I sit up in the chair I'd crashed out in while waiting for a return call from Stone. I stifle a yawn and look at the caller ID; I frown when I see it's from a restricted number. If I wasn't waiting for Stone to get back to me, I would have let it go to voicemail. But this could be a number Stone keeps private, so I connect the call and press the phone to my ear.

"Wilder," I say.

"Did I wake you?"

It's a man on the other end of the line—but it's not Stone. I don't recognize the voice at all, which immediately puts me on edge. I get to my feet and start to pace.

"Who is this?" I ask.

"Somebody you're going to want to talk to," he replies. "Or rather, somebody you've been asking to talk to."

"Mr. Keller?"

"No. I'm not Brad Keller."

"I don't have the time or stomach for games," I snap. "Who is this?"

"A friend of your ADIC," he clarifies. "I got off the phone with him just a little while ago."

"All right," I say, feeling the first stirrings of excitement in my belly.

"If you want to talk, meet me at the Cathedral Basilica of the Immaculate Conception."

"When?"

"Twenty minutes."

I glance at my watch. "It's almost midnight."

"It'll be open. You've got one shot," he tells me. "If you're not there in twenty minutes, I'm gone, and your investigation goes nowhere."

"All right."

"One more thing. Come alone," he says. "And I do mean alone. I see another warm body with you, I'm gone, and again, your investigation is dead in the water. Capiche?"

"Understood."

There's a click, and the line goes dead. I look at my phone for a minute then spring into action. If I've only got this one shot, I'm sure as hell not going to blow it.

CHAPTER SEVENTEEN

Cathedral Basilica of the Immaculate Conception; Denver, CO

I MOUNT THE STEPS AND GRAB HOLD OF THE HEAVY FRONT door, surprised to find it unlocked. I pull the door open and step into the hushed interior of the cathedral. Built in the French Gothic style, it's the seat of power for the Denver Archdiocese. The building itself is gorgeous but is an imposing place made of white stone with soaring spires, lots of leaded glass windows, and stained glass depictions of biblical scenes set high into the walls.

The interior is dimly lit but bright enough for me to see it's as elaborate and beautiful as the exterior. The inside is made of the same pristine white stone and has soaring arches and thick, fluted columns. Two rows of dark wooden pews fill the nave and are separated by an aisle that runs down the center of the cathedral. The aisle down the center of the church ends at the rounded chancel and apse that holds an even more elaborately carved altar. And in the center of the altar stands a golden crucifix.

One thing's for sure—this is a long way from the Pulpit back home.

The incense-tinged air is so perfectly quiet that it feels like the silence is physically pressing down on me. It's been a long time since I've been in church, and just standing there looking at the interior of the cathedral triggers a tsunami of memories inside of me. I remember being a little girl and going to Mass with my parents and Kit. I remember being in awe of the beauty of the place and the power I felt within its walls. The sound of the choir was always beautiful, and the sermons of Father Jackson never failed to move me.

After my parents were murdered, though, I stopped going to church. I don't know that I've ever fully stopped believing, but my relationship with God is… complicated. Doing what I do, I've borne witness to some of the evilest things imaginable, and I have a hard time believing in a deity that allows the sort of cruelty I see on a daily basis. I have a hard time believing in a God who will allow a little girl's parents to be slaughtered. I know people like to tout the whole "free will" of humanity thing when talking about the evil that seems to flourish in this world. But to me, that excuse has always been a cop-out. If God can perform some of the miracles He's credited with, why can't he prevent the evil that makes my job necessary?

I'm not here to revive my debate with God though. I look around, searching for the man who called me, but don't see anybody. I assume he's going to want to make a dramatic entrance, so I settle the weapon on my hip and loosen my coat just in case he gets a little too dramatic. Shedding blood in a house of God isn't ideal, but I won't hesitate to put a few into this guy if he gets a little too frisky.

I walk down the center aisle and take a seat in the front pew and use the time I'm waiting to contemplate the crucifix and other religious items up there on the altar. As I stare at the face of Jesus on the cross, I find myself lamenting that I don't feel the power in this building I did as a child. I find that I don't feel the Spirit moving through me.

Faith came so easily to me as a child, but sitting here, contemplating the nature of God and religion as a whole, all I feel is… empty. Hollow. And I don't feel like immersing myself back into the mysteries of Catholicism is going to fill that hole. I feel like I've seen far too much evil in this world to let myself become a true believer ever again.

The soft creak of the pew behind me alerts me to his presence. "I know that look," he says. "That looks like the guilt-ridden face of a lapsed Catholic."

I turn around to find the man sitting there with a smile on his face and his hands up, his palms toward me. I'm already on edge, though, and my muscles tense as my hand strays toward the weapon on my hip.

"No need for that, SSA Wilder," he says. "We're all friends here."

"Are we?"

The man has soft lines at the corners of his eyes and mouth and looks to be in his early fifties. His salt-and-pepper hair is cut stylishly short, and he's got dull green eyes behind a pair of round, rimless spectacles. I'd estimate him to be about six feet tall, and he's got a lean build. But everything about the man is average. There is not one thing about him that stands out. He's the kind of person you'd completely forget about five minutes after meeting him. I suppose that's probably a good thing in his line of work.

But he seems friendly enough, and I feel my body start to relax. There isn't anything about him that sets off warning bells or triggers my fight or flight response. I don't necessarily trust him, but I don't get the feeling that he's going to kill me, which is a good thing. The last thing I want to do tonight is to desecrate a church.

"Doyle Kalfus," he says.

"So, is that your real name or your made-up, superspy name?"

He shrugs. "Would you believe me if I said it's my real name?"

"Probably not," I admit. "So, we'll just go with Doyle."

"Fair enough," he says, then gestures to the altar. "Are you contemplating the mysteries and wonder of organized religion? Perhaps pondering a return to the fold?"

"No, I was just remembering growing up in the Church," I tell him. "And thinking about why it is I can never come back."

He nods and gives me a sympathetic look of understanding. "Yeah, well, faith can, unfortunately, be an unintended victim of what we do for a living."

"Seeing the horrors and evil people commit day in and day out certainly doesn't help me believe in the divine," I agree.

"I know people who lean harder into their faith as a result of what they see on the job."

"I'm not one of those people."

"Neither am I," he replies.

I can see him working to build a rapport. He's sympathizing and trying to relate and find some common ground with me. What I don't know is whether he's been doing it so long it's become second nature to him, or if he's trying to work me like a mark. Like he thinks he can turn me into one of his assets. Unfortunately for Doyle Kalfus, I'm not a mark and know how to play the game— because I play it too.

"So, is that what Brad Keller was? An unintended victim?" I ask. "I mean, he was employed by the Agency, was he not?"

A gentle smile curls the corners of his mouth upward. "I've been told you are unfailingly blunt and direct."

"I am when I need to be."

"I appreciate the directness. There's not a lot of it in my world, as I'm sure you can imagine," he says. "And yes, Brad was one of ours. Unofficially speaking."

I look at him for a moment, trying to see into him. But the man is well-schooled in controlling his facial expressions and giving nothing away. Most people aren't able to keep their faces completely blank and unreadable. It's usually their eyes or some small tic they can't control that gives them away. Unless they're sociopaths, most criminals don't have the control to keep from giving themselves away. The questioning doesn't even have to be all that intense. It's good when you're interrogating somebody.

But Kalfus is something entirely different. His face is smooth and unyieldingly plain and expressionless. He's as readable as a stone and will only show me what he wants me to see. He could be sitting there thinking about the best way to kill me or the box scores from last night's Lakers game, and I can't tell which it might be. Not even microexpressions give him away. It's impressive. And unsettling. I wouldn't go so far as to say he's a sociopath, but I think he shares some tendencies with one. I suppose to do the job he does, he'd have to be.

"I'm not going to be able to tell you everything. Some details are too sensitive. Even still," Kalfus begins. "And I wouldn't be telling you anything if not for Max Stone. I owe the man my life. He says I can trust you, but I want your word that my name will never, ever cross your lips after tonight."

"That's fine. I don't need the fine details. I just need the broad strokes," I reply. "And you have my word. You will not be connected to this in any way, shape, or form."

"All right," he says.

He sighs heavily, and for the first time, I see a flash of emotion on his face. He quickly gets it back under control, but it's enough for me to see that this is weighing on him. It's enough for me to see that he likes Keller, so I decide to start with some softballs rather than get into the meat and potatoes of this chat. It's better to get him into a more positive frame of mind than start with the emotional stuff.

"How did you go about recruiting Mr. Keller? What put him on the Agency's radar in the first place?" I ask.

A wry smile twists his lips. "I shouldn't be giving away Agency secrets, but this one is probably benign," he says. "We host job fairs at high schools around the country. Obviously, the Agency isn't connected to these fairs. Not directly. There are real recruiters for real post-high school careers, including the military, but the fairs themselves are a front for our true purposes, which is to identify talent we might want to groom."

"And how do you identify this talent?"

"We give kids who attend the fair an aptitude test of sorts," he tells me. "Brad scored off the charts. He also fit a certain personality profile we want in our recruits: he was intelligent, adaptable, great at improvisation, and above all, he was loyal—incredibly loyal to those things he cares about, and lucky for us, he cared about this country. A lot. When we got to know him, we knew he would be a perfect fit for NOC training."

I nod as I absorb the information he's giving me. I'd always heard the Agency recruited like that, but I always thought that was just a rumor. It was hard for me to believe they were targeting kids like that. But, as I think about it more, I suppose the Bureau isn't any different—we're just more upfront about it. The Bureau hosts job fairs as well, but at least we don't hide the fact that they're being recruited by the FBI.

"Anyway, we recruited him hard. And for his part, he was eager to serve," Kalfus goes on. "We helped get him through college, helped get him established—"

"I recall seeing that he worked for HUD for a time," I interrupt. "But he never took an official role in the department, did he?"

Kalfus shakes his head. "No, his post with them was a cover, but it required him to temporarily move to the east coast while Bridget stayed here in Colorado. He was training at Langley. At the time, he and Bridget were getting serious, so we needed to provide him a reason to be away for as long as he was," he admits. "Once he finished with his training, we helped establish his architectural firm, made it famous, and deepened his cover. Having to travel for work became the norm. It was a helpful excuse to explain his absences from home."

"Wait… are you telling me his wife doesn't know what he does for a living?"

Kalfus shook his head. "No. Brad wasn't allowed to tell her. The Agency demands absolute secrecy, which requires you to lie to your loved ones. So, no, she never knew. Brad Keller was never connected to the Agency in any official capacity. He operated under a pseudonym when dealing with us in an official capacity—Brad Hewitt. And, of course, he also operated under the four cover IDs you found as well," he says softly. "Unfortunately, living a double life is a requirement to do what he did. What we all do. I expect that even you have something of a dual life, SSA Wilder."

"Jesus," I whisper, wondering at the depravity of it all. "And, no, I don't have a dual life."

"No? There isn't one face you wear at work and one face you wear for your loved ones?"

I shake my head. "I'm the same for both. I am the job."

"I think you have a talent for deceiving yourself," he says. "Not that I think it's a bad thing. I just have a hard time believing you are the same hard-ass with your boyfriend that you are with the perps you interrogate."

I give him a wry grin. "I don't have a boyfriend. Probably because I'm the same at home as I am at the shop."

"No boyfriend? Interesting," he notes. "So, who is Charles Kragen?"

My mouth falls open and I glare at him. "You dug through my life?"

"As much as I love and respect Max, when he asked me to meet with you, yes, I did some digging," he admits. "I don't go into meetings blind. I always do a background before I agree to sit down with somebody. It's one reason I've stayed alive in this business so long."

I open my mouth to protest but then close it again. I suppose as a spy, it's prudent. He probably has to be even more paranoid than I am. It's a job requirement. So, I can't blame him for wanting to know who he was sitting down with. Still, it feels like an invasion of my privacy. But I guess I see what he's saying about not being the same person. Though we're only seeing each other casually, Charles is somebody I feel like I can let my guard down around. I'm more relaxed when I'm with him.

"Charles is just somebody I see from time to time. It's nothing serious. And I suppose you've made your point about wearing a second face," I say grudgingly. "Anyway, we're getting off track. Tell me more about Keller."

"Right. Brad was a good man. He always did the right thing and handled his business the right way. And he was devoted to his family—that's the loyalty I mentioned. He truly loved them more than anything," he tells me. "And he was damn good at his job. One of the best I've ever worked with. He managed his double life better than anybody I've seen."

It's stunning to learn just how things operate in the Agency. The fact that Keller had to lead a double life, never telling his own wife what he did for a living, is mind-boggling. And I thought I had it bad. I have no idea how a person can compartmentalize so well—how they can be two different people like that. That's not something I could do. I may be a different person around Charles, or even Astra when we're not in the shop, but I don't have to lie to their faces about who I am.

I clear my throat. This is all good background, but now I need to start asking the tougher questions. Kalfus looks at me with an expression that says he knows I'm working him the same way he's working me. He seems to appreciate the effort.

"So, you ran ops in the Middle East with him?" I ask.

He shrugs. "Yeah. I was his case officer on quite a few ops. Almost died in the field myself, so I opted for a different career path."

"Understandable," I say. "So, what we know is that Brad is on the run. He left his alternate passports behind—I can only assume that's because those cover IDs are burned. Are you aware of any other IDs he might have? Something we can use to track him?"

Kalfus shakes his head. "No, those four IDs you have are the only ones I knew about. It wouldn't surprise me, though, to learn he had another secret ID. Brad always had great foresight and instincts. He'd have a way out."

"Can you tell me about what Brad did overseas? Just—broad strokes," I say. "Can you tell me who he might have pissed off enough that they'd come after his entire family?"

A wry chuckle passes his lips. "Take your pick. ISIS, the Iranians, Pakistanis, Afghans, hell, throw the Chinese and Russians into the mix as well," he says. "Brad had a real knack for this work. He was highly effective at breaking up terror rings, spoiling arms sales, and even took out a few human trafficking rings. The man was one of the most effective field operatives we've ever had. Which earned him one hell of a list of enemies. Any one of those groups would love to put him in a ditch."

I frown. That doesn't narrow down the suspect pool any, but it is useful information, nonetheless. At least, it is if I can figure out how to use it. But it's the first breadcrumb on a much longer trail that I intend to follow. Kalfus is staring at me, and I can see that he's wrestling with something. But then he gives himself a brief nod, the internal debate over.

"Look, I shouldn't be telling you this, but we've been tracking a team of Saudis who entered the country a few days before Brad went missing," he tells me. "The team was dispatched by the GID. They're here in Denver."

That news hits me like a punch to the gut. At the same time, though, it fills me with a rush of excitement. It means I was right. The GID—the General Intelligence Directorate—is the Saudi version of the CIA. Like the Agency, they've got field operatives all over the world. And also like the Agency, they've got kill squads tasked with eliminating threats. The fact that a GID team is here in Denver lends heavy credence to my theory if not proves it outright. And I think that means that Keller and his family are indeed on the run. At the very least, Kalfus has given me a solid place to start.

I've gotten what I need, but there is one thing that's been nagging me throughout this entire conversation. I know that CIA spooks are known for double-speak and twisting words around to conceal the truth of things, and I can't help but wonder if Kalfus knows more than he's telling me.

"One more thing, Agent Kalfus," I say. "I noticed that you keep referring to Agent Keller in the past tense. Do you know something I don't?"

"I know a lot of things you don't, SSA Wilder."

"Fair enough. But specifically in regard to Agent Keller, why do you keep referring to him in the past tense? Do you know that he's dead?"

He shakes his head. "No, I don't know. But GID teams are among the best in the world," he says. "If there is a Saudi kill team on his tail, Brad's as good as dead. It's an unfortunate reality, but it is a reality."

I give his words a moment to soak in. The Agency may have already thrown in the towel, but I'm not ready to do that just yet. I'm not convinced Keller and his family are dead. Maybe I'm being overly optimistic, or underestimating the GID team, but my gut is telling me that Keller is still alive—at least for the moment.

"Thank you for speaking with me, Agent Whatever-Your-Name-Is," I tell him. "I appreciate the intel that I didn't get from you."

He gives me a small smile. "Do me a favor."

"Name it."

"Find the men who did this," he says, his voice tight. "Find them and put them down."

"I intend to."

CHAPTER EIGHTEEN

Rocky Mountain Inn & Suites Conference Room; Denver, CO

"HAVE YOU GONE COMPLETELY OUT OF YOUR MIND?" Astra practically shouts at me. "What in the hell were you thinking, Blake?"

"I was thinking that we might get some useful intel on Keller. Turns out I was right."

Astra paces angrily around the conference room, her face a mask of irritation. Mo and Lucas are pointedly avoiding looking at us, neither of them wanting to get caught up in Hurricane Astra. Can't say I blame them.

"That was the stupidest thing you've ever done," she seethes. "And you've done some really stupid stuff before."

"Look, I'm fine. Not a hair out of place."

"Lucky for you," she fires back. "I mean, what would you be saying to me if I'd gotten a call from a stranger in the middle of the night asking to meet at some sketchy, shady place?"

I laugh. "It was a church. A very public church."

"As I said, a sketchy, shady place," she retorts. "If I'd done what you did, you would be reading me the riot act right now."

I run a hand through my hair. She's right. I know she's right. And I know she's tearing into me simply because she cares about me. Yeah, I could have been walking into a trap. I could have ended up taking two to the back of the head. And I know if she or any of my team had snuck off in the middle of the night for a clandestine meeting, I'd be ripping them a new one for it right now too. But I'm fine. Plus, I'm holding an ace in the hole.

"It was ADIC Stone who set up the meet for me," I say. "He and this guy are friends. I get the feeling they go way back."

"That's really not the get-out-of-jail-free card you think it is."

"Look, it was the only way he was going to meet—if I was alone," I insist. "He's a spook and was watching me arrive. He would have noticed if I'd left you in the car or had anybody shadowing me. I couldn't risk it."

"But you could risk your life. Yeah, that makes sense," Astra counters.

"What could I have done? It was the only way I was going to get the intel I got."

"You could have called me and told me where you were going, that way if you didn't come back, I'd know where to start looking for your bullet-riddled corpse."

I laugh again, but her point is taken. I probably could have let her know where I was going just in case something happened. In my defense, I didn't have much time; plus I was on such an adrenaline rush, I wasn't thinking clearly. That's an excuse I wouldn't accept from her, though, so I keep it to myself.

"Fair enough," I tell her. "If it ever happens again, I'll be sure to tell you where I'm going to be. I promise I won't do that again."

Astra stops pacing and turns to me, her arms folded across her chest and a scowl on her face. She stares at me for a long minute, and it's not hard to see how much I scared her by what I did. But she finally relents, and her shoulders relax. Slightly.

"If you do anything like that again, I swear to God, I'll kick your ass, Blake. I'm serious," she snaps at me.

"I promise."

"Fine," she huffs as she takes her seat. "Now, tell us what you found out."

Leaning forward in my seat, I tell them everything Kalfus told me last night—except for his name. I gave him my word I'd never out him, and I intend to keep that promise. They listen with expressions of surprise on their faces, and I can see the questions in their eyes, but they don't interrupt. When I'm done with my story, silence descends over the room. They all look at one another as if they're waiting for someone else to speak first.

It's not quite the reaction I expected. To be honest, I expected them to be a little more excited about the information since we finally have a solid lead to follow.

Lucas clears his throat. "Well, I guess since I'm the resident skeptic, I'll ask," he says. "Can we trust what this guy says? I mean … he's a spy. They get paid to lie."

"He's got no reason to lie. He thinks Keller is already dead— or soon will be," I reply. "The Agency seems to be positioning themselves to sweep this under the rug, which tracks since Keller was a NOC anyway. I think they know if they go after this GID team, they'll very possibly create an international incident. At the very least, they'd be faced with questions about Keller's activities they won't want to answer."

"And since he's a NOC," Astra notes, "the Agency will have already disavowed him, so even if we do find him—or his body— they're going to be insulated from questions."

"Exactly. My source loses nothing by telling us what he told us," I add. "But if we find the actual killers, I have no doubt they'll disappear shortly after we take them into custody, and the Agency will very quietly get to congratulate themselves."

"But won't that create an incident?" Mo asks. "I mean, if this is a GID team, surely, the Saudis are going to miss them if they're disappeared."

"It's high-level spy games," I tell her. "Even if the GID team disappears, the Saudis won't make too big of a stink of it. If we catch them and prove they murdered Keller, I'm sure the GID would prefer their team disappears. Without the team in custody, they wouldn't have to answer some uncomfortable questions about Keller, or what one of their kill squads was doing on US soil in the first place. After that, it'll probably never be spoken of by anybody. No harm, no foul on either side. Nothing but missing people nobody is looking for."

"That's cold," Lucas remarks. "Really cold."

"That's the life of a spy," I shrug.

I can't help but see the slight parallel between that situation and my running feud with Lucas. Neither of us has mentioned our mini-blowout yesterday and likely won't. He probably knows he pushed too far, and I know I probably overreacted. A little bit. Anyway, it's water under the bridge, and we're just moving on like it never even happened, an uneasy and unspoken truce between us.

"And Brad Keller would have died for his country without getting the respect of a proper funeral for his service," Astra says.

"He'll get a star on the wall at Langley," I reply with a shrug. "These guys all know the life they're signing up for when they do it. They know they'll never get the accolades or even a proper burial for what they do. But they do it anyway."

"If your source is right, and Keller and his family are already dead and gone, doesn't that close the case on us?" Mo asks.

I shake my head. "That's the thing: I don't think Keller's dead. Not yet anyway."

"What makes you say that?" Astra asks.

"One, my gut is telling me he's still alive," I say. "But two, the fact that the GID team is still in Denver. If they'd completed their mission, they'd be gone already. That tells me they're still in Denver because they're looking for him. And they must think he's still local too."

"I can't think he'd be here," Lucas chimes in. "If he got wind of a Saudi team coming for him, surely, he would have gotten his family out of Colorado already."

"Not if his four established alternate identities were burned. It's possible he already has papers under a different assumed name, but if he didn't, that takes time to put together," I say. "I tend to think he's still in the area. Saudi Intelligence is very good. I don't think they'd waste time in Denver if they didn't think he was still here."

Silence fills the room as we take a couple of beats to consider the situation. I look around the table at each of them, watching them process everything I've told them so far. There are still a lot of disparate parts to consider before I'm comfortable putting them all together and forming one complete picture. There are still some holes in my theory, and even though everything seems to be lining up to support it, I learned long ago to never take anything for granted.

"All right, so the question is, what are we going to do with this information?" Astra asks. "I have a feeling Ayad is going to be more concerned with how we learned there's a GID team in Denver than the fact that there's a kill squad operating on US soil."

"We're going to tell Ayad as little as possible," I say. "Just leave him to me."

"What are you going to tell him?" Mo asks.

"As little as I can," I reply then cast a pointed glance at Lucas. "If you're not comfortable with where this conversation is headed, you should probably head out. I'll have an assignment to give you later—"

"I'm fine," he says. "I'll stay."

I look at Lucas and see something different in his eyes. I wouldn't say he's come around to full-blown acceptance of my methods or how I run my team, but I think there's a grudging respect starting to bloom. All I can assume is that he came to his own personal crossroads after yesterday and has decided to throw his lot in with us. For good or ill, he seems to be putting his chips on our little unit.

"Are you sure?" I ask.

He nods. "I am. I joined your unit because I wanted to work in the field. I wanted to learn from the best," he says. "And I'm coming to understand that out here in the field, there are a lot more shades of gray than I believed before."

He and I smile at each other, and I nod to him. Maybe I underestimated him after all. Lucas may never completely fit into our unit. I have a feeling there are always going to be some sharp edges and that he will forever be the square peg in the round hole our team is. But I see in his face there's a renewed commitment. I see determination. And though I know he's going to challenge me at times and that we are going to clash now and then, I can also see he's open to learning. His attitude seems to have changed overnight, and judging by the glance he shared with Mo, I have a feeling she had a hand in his coming to the light.

That's good. I'm happy about that. We don't have the time to explore it right now though. With a Saudi kill team in town, we are most assuredly on the clock. Or rather, Brad Keller and his family are on the clock. And I'm determined that we're not going to let anything happen to them. Not if we can help it.

"Good to have you on board, Lucas," I say, then turn to Mo. "Can you please video conference with SAC Shelby Locke?"

"You got it," Mo says.

Astra looks at me. "Pulling Homeland into this?"

I shrug. "I'm going to pull in anybody I have to because we are not going to stop until we either find Keller and his family—or find their bodies."

Shelby Locke is the SAC of Homeland Security's Seattle field office. She's good people, and a tough agent I got reacquainted with on the recent serial bomber case. She put Winslow in check a couple of times on my behalf—and I have a feeling she had a hand in his demotion and exile. She's not a woman without connections herself. And since I already know the Agency isn't going to help us, I'm hoping Homeland will.

The screen flashes, and SAC Locke's face fills the screen. She's got a couple tense lines on her face, and she's got a little more gray throughout her short hair than I remember, but otherwise she looks every bit the college athlete she was decades ago. Even through the screen, her dark eyes burn with intensity.

"Blake," she says. "Nice to see you again. How are you?"

"I'm doing well, thank you," I reply. "How are things at Homeland?"

"Busy. Things are always popping off all over the place. I'm sure I'm not telling you anything you don't already know."

"No, I know that all too well," I say.

"So, what can I do for you?"

"I was hoping that you might be able to help us with something."

"I will if I can. What is it you need?"

I trust Locke wholeheartedly, but know that I need to tread lightly. I don't want to reveal too much, but I know I have to tell her enough to convince her there is a very real threat and that we need her help with it.

"Well, it seems that we've got a team from the GID in town," I say. "And we believe they are hunting somebody who's done a lot of work in the Middle East."

A wry smile touches her lips. She's no fool; I can see by the look on her face that she knows what I'm talking about. But she's also discreet and knows she shouldn't push too hard.

"The GID, huh? This person must have kicked a real hornet's nest to move the Saudis to send a team to take him out," she comments.

"I don't know the specifics, but it certainly seems to be the case," I tell her. "My source tells me this GID team landed here in Denver at some point in the last couple of weeks. If you could work your sources to get me some names, I'd appreciate it."

She frowns and looks down at something on her desk, obviously taking a moment to think about it. I can see she doesn't necessarily want to involve herself—or Homeland in general—with Agency business. I can't blame her. If the Agency got wind of Homeland looking into this in any sort of official capacity, the crapstorm it would stir up would be intense and terrible.

"I'm sorry, Shelby," I say. "I wouldn't ask if this weren't important. There are two small children caught in the crossfire, and I want to bring them home safe if I can."

Locke's eyes soften and she nods. She gets it. There are some things bigger than government agency turf wars or the egos of the people who make some of the decisions that keep our agencies at each other's throats.

"Give me a little time to see what I can find and put it together. I need to be discreet about it," she says. "I can't afford any blowback."

"Understood," I nod. "And thank you. I appreciate it."

"You're welcome," she replies. "Just bring those kids home."

"That's my plan."

CHAPTER NINETEEN

Rocky Mountain Inn & Suites, Room 312; Denver, CO

A FTER GETTING BACK FROM DINNER WITH THE TEAM, I took a decadently long and hot shower. Surprisingly, the hotel has good water pressure. I stand beneath the water, letting the warmth work at the tight knots in my shoulders. I'm holding more stress than I even realized. Eventually, I get out and towel off, wishing I had a bottle of wine with me. Unwinding with a book and some wine sounds ideal right now.

Dinner was unexpectedly nice. It was the first meal we had all taken together since arriving in Denver, and it was a good bonding session for us all. Even Lucas. He still doesn't smile much or joke around like we do—he's still got that square peg/round hole thing happening. But I can see he's making more of an effort to engage us and be part of the team. It must have been quite the talk Mo had with him.

I climb into bed and pull my laptop over to me. There's nothing in my email that can't wait until later, so I set it aside and grab my book. I haven't had much time to read lately, and I've got the itch to get into this book. Before I can crack it open though, my laptop chimes with the sound of an incoming video conference request.

With a sigh, I drop my book, grab my computer, and open it up. When I see it's Locke calling, my sense of dread fades and is replaced with a bolt of excitement. I hit the button to connect the call, and there's a pause as the encryption kicks in. A moment later, the speakers chime, letting me know the line is secure, and Locke is there on the screen, her face tight.

"Well, that was quick," I note. "I didn't expect to hear back from you until tomorrow at the earliest."

"What can I say? I'm a paragon of efficiency."

I laugh. "I hope I'm not the reason you're at the office so late."

She shakes her head. "No, there are always a thousand different fires to put out," she says. "I'm sure you know how that goes."

"I think, on the whole, you've got it ten times worse than I do."

She laughs. "Yeah, maybe so," she says. "Anyway, I got the names you were asking me about. But you need to promise me your discretion. I can't have my name pulled into this."

I grin. "Don't worry. I'm getting good at keeping secrets," I say. "Nobody's ever going to know you gave me anything. You have my word."

"Fair enough," she says. "Four Saudis flew into Denver on diplomatic passports about two weeks ago. They're posing as representatives for an oil company, and they're attending a green energy conference."

"Those have to be our guys."

"Stands to reason," she says. "Your guys are Hamsah Saleh, Jalil Alam, Karam Saeed, and Malik Eid. They're all known to be GID operatives. We had a tail on them, but State told us to back off. They told us because they're on diplomatic papers, we need to leave them alone."

I grab the pad of paper from the nightstand and a pen, jotting down the names. We'll need to do a deep dive into them in the morning. I'm not sure exactly how to go about that with Ayad looking over Rick and Nina's shoulders, but I file it away as yet another bridge to cross in the distant future.

"So, State wants you to back off… even though they're a kill squad."

She shrugs. "We can't definitively prove they're a kill squad," she says sardonically. "Those are their words. Not mine. But they told us harassing Saudi diplomats would put a strain on our relations with one of our allies."

"Unbelievable."

"Right?" she asks with a wry chuckle. "Anyway, that's why I can't afford to have my name connected to this in any way."

"I understand. Trust me, nobody is ever going to know you gave me these names," I say. "And I appreciate you going out on a limb for me like this. And, hey, State never gave me a directive to back off, so I'm going to run with this."

"Not a problem. And please run with it. Run far and run fast with it. If they're here with bad intentions, we need to be able to stop them, diplomatic relations be damned," she says, her voice tight with anger. "We can't let US citizens be targeted and killed by hostile elements—even if their government is allied with ours."

"I agree. One hundred percent," I reply.

"Good. Do what you have to do," she says. "But do it quickly and quietly. You don't want State getting wind of what you're doing, or they'll rain hell down on you."

"I will. And thanks again, Shelby."

"No problem. And, hey, I meant to tell you before that I was sorry to hear about the reshuffling at the Bureau. Heard they took your team from you. That sucks, Blake."

"Yeah, thanks," I say and try to strike a more diplomatic tone. "I get it. The new president wants new people in new places. It's not ideal, but it is what it is."

"Yeah, it's not ideal. It'd be nice, though, if you didn't have to deal with their cronies whispering in their ears on top of it all," she says. "I hate that somebody like Senator Hedlund can impact your life like that."

That's a name I haven't heard in a while, and when Shelby mentions it, I feel the blood in my veins turn to ice. We worked a case a while back that involved Hedlund's daughter whom she thought had joined a cult. It turned out that it wasn't a cult but a group of people who just wanted to live a simpler life free of society's constraints. The case ended with Hedlund ordering a raid that killed a handful of the community members—including her own daughter. The Bureau took as much heat for it as we did for Ruby Ridge and Waco.

My reputation took a beating because Hedlund lied and threw me under the bus. Even though she was the one who ordered the raid, I somehow took the brunt of the blame for it and found myself in real trouble with the Bureau brass. In the end, the truth came out, and I was cleared. Somehow, though, Hedlund not only avoided trouble, she got a damn promotion. She took advantage of the chaos that unfolded when we busted the Thirteen and pressed a hard-line anticorruption campaign, and the voters of West Virginia made her a senator. The only silver lining is that I haven't seen or had to deal with her since then.

Until now, apparently.

"Wait. What do you mean? What does Kathryn Hedlund have to do with any of this?" I ask tentatively.

Locke's eyes widen and an expression of surprise crosses her face. "Oh, I thought you knew," she says uncertainly. "I'm sorry, I didn't mean to start something—"

"No, it's fine. It's not your fault. But what does Hedlund have to do with anything?"

Locke clears her throat and looks away for a moment. Her expression is tight, and she looks like a woman who knows she just stepped in something.

"Dammit. I thought you knew. I'm so sorry, Blake. If I'd known you didn't know—"

"What am I supposed to know? Or rather, what am I not supposed to know?"

She runs a hand through her hair and turns away. The frown on her face tells me she's not thrilled about having opened this can of worms with me. Locke isn't a woman who sticks her foot in her mouth very often and is usually very measured when she speaks. She's not a woman who rattles easily, but right now, she looks shaken.

"Whatever you've heard is fine. I've made my peace with it all," I tell her. "I'm just curious. It seemed like there was more going on behind the scenes that I wasn't aware of, and I would kind of like to know."

"I suppose you have a right to know," she says. "Senator Hedlund has ingratiated herself with the right people. She's also a good friend of President Miller's, and most believe she has his ear on important things. Hedlund chairs the Judiciary Committee and is also heading up a new domestic oversight committee. That makes her a very powerful woman."

"Maybe the most powerful woman in the Senate," I note.

On the screen, Locke nods. "I don't think there's any maybe about it. But that doesn't mean everybody's happy," she says. "There are some in her party who are bitter as hell that she skipped the line straight to a leadership role."

"That's going to happen when you have connections like she does."

"Unfortunately, so."

I blow out a long breath. I'm normally pretty up to date with current events, but Hedlund's appointment to chair Judiciary and this new oversight committee is something that didn't ping my radar. It's also horrible news for me. Nothing good will ever come of having somebody who hates me as much as Hedlund does have the sort of power she has. Nothing good for me, anyway.

"So, are you telling me that Hedlund had some role in this shakeup at the Bureau?" I ask. "That she had something to do with my team being stripped from me?"

"Well, the final decision comes from POTUS, obviously. But yeah, he had some help making that decision," she says. "And word 'round the campfire is that it was Hedlund who suggested shaking things up."

I groan and shake my head. If that's true, I don't doubt that's the last I'll be hearing from Hedlund. It could also explain, though, the reason Ayad has been on me from day one. I have a feeling if we start looking deep enough, we're going to find a connection between Hedlund and Ayad. It explains everything.

"I'm sorry, Blake," Locke says.

"You've got nothing to be sorry for, Shelby. I appreciate the heads up," I tell her. "Let me know if you hear anything else."

"Count on it," she nods. "And, hey, good luck out there. Be safe."

"Thanks, Shelby."

The screen goes dark, leaving me sitting here staring at my reflection on the screen. I've long suspected that Hedlund was part of the Thirteen. I simply haven't had the proof to back up that theory. But now that Hedlund is back on her feet and in a much more influential position, she has even more power to screw with my life—which seems to be one of the Thirteen's primary goals. Well, that and to kill me.

I set my computer aside and stand up. Clasping both hands atop my head, I start to pace the room, my mind spinning. As if things aren't already bad enough with having to deal with a guy like Ayad and this shuffling at the Bureau—but knowing now that Kathryn Hedlund is running amok behind the scenes, pulling strings like some deranged damn puppet master, things have gotten exponentially worse for me.

Petty revenge seems to be the most basic answer to the question of why Hedlund would do this to me. Though she ultimately recovered and now seems to be flourishing, her reputation took a slight ding when we butted heads. She's maybe not seen as the golden girl she once was. Whereas she was once considered a likely front runner whenever she jumped into the presidential race, it might take her a little more time to reach her goals.

I took my shot at her, and much to my detriment, she's come back even stronger than before. She's ruthless, and now she not only has me in her sights, but she's also got the clout and political capital to back up whatever her grand plan is. I hope that seeing me knocked off my perch and stripping my command from me will be enough for her. But my gut tells me it's not. My gut is telling me that she's coming for her pound of flesh.

What my gut can't tell me, though, is whether this is part of a plan devised by the Thirteen. My sister and I weakened their regime, but they were not annihilated. Elements of it remain and have been dormant for a while now. They've been quiet. But I'm starting to get the feeling that they've reformed and reorganized enough now to start moving pieces around the board again. And I fear that Kathryn Hedlund is one of those players making moves. It's the only thing that makes sense to me right now.

There's an old saying that's been passed down over the centuries, from Machiavelli's *The Prince* to Emerson, but the gist has remained the same in all its iterations through the years. My favorite is from the late, great Michael K Williams's character in the show *The Wire*:

"You come at the king, you best not miss."

Kit and I took our shot at the king. We missed. And now, the king has gotten back up off the ground and is coming for us.

CHAPTER TWENTY

Javaland; Denver, CO

"WHERE ARE MO AND LUCAS?" ASTRA ASKS pointedly as she takes a seat across from me.

"They'll be along. I sent them a text telling them to meet us here."

She looks like she wants to admonish me, but I hold both my hands up in protest. "I swear. No further subterfuge."

"Why here and not in the conference room?"

"Needed a change of scenery," I reply. "And while this isn't exactly beautiful and scenic, it's better than staring at those same four walls again."

Astra stirs three packets of Splenda into her mocha and looks at me, a curious expression on her face. I take a sip of my drink, my mind spinning with everything that's going on. The coffee house is only about half full this morning, and nobody is sitting at the tables directly around us, which should allow us to speak freely.

"You all right?" she asks.

"Yeah, I'm fine."

"You don't look fine," she replies. "You look rattled. What happened?"

"Nothing happened."

"Something happened. You're not yourself right now."

I take another sip and set my mug down as I try to put some sort of order to my thoughts. Honestly, I feel like I've been on a roller coaster since speaking with Locke last night. And after a mostly sleepless night, I'm still not sure what to think about any of it, let alone what to do about it. Not that there's a whole lot I *can* do about it.

"Talk to me," Astra presses. "What's going on?"

Astra won't relent until I tell her what's going on, so I give in and tell her about my conversation with Locke last night. I tell her everything. And as I speak, I see her face growing tighter and darker. When I'm done, I sit back and take another sip from my coffee mug and give her a small shrug.

"That's where we're at," I say.

"How in the hell did Hedlund get the juice to make this happen?" Astra muses.

"She knows the right people," I say. "The fact that she not only survived the scandal but came back from it even stronger makes me surer than I've ever been that she's part of the Thirteen. She has to be. Only somebody connected to a group like that could have come back from that scandal."

"Maybe. You might be right. But this world is so cynical anymore, people survive scandals all the time. She would probably have to eat a baby on live TV to sink her career," Astra replies. "In this day and age, everything is so cynical, so polarized. I don't know what it would take for a scandal to drop any politician anymore."

"Yeah, that's true. I know you might be right," I admit. "But I know she's up to something. Even if she's not connected to the Thirteen, she's got something in the works. I can feel it, Astra. She's coming for me."

"I think it's a good idea to do a dig deep into Hedlund, don't get me wrong. See what sort of connections she does have," Astra says. "But don't be surprised if she doesn't have any links to the Thirteen. We just live in a really screwed up world."

"You're not wrong. And I will have a deep dive done on her. My gut is telling me she's part of it though."

"She very well may be. But you need to have a plan to deal with her if she's not. If she's just a run-of-the-mill, spineless politician who cares more about the size of her bank account than she does about her constituents. Of course, she's hardly unique in that regard. Politics is full of people just like her."

"Right now, I plan to work this case and deal with Hedlund when we get back to Seattle," I say. "We can't afford for me to be distracted right now."

"No, we can't," she replies. "But you've got some heavy crap raining down on you—"

"I'm fine. I'll deal with it later," I tell her. "We've got a lot on our plates already without adding that psychodrama to the pile."

"Fair enough."

We sit in silence for a moment, each of us drinking from our mugs, both our minds caught up in thought. I can see that Astra is worried about Hedlund having as much pull as she does. But it's not something we can worry about right now. We'll handle Hedlund later. Right now, we have a family to find—before a squad of highly-trained killers does.

As if that thought firing through my mind was their cue, Mo and Lucas arrive and take seats across from each other at the table. They've already gotten their drinks, too, so we all take a moment to settle in. Lucas gives me a look though—one that says he's glad I didn't cut him out of this meeting, and I offer him a gentle smile in return. I'm trying here. My paranoia is in high gear right now, but I'm doing my best to keep it in check.

"All right," I start. "Thanks for meeting here."

"It's a good change of pace," Mo offers with a chuckle. "I was starting to feel like the walls in the conference room were closing in on me."

"I hear that. I was just saying the exact same thing," I tell her.

"So, what do we have?" Lucas asks. "Did SAC Locke get back to you with those names you asked about yesterday?"

"She did," I nod. "And it's not good."

"What isn't?" Mo asks.

"Everything right about now," I reply.

I tell them everything Locke shared with me last night—all except the bit about Hedlund. That's my cross to bear right now. When I'm done relaying all the information, they all look every bit as unsettled as I feel.

"If these guys are known GID operatives—assassins, really—why were they let into the country to begin with?" Mo asks.

"Because the State Department wants to avoid any semblance of conflict with a regional ally like Saudi Arabia," I say.

"State is so worried about covering their asses and avoiding any sort of dustup, they're letting kill teams hunt US citizens," Astra adds. "It's repulsive. It's cowardice."

I nod. "You're preaching to the choir."

"So, if State has already told Homeland to back off these guys, what does that mean for us?" Lucas asks. "I mean, shouldn't we be operating under the same—"

"State never gave us that directive," I interrupt. "And because I didn't hear any of that from Locke, I've heard nothing about a directive to steer clear of the Saudis."

"But you just told us that Locke..."

Lucas's voice trails off, and a sheepish smile crosses his face. "Oh, okay, I got it," he says. "You never spoke with Locke. I get it now."

I laugh. Lucas seems like he's starting to come around—like he's starting to understand how we operate in those gray areas we spoke about. It's not hard to see that he's still not entirely comfortable with doing things the way we do things, but I can see he's doing his best to overcome it. Or at least hide his discomfort with bending the rules. I make a mental note to ask Mo what she said to him, because it must have been one hell of a talk. We might want to put Mo on the Ted Talk circuit.

"I think we might make a real field agent out of Lucas yet," Astra comments.

Lucas grins, and frankly, I'm surprised he didn't take offense to it. But there is something different about him this morning. He seems marginally more relaxed and slightly less uptight than he has been since transferring into my unit. That's a good thing. Maybe Astra was right and the fact that I showed him a little trust and didn't freeze him out this time made him feel like part of the team.

"Do we know anything about these GID operatives?" Mo asks.

"Not much other than their names just yet," I say. "I asked Rick and Nina to do a deep dive on them for us. I'm hoping to hear something back from them soon."

I'd been reluctant to ask them to do the workup for me, knowing it could lead to some questions from Ayad that I don't want to answer. But I couldn't reach Brody last night, and time is of the essence, so I had no choice but to roll the dice and hope Ayad doesn't get wind of it.

"So, what's our plan?" Astra asks.

"First things first," I say. "We need to talk to Rick and Nina and see what they've managed to dig up for us."

"Back to the conference room?" she asks.

"Unfortunately, so."

CHAPTER TWENTY-ONE

Rocky Mountain Inn & Suites Conference Room; Denver, CO

ASTRA AND LUCAS TAKE THEIR SEATS AT THE CONFERENCE table as Mo gets the video connection set up. Crossing my arms over my chest, I pace back and forth at the foot of the table, frowning at the walls all around me. I am tired of looking at these things. And I think the reason for having such a visceral reaction to the room is because I know we should be out there, pounding the bricks, searching for Keller and his family. Every minute they're out there, alone and unprotected, is another minute the GID team has to murder them.

The screen crackles, then comes to life, giving us a view of the empty bullpen. A moment later, a hand enters the screen, and the camera is turned around, giving us a view of Rick and Nina, both with wide smiles on their faces.

"Afternoon, fellas," Rick chimes.

"Hey, guys," Nina adds. "How are things going out there?"

"We've got some things in motion here," I tell them. "We're hoping you can help us keep the momentum building."

"Well, I'm going to have to burst your bubble," Rick says. "There is nothing on the names you gave me. No red flags. No—nothing."

"How is that possible? They're GID operatives," Mo asks.

"Not according to their official dossiers. According to what I've been able to dig up, they're all executives with the Faisal Oil and Gas Company," Nina says.

"Well, that's a load of crap," I say.

"But solid covers," Astra replies. "And we have no way of disproving them. Not unless we want to get into a pissing match with State."

"We do have a way to try and disprove their covers, but that's not a trigger I want to pull just yet," I say. "It's not a trigger I want to pull at all if we can help it."

"I dug a little deeper," Nina says. "And all four of them supposedly went to the same college—King Abdullah University of Science and Technology—different years, of course. But a quick look at their academic records shows that it's all a front. Their records aren't worth the paper their diplomas were printed on. It's like whoever put these things together weren't even trying to make it look credible."

"They probably didn't expect anybody to look so closely at them," Mo offers.

"And how did you get their academic records?" I ask, raising an eyebrow at her.

Nina laughs. "Some questions are better left unasked," she tells me. "But don't worry, I wasn't using Bureau equipment to do my sleuthing."

I give her a grin. "Just… be careful, you two. I appreciate the initiative, diligence, and effort, but I don't want either of you to get into trouble. New regime means new rules, and we've got to appear to be complying with them."

"But only *appearing* to be complying," Astra adds with a laugh.

"My view is, what certain folks don't know won't hurt them," I reply.

Lucas shifts in his seat, and a frown crosses his lips. This is hard for him. It's not easy to go from a world where things are black and white, where there are good people and bad people, and land in a world where nothing is what it seems. Where there is no black or white, and everything is gray. On one hand, I understand what he's feeling—and to some extent, sympathize with him. On the other hand, I am going to use whatever tools I deem necessary—without fully breaking the law, of course—to protect innocent people like the Keller children.

To his credit, though, despite his obvious discomfort, Lucas gives me a nod, a non-verbal signal that he's with me. Rick clears his throat, drawing my attention back to the screen.

"So, does that mean I shouldn't be trying to ping their phones?" he asks.

"Do we have a warrant to ping them?" I ask.

"No?"

"Then probably not—"

"Damn," Rick mutters.

His face blanches, and he's looking at something off-camera. There's only one reason Rick would be looking like somebody just walked over his grave—and that reason turns the camera around to face him. Even through the screen, his eyes are intense. They feel like they're burning holes through me.

"Chief Ayad," I say dryly. "What a pleasant surprise."

"What do you think you're doing, Wilder?"

"Conferring with my team, sir, and trying to make some headway on our case," I say. "In other words, trying to do my job."

"Don't get cute with me. Why are you attempting to ping the phones of four foreign diplomats? That question seems especially important, given that I haven't seen an application for a warrant to take such action."

From off-screen, I hear Rick's voice. "Sir, that wasn't—"

"I asked Supervisory Special Agent Wilder," Ayad says coldly.

Yeah, Rick took a little too much initiative. But that's my fault. He was only anticipating my needs and doing what he thought I was going to ask him. And to be fair, at any other time, I would have asked him to do exactly what he was in the process of doing. As we're all learning, though, the times are changing—and we're going to need to learn to change with them.

"One thing I would like to know is how you know what my tech is doing, Chief Ayad," I ask. "Are you spying on us?"

"I am monitoring your activities, yes, since it's my job," he says, his voice tight, his expression dark. "Part of my job is to ensure that laws are being obeyed as we conduct our investigations, SSA Wilder. The Bureau cannot afford to have loose cannons running around, running roughshod over the law and the Constitution. What you're doing by having your tech ping their phones violates—"

"The Fourth Amendment. Yes, I know," I say. "It was a mistake. My mistake. I miscommunicated with Rick, and he believed I had a warrant. He was acting in good faith. It was my fault, sir. I take full responsibility."

"Can you tell me exactly why the warrant request was never filed?"

"Because I realized I didn't have enough for probable cause," I say. "I looked at what we had and knew no judge would ever sign off on it, so I pivoted to a new angle of investigation and forgot to tell Rick. So, as I said, that's my fault."

It's as plausible an explanation as any, and Ayad seems to buy it. Clearly, I have a talent for deception. Maybe I should have opted for the Agency instead of the Bureau.

"That's quite a mistake, SSA Wilder," he says, seemingly to be reveling in my admission of a mistake. "One that could have tanked the entire case—if you ever bring one."

"Yes, sir, I'm aware," I reply. "Apologies. It won't happen again."

"It better not, SSA Wilder," he says. "And believe me when I say that you and I will be having a long conversation about your investigative methodology—as well as your attitude—when you return."

I hope the sheer rage I'm feeling doesn't show up too much on my face right now.

"Looking forward to it, sir."

The screen goes dark, and I grab the bottle of water sitting in front of me, turn, and with a primal scream of frustration, fire it at the wall of the conference room as hard as I can. The bottle explodes on impact, sending a spray of water high into the air. Streams of water run down the wall and form a small puddle on the carpet.

"If you wanted something else to drink, all you had to do was ask," Astra cracks with a mischievous grin.

Astra's joke has the intended effect and immediately lightens the mood in the room as everybody laughs. It even gets a grin out of me. But I'm currently feeling a little too bitter and salty to laugh along with them. Their good cheer tapers off after a minute, though, and some of the heaviness returns.

"Sorry for the outburst," I say. "That was… unprofessional."

"If nothing else, at least you know you're right about Ayad spying on us," Mo offers.

Lucas looks at me nervously. "I hate to say it, but Ayad isn't wrong about needing a warrant to ping those phones. Like you said, new regime, new rules."

"I know, I know," I say. "And because of that, I wouldn't have asked Rick to ping them simply because I suspected Ayad was monitoring the electronics in the shop. I wouldn't have wanted him to get into trouble for it. I didn't need him to anyway."

"So, what now?" Astra asks. "Denver's a big city. How are we going to find four guys in a metro area of three million people?"

That finally allows me to break out a grin—a genuine one. "Because we know where to start looking."

CHAPTER TWENTY-TWO

Colorado Convention Center; Denver, CO

AN ARTFUL, MODERN MASTERWORK OF GLASS AND STEEL, the Colorado Convention Center has more than two million square feet of space with meeting rooms, ballrooms, and space for exhibits. There are all sorts of amenities crammed into every corner of the cavernous space. It's even got a sizable public art collection both inside and outside the center that's the focus of the many cultural tours that run through the city. It's an impressive building—the kind I'd expect from the oeuvre of Brad Keller—or I suppose

Daniel Waters, in truth. And it is currently hosting the Green Energy Expo.

We're standing beside the sculpture known as the "Big Blue Bear," watching hordes of people moving in and out of the convention center. The sculpture of the bear is nearly forty feet tall and has its paws and nose pressed to the glass wall, appearing to be peering into the main lobby. It's a fun and whimsical piece that people love snapping pictures with. Outside the hall, there are knots of people standing around talking while others seem to be moving about with a purpose. Finding four men in this sea of humanity isn't going to be easy.

"Talk about a needle in a haystack," Mo says.

"Most Saudi men, even here in the west, will wear the traditional *ghutra* and *iqal* on their heads," Astra tells us. "It's likely going to be either white or red-and-white checkers. The *iqal* will be two black cords around the head to help keep it in place. That should hopefully narrow it down some."

"Well, look at you being all knowledgeable about other cultures," Mo teases.

"Hey, I ain't just a pretty face," Astra replies.

"I think it'll be more efficient if we split up and search," I say. "Does everybody have the photos of the men on their phones?"

They all nod and hold up their phones displaying the four-pack of pictures of the men we're looking for.

"Good. Each of us should take a hall," I say. "Mo, take the west hall. Astra, the north. Lucas, take the south hall, and I'll take the east. We'll meet back here at the bear in—what, two hours? After that, if we haven't found them, we'll reassess."

"There might be an easier way to do this, you know," Astra comments.

"Yeah? What's that?" I ask.

"Why not have Rick and Nina start calling the hotels in Denver? Find out where they're staying," she offers.

I think about it for a moment and nod. It's not a bad idea. "There are more than a hundred hotels in Denver, so that's going to take some time. Might as well use it to do an eyeball search," I say. "If we come up empty, we'll hopefully have something from

Rick and Nina. Or we can go back to the conference room and wait for them to get back to us."

"God, no. I'm good with walking around here," Astra says with a laugh.

"That's what I thought," I reply and smile at her.

"What should we do if we spot one of them?" Mo asks.

"Detain them and call me," I reply.

"Can we legally detain them?" Lucas asks.

"Don't use the word detain," I offer. "Just have them wait with you until I can get there to ask a few questions. Just tell them we need their help with something. Be as vague as possible. Don't mention Keller or anything specific."

Lucas grimaces, obviously not a fan of the plan. Legally, no, we can't detain them. They're not a suspect in a crime. At least, not one we can prove. But if we frame it as simply needing their help with an ongoing investigation and make it seem like their cooperation is voluntary, then we dodge all the land mines these new rules are putting in our way.

"And if they refuse to stay?" Lucas asks. "It's not like we can arrest them."

"No. If they refuse to stay, then we'll have to figure out what our next steps will be," I shrug. "But we'll cross that bridge when we come to it. For now, do everything in your power, be as persuasive as you can be, and get them to voluntarily wait for us."

"We'll do our best," Mo says.

"All right. You've got your assignments," I say. "Let's get to it."

We scatter and head for our assigned halls. I weave my way through the crowd, doing my best to avoid bumping into anybody. It's not an easy feat. The Green Energy Expo is very well attended, and just walking through the lobby, I hear at least twenty different languages being spoken. I keep my eyes moving, though, looking for the head covering Astra described. In theory, it will make them stand out. And I would think, if they're traveling on diplomatic papers, they'd be wearing it just to keep up appearances that tie them to their culture.

As I stare across the hordes of people filling the lobby, though, I'm having a hard time seeing anything. I dart around a cluster of people speaking German and find my way to a staircase. I climb halfway up and scan the lobby, looking for the head covering or anybody who looks like they might be Saudi. Yeah, some would call it racial profiling, but I'm looking for specific people, not people of a specific color.

But the lobby is a dry hole. I don't see anybody matching the photos on my phone, so I come down the stairs and head into the east hall. As I walk down the carpeted path, I crane my neck at the booths on either side of me, all of them filled with some machine or gadget that is somehow related to green energy. There's no doubt some would think me a horrible person, but I don't know much about the environment or green energy. It's just never been something that holds a lot of interest for me—mainly because I don't understand most of what people are talking about.

I mean, I get that it's important and that a changing environment can change the world for all of us—and not in a beneficial way. I have a rudimentary understanding of climate change, melting polar ice caps, warming oceans, and the like. I try to use canvas bags at the store, and I buy those energy-efficient lightbulbs, and I grumble about those paper straws at coffee shops, but I put up with them. Honestly, I couldn't tell you anything remotely intelligent about the large-scale science behind it. Mostly, I think it's probably better to leave it to people who are smarter than I am to figure out while I do what I was put on this earth to do—put bad people in small cages for the rest of their lives.

I walk the entire hall, not seeing the men I'm looking for, and blow out a frustrated breath. It was probably a stupid idea to think we could find them in this mass of humanity in the first place. I give myself a mental kick to get out of that mindset. That's never helped anything. I glance at my watch and see I still have time to make the circuit through the hall again before I need to meet the others at the bear.

I'm just about to set out when my phone buzzes. Pulling it out of my pocket, I see that it's Lucas and feel a bolt of excitement. I connect the call and press the phone to my ear, clamping my hand over the other one to shut out the noise so I can hear.

"Yeah," I say. "What do you have, Lucas?"

"I've got two of our targets in sight," he tells me. "They're out here in the lobby near the coffee cart outside the south hall."

"I'll be right there. Do me a favor and text Astra and Mo. Let them know," I say. "And for God's sake, don't let those two out of your sight."

"Copy that," he replies.

I disconnect the call and drop the phone into my pocket then start off, walking at a brisk pace, but not quick enough to draw attention to myself. An excited energy surges through me. It's a massive stroke of luck that Lucas was able to find these guys—two of them anyway. And I hope that it's a portent of something good. I'm hoping that talking to these two will break the case wide open for us. At the very least, I'm hoping that it will point us in the right direction and give us a viable investigative path to follow.

These guys are GID and, presumably, will know what they're doing. They'll know to not give anything away. Which means I need to be on top of my game and use all the tricks in my arsenal to trip them up. An eye twitch, an involuntary smirk—I need to keep a close watch on them for the slightest tic or tell. There's part of me that's worried they'll be as unreadable as Kalfus was. And if they are, I'll deal with it. Right now, being face to face with them and getting some answers is all that matters.

I spot Lucas standing off to the side, pretending to be looking at his phone. He's casual and cool. He's good. He looks up when he sees me coming and cuts a glance to his right. The two Saudis are standing at a table near the coffee cart enjoying a cup and talking with one another. Aside from the ghutras on their heads, they blend in exceptionally well with everybody else in the crowd.

The whole scene is surprisingly... normal. Lucas starts to push away from the wall, but I give him a subtle gesture to stay where he is. I don't want to give these two the faces of everybody on my team. I have a feeling we're going to need to keep some anonymity to move against them. Astra must have been reading my mind because she and Mo are standing at a table off to the side about ten feet away, looking as casual as anybody else. They don't even bother looking at me when I pass their table. I love that we have that innate connection.

The Saudis are dressed in dark blue suits. Hamsah Saleh, who I figure to be the leader of the team since he's the oldest, has dark, olive-colored skin and eyes blacker than midnight that are piercing—and a little unsettling, truth be told. Eyeballing it, I'd say he's an inch or two taller than me, so not quite six feet tall. But he is athletic-looking. He's got a blue shirt beneath his jacket and a yellow tie. There are fine lines at the corners of his eyes and mouth, and his goatee is more gray than black.

Malik Eid, the other man at the table, is just twenty-nine years old and the youngest member of Saleh's team. He's tall—six-three or six-four—and has terra-cotta-colored skin. His eyes are green, he has a neatly trimmed beard, and he's got a smooth, youthful look to him. Like Saleh, Eid is lean and fit. He looks like a man who knows how to handle himself. His shirt is white, and he's wearing a dark tie. A white pocket square completes his outfit, making him look very refined, but he's got the eyes of a killer.

They both look at me, surprise on their faces when I step to their table. We exchange glances in silence for a long, awkward moment.

"Can I help you?" Saleh finally asks, his voice richly accented.

I finally flash them my credentials, which doesn't seem to impress them. Once they've gotten a good look at them, though, I put my creds back in my pocket and lean forward on their table, clasping my hands together.

"Perhaps you can help," I start. "I was hoping you might tell me where Brad Keller is."

Saleh frowns. "I'm sorry, who?"

"Keller," I reply. "Brad Keller."

"I'm afraid I don't know who you are talking about," Saleh says.

"No?" I ask. "I mean, that's who you and your boys are here to murder, isn't it?"

Saleh stares at me for a long moment then bursts into laughter and looks around. Eid stares at me with those dead eyes, his face completely expressionless. Saleh slaps him in the arm as he laughs, as if to remind Eid to smile. And when he does, it looks more vicious than joyful. The man's smile is even more unsettling than his dead, blank stare. Saleh is a much smoother, more natural operator than Eid. It's clear he still needs some seasoning.

"Is this one of those practical jokes you Americans like to play and film then put on television?" Saleh asks. "Where is the camera?"

"No camera, sir," I reply. "But we have it on good authority that you, Mr. Eid here, as well as Mr. Saeed, and Mr. Alam are here in town to kill a man and his family."

Saleh is still smirking at me but gives me a shrug. "Your good authority has made a mistake. We are executives with Faisal Oil and are attending this conference to learn more about green energy. It would be a prodigious investment for our company."

"Uh-huh," I reply. "That almost sounds convincing. You're good."

"I'm afraid I don't know what you're talking about," Saleh says.

I turn to Eid. "What about you? Do you know what I'm talking about?"

Eid cuts a glance at Saleh. Saleh responds with an extremely subtle shake of the head I only catch from the corner of my eye. Eid smiles at me and then starts speaking in Arabic.

"I'm afraid my colleague doesn't speak English," Saleh says.

"Convenient," I note. "You'd think that an oil company executive would be able to speak English, what with all the western countries you deal with."

Saleh's jaw clenches. He'd made his first mistake, and he knows it. But he quickly smooths out his face and offers me a smile.

"Agent Wilder," he says. "Are you accusing us of something? Do you believe we've done anything but attend this conference?"

"Where are Saeed and Alam?" I ask.

"I believe they're attending a seminar on solar power," he says. "I know they're both very passionate about bringing solar power into the mainstream at home. We certainly have enough sun, don't we?"

He laughs at his own joke and even Eid cracks a smile. I don't though. I just look at him, trying to give him the sort of dead-eyed stare Eid has been giving me since I stepped to their table. He's better at it.

"Brad Keller," I press. "Where is he?"

ELLE GRAY

"I do not know who this is or why you think I want to kill him," Saleh says.

"Let me try it this way. You might know him as Drake Weathers, Thomas Cooper, Charlie Mullins, or August North," I say, flashing them the picture of Keller I have on my phone. "Look familiar? Ring any bells yet?"

As I list off the names, I watch them as closely as I've ever watched any suspect. All I get is a slight twitch of the eye from Saleh when I flash the photo. It isn't much, but it's enough for me. It confirms for me, the Saudis know Keller. They recognize him. It leads me to believe the intel is right, and they're probably here to kill him.

"I'm afraid none of those names mean anything to me, Agent Wilder," Saleh finally says.

"Are Mr. Saeed and Mr. Alam out there hunting for him now?" I ask.

"I told you, they are—"

"That's crap, and we both know it," I cut him off. "The four of you are with Saudi Intelligence. Don't even try to convince me otherwise. I know who you are and what you're really here for."

"I'm afraid your information is incorrect, Agent Wilder," he replies. "And if you have any further questions for us, you can relay them to our consulate. We are done here."

Saleh and Eid turn and walk off together. I watch them go and wait until they melt into the crowd before I turn to Astra.

"Well, that seems like a bust," she says.

"Nah. I just want to get them feeling some heat. Had to kick the hornet's nest to do that," I say. "Mo, I want you and Lucas to run loose surveillance on them. Now that they know we're on to them, that's going to force them to alter their timeline. If we're lucky, it will lead them to make a mistake that we can arrest them for. It's not ideal, and with their diplomatic status, they'll be out sooner than later, but it might give us the time we need to find Keller."

"Smart," Mo says.

"That's why I make the big bucks," I reply with a grin.

"Yeah, until Ayad fires you for this," Astra adds.

174

"Yeah, there's that," I say. "Until then though, we've got a job to do. So, let's get to it."

CHAPTER TWENTY-THREE

Rocky Mountain Inn & Suites Conference Room; Denver, CO

WITH THE INVESTIGATION STARTING TO FEEL LIKE IT'S gaining a little traction and momentum, I hate coming back to the conference room. I'd much rather be out there developing leads or running down clues. But the truth is, we've got a disturbing lack of either. Plus, about an hour after we left the convention center, Ayad called and said he needed to talk. He gave me the impression it wasn't optional.

"He say what he wanted?" Astra asks.

I shake my head. "No, but he didn't sound too happy."

"Does he ever sound happy?"

"No," I reply. "But there were definitely extra notes of peevishness."

"What did you do now?" Astra asks with a grin.

"I haven't had time to do anything."

As if speaking his name cued him to call, the request to join a video chat comes through. Astra and I share a glance.

"Think I should let it go to voicemail?" I ask.

"How much do you like your job?"

I sigh dramatically. "Fine."

Astra makes sure she's out of the line of camera sight as I connect the call and the video screen comes on. Ayad is sitting in his office, his face not just stern, but dark with anger.

"You must not like your job very much, SSA Wilder."

"I love my job," I reply. "I'm just not so fond of a few of my coworkers."

His jaw flexes, and the darkness in his eyes deepens. Astra looks at me like I've lost my mind and shakes her head. She tries but can't keep the smile from flickering across her lips, but her point is made. I should probably take this a little more seriously. Ayad isn't the kind of guy you want to screw with. He's got enough friends in enough high places to bring down the hammer. Anything I do to him, he'll revisit upon me tenfold. There's just something about him that brings out my own petty, snarky side, and it's difficult to contain.

"What has you so upset this time, Chief Ayad?" I ask. "I didn't do anything that required me to get a warrant—"

"Do you know who I just got off the phone with?"

"I'm a woman of many exceptional skills, but I'm afraid that clairvoyance isn't among my talents," I reply. "Sir."

"We are going to have a long talk about your attitude, Wilder," he snaps.

"I'll be sure to clear my schedule," I say. "So, what can I do for you, Chief. I have an investigation—"

"What in the hell do you think you're doing down there?" he growls.

"Investigating the disappearance of Brad Keller and his family. You do remember giving me the file and telling me to get to Colorado and find them, don't you?" I ask. "I mean, if you don't, that's all right. I would suggest, though, that you take a cognitive test—"

"Enough!" he shouts, slamming his fist down on his table to emphasize his word.

Ayad draws in a deep breath, seems to silently count to ten, then lets it out slowly. It doesn't work though. He doesn't look any less angry. I know I shouldn't be antagonizing Ayad. He's my boss. But he rubbed me wrong from the jump. That conversation we had after Stone left my office that first day told me everything I need to know about the man.

He's a climber. He's willing to kiss the right asses, but when it comes to the people working under him, he's more than happy to dump all over us. I despise people like that. Like him. And that's why I can't seem to keep my snark and contempt for him under wraps. It's as involuntary a reflex to me as blinking or breathing. I catch Astra's eye and she's giving me the sign to knock it off, so I frown and look down, doing my best to put a contrite expression on my face.

"Apologies, sir," I say.

"I just got off the phone with State. It seems they got a call from the Saudi consulate," he says, his voice quivering with anger. "They wanted to know why you and your team are harassing Saudi diplomats here for a conference on green and renewable energy."

"Sir, we have reason to believe that's a cover. These four men are here as a kill squad, and we believe they are hunting Brad Keller."

"What reason?"

"Excuse me?"

"Your reason for believing they're assassins. What is it?"

"They're with the GID, sir, and—"

"Being employed by Saudi Intelligence doesn't make them assassins."

"It also means they're not oil executives—which is their cover," I point out. "They're attending that conference as cover. When I spoke with them—"

"SSA Wilder, they may or may not be with GID. We don't know. The papers State has on them backs up their story that they're oil executives here for a conference," he says. "Not here to hunt and kill a US citizen."

As badly as I want to tell him what Kalfus told me and Locke echoed, I can't. I was sworn to secrecy. Not only that, but I also can't have Ayad finding out this investigation is being based on the words of a spy. So far, everything Kalfus told me has checked out. But that won't be good enough for Ayad. Frankly, it's not good enough for me right now. We have zero physical evidence. Hell, we can't even prove a crime has been committed. Right now, all we have is a missing family.

I know there's something here though. I know that underneath all this smoke, there's a raging forest fire. I can feel it in my bones. The trouble is, I can't get through the smoke to get to the fire underneath. And having Ayad looking over my shoulder every step of the way isn't helping me cut through the smoke either. If anything, all he's doing is making more smoke. If I didn't know better, I'd say it's almost like he wants me to fail.

It's a thought that sends a cold shiver down my spine. Why would Ayad want me to fail? Because if the Thirteen can't kill me, tarnishing my reputation and tearing me down is the next best thing. From their perspective, I'd imagine that seeing me laid low and rendering all my accomplishments meaningless, turning me into a punch line or a cautionary tale, would be even better than taking my life.

"Sir, I looked them in the eye, and I've been doing this job a while now," I say. "I know a killer when I see one, and those men—"

"SSA Wilder, I am ordering you to stand down," he cuts me off. "You are not to approach the Saudis. You are not to talk to them. I don't even want you thinking about them. State is already having to smooth ruffled feathers because of your stunt. You are to stay away from them. Do you understand?"

"Sir, my path of investigation has led me to them. Are you asking me to ignore viable suspects—"

"I'm not asking you to do anything, SSA Wilder," he interrupts me. "I'm *ordering* you to stay away from them. Do you understand?"

"To be honest, no, I don't."

"Well, that's unfortunate. But you don't need to understand. All you need to do is follow my order. And if you can't do that, you're going to end up exiled to a field office in Montana chasing… cattle rustlers," he snaps. "I know you think you're special and the rules don't apply to you, but I'm here to tell you that they do, Wilder. And it's well past time you fall in line and do as you're told. Do you understand?"

"Sure, but I'm not sure cattle rustling is still a thing, sir."

His face darkens again, but rather than blow me up, he cuts the feed, and the screen goes dark. I sit back in my seat and blow out a long breath. I'm so angry I'm trembling.

"Blake, you know I'd never tell you to back off an investigation, but…"

Her voice trails off, but she doesn't need to finish the statement for me to know what she's trying to say. She's telling me that we need to do just that. Back off. Never in my career have I ever backed off a suspect or an investigation.

"This is what happens when you put climbers and politicians in positions of authority," I tell her. "It makes me sick to my stomach that politics get in the way of viable leads and suspects."

"How viable is the lead though, Blake?"

I turn to her, surprised. "What do you mean?"

"I mean, just because it's our only lead, it doesn't mean it's all that viable," she points out. "What if Ayad is right and these guys really are just oil guys?"

"I looked them in the eye, Astra. They're cold, and they're calculating," I say. "They're killers. Assassins."

"Yeah, maybe. You very well may be right," she says. "But, what if you're wrong? What if they're not? All sorts of oil executives could be just as cold and calculating as any killer. Maybe they're just extremely cutthroat businessmen."

"But they're known—"

She holds up a hand to stop me. "I know. And that's the other thing. Even if they are known assassins—what if they're not here chasing Keller? Let's say they are GID, and they're here on assignment. Is it possible they're here for some other reason? I mean, a green energy conference is a strange place to be hanging out when they're supposedly hunting a CIA spook who's gone off the grid. Isn't it?"

I run a hand over my face and look down at the table. As much as I want to refute her words, to prove her wrong, I can't. She's not wrong. But that doesn't necessarily mean she's right. I don't care what Ayad says—these guys are trained killers. When you've been around killers as much as I have, you get to know what they look like. They all have something in their eyes that marks them as different from other people.

I can't explain it in any way that makes sense, but it's like Supreme Court Justice Potter Stewart said in an opinion on pornography back in 1964: *I know it when I see it.* Standing there with Saleh and Eid and looking them in the eye was enough for me to know they're killers. Without a doubt. It's the same gleam I've seen in the eyes of every single killer I've ever dealt with. It's… an emptiness. It's the only way I can describe it. There's a void behind their eyes and a complete lack of humanity.

But I have to admit that Astra's suggestion they might not be here for Keller is something I hadn't considered before. That might explain the strange look on their faces when I mentioned his name. Maybe it was confusion. Maybe they weren't lying about not being here for him. But if they're not here for Keller, what are they here for?

My phone rings, and I see it's a Skype call from Mo. I quickly open it but am surprised to see it's not Mo on the other end of the call. It's Saleh.

The iceberg that drops into my gut at that moment is about a thousand times bigger than the one that sunk the Titanic.

"We should talk, Agent Wilder," he starts.

My heart is racing, and it's all I can do to prevent a torrent of rage from spilling out.

"Where are my people?" I demand.

He turns the phone to show Mo and Lucas sitting in the SUV, both with sheepish expressions on their faces. They're not cuffed and seem unharmed as far as I can tell, which lets me exhale the world's biggest sigh of relief. Saleh made them—then got the drop on them. The phone turns back, the screen filled with Saleh's face.

"They are safe, as you can see," he says. "I am not going to hurt them. I merely wanted to speak with you."

"So, speak."

"Not on the phone," he says. "You just never know who's listening."

"Fine. Where and when?"

"There is a fair in town. Near the Botanical Gardens," he says. "Meet me near the carousel in an hour."

"I'll be there."

"And please, come alone. What I have to say is for your ears alone."

"I'll see you in an hour."

CHAPTER
TWENTY-FOUR

Centennial State Carnival; Denver, CO

A S FAR AS CARNIVALS GO, THE CENTENNIAL STATE version is a little disappointing. Set up in Congress Park, across the street from the Botanical Gardens, it's more like a stripped-down county fair or maybe a pumped-up flea market than an actual carnival. There are a handful of rides, carnival games, and a petting zoo, but it seems like local vendors are the main attraction. There are about a hundred booths of local artisans hawking their wares.

It took me half of the hour Saleh gave me to talk Astra into letting me come alone. I rejected the wire she wanted to put on me and only consented to a tracking device in my shoe. Saleh is smart and knows his craft. I'm sure he's going to take steps to neutralize any possible surveillance equipment, and I have no doubt his guys will be there, shadowing him and making sure I don't get too frisky.

Not that I'm planning to. Mo called us after I hung up with Saleh and reported they were on their way back to the hotel without a hair on their heads out of place. Saleh got the drop on them but seemed content in making his point. If he'd wanted to kill them, he could have. That gave me confidence that he wasn't looking to kill me and that he simply wanted to, as he said, have a conversation.

And so, here I am, standing at the fence that surrounds the carousel, watching it slowly turn in circles to the delight of the small children sitting on the unicorns and in the frogs. The tinkly music from the carousel is loud and about as soothing as the music on "It's a Small World" at Disneyland. I can't imagine working here and having to listen to that for hours on end. A group of mothers stands off to the side looking equal parts grateful for the break from their kids and terrified of them falling off the carousel.

"I don't suppose you've tried the fried butter," Saleh says as he steps up to the fence beside me.

"God no," I say. "I think just saying the words fried butter clogs your arteries."

Saleh chuckles. "You Americans will fry anything. Butter has to be one of the worst things I've seen. It sounds disgraceful."

"I agree with you. And don't lump us all into the same category. Not all of us like fair foods," I say. "And some of us think they're crimes against humanity. Though I would suggest you at least try the fried Twinkie before you go. It shames me to admit this, but they are surprisingly good."

He smiles at me. "I'll try that," he says. "Thank you for coming."

"Thank you for not hurting my people."

"I have no desire to hurt your people, Agent Wilder," he says. "I am not here for that."

"Then why are you here?"

He looks around and given the slight frown upon his lips, doesn't like what he sees. There are clusters of people who've moved closer to us, and it seems he would rather speak privately. While I appreciate him wanting to meet in public to keep tensions low—and make me feel better about meeting with him in private—it's not very practical when you want to have a quiet word with somebody.

"Come," I say. "I see a place we can get away from people and talk."

"Thank you," he nods.

On our way toward a bench beneath a small thicket of trees well off the path of the fairway, I stop at a small booth and order a pair of fried Twinkies. Saleh laughs as I hand one to him but gives it a try. He nibbles delicately at the edges at first but then takes a real bite and makes a sound I can only interpret as approval.

"I must admit, you have surprised me," he says with a smile. "It's no *kunafah*, but it is not bad."

"Right?" I reply with a laugh.

We sit down on the bench, taking a minute to finish our fried treats. When we're done, he takes my wrapper from me and throws it into the trash can next to the bench.

"Thank you for the treat," he says.

"You're welcome," I reply. "Couldn't let you leave without giving you something horrible to eat. It wouldn't be American."

He laughs. Saleh is a surprisingly easygoing man. I'd go so far as to say he's even somewhat likable. He has a quick smile and an infectious laugh. He is not what I expected of a hardened spy and assassin. But then, Kalfus was much the same way. Maybe when you see and do the things these men have to do, you find refuge in humor. No matter how long you've been doing the job, it can't be easy to kill other people for a living. You would have to find some way to cope with it.

But that's just my armchair shrink's take on it. Some people are just cold and hollow inside and take pleasure in killing. It's the only thing that brings some people any sense of joy. Which is sick, of course. But they've got such a hole inside them, swallowing the suffering of others is the only thing that fills it. Albeit temporarily. I don't get that sense from Saleh though. I think he sees what he does as his patriotic duty.

"You were right. I do know Brad Keller. Though, I knew him as Brad Hewitt," he starts. "I have known him for more than ten years."

"How did you meet him?"

"He was on loan to us from your CIA, and we worked together in Yemen many years ago," he tells me. "He saved my life, and we became friends after that. He is a good man."

"So, why does the GID want him dead?"

He looks at me with an expression of confusion on his face. "The GID does not want him dead. We've received no orders to eliminate him. I give you my word."

"Then why are you here?"

"We are seeing to… other matters," he says. "Your State Department asked us to assist them with a matter that has nothing to do with Brad. That is why we are here. If somebody is trying to kill him, I assure you it is not the GID. I would have gotten word. And I promise you that it is not my team. I have no reason to want to see him dead. Nor does the GID. Brad has been a valuable ally to us over the years. And a good friend to me."

I search his face, looking deeply into his eyes for the barest hint of deception. I know spies are well trained to never give anything away, but I don't get the sense that Saleh is shielding his emotions from me. If anything, I see fear and grief over the potential death of somebody he considers a friend. There are times when you have absolutely nothing but your gut to go by and you have to listen to it. This is one of those times. When Saleh says he cares for Brad, I believe him. His words ring true, and his voice is sincere. I don't think he's lying to me. I'd bet my pension on it.

While hitting a dead end in the course of an investigation sucks and is frustrating, I have to admit to feeling a sense of relief washing over me that it's not the GID trying to kill him. Of course, this means starting from square one again and having to figure out who's trying to kill Keller. And, of course, to find him. Dead or alive, I'm more determined than ever to find Brad Keller and his family.

"When was the last time you spoke with Mr. Keller?" I ask.

"I would suppose about a month ago," he replies.

"Did he say anything to you? Did he mention he thought he was being watched? Or that somebody might be after him?"

Saleh frowns and looks away, and I can tell he knows something. I give him a moment to gather himself to see if he'll tell me, but his silence drags out, and I know he's not going to. Not unless I push him.

"What is it?" I press. "What did he say?"

Saleh's face darkens, but he finally turns back to me and runs a hand over his face.

"Mr. Saleh? Please," I say. "I need to find Mr. Keller and his family. And whatever you know might help me do that."

He lets out a long breath. "No, he never was in fear of being followed or targeted. Not that he ever said to me."

"Then what did he say?"

"He asked me to help him get out of the United States," he replies. "He wanted me to arrange passage to Saudi Arabia. Help him obtain a new identity and citizenship once there."

"Did he say why he wanted those things?"

He shakes his head. "He didn't. He said he would explain everything, but he needed to arrange things here first," he tells me. "All he said was that he had to finish collecting evidence and get it to somebody he could trust."

"Evidence? What was he collecting evidence of?"

"He did not say. Brad said he didn't want to get me mixed up with his problems," Saleh goes on. "But he said that once he had gathered whatever it was he was seeking, he would need my assistance to get out of the country. I thought perhaps it was just paranoia speaking. Paranoia is very common in our line of work, as I'm sure you can imagine."

"Given the fact that he hasn't been seen in a while now, I'd say his paranoia might have been well-founded," I say.

"So it seems," he replies, his voice colored with sadness.

"And he didn't give you any hint of what he was gathering evidence of?"

"Unfortunately, no. Nothing. He said it was for my own protection," he says. "It seemed to be something very large. Something delicate. Brad was not one for half measures. And I could tell that he was very frightened about whatever this thing is."

"Did you know of any place he might go to hole up? Did he ever mention a hideout?"

"No. Nothing of the sort. He believed in keeping his circle of information small. Very small."

"His paranoia at work again."

Saleh nods. "In the circumstance, I suppose I cannot blame him."

"I suppose so."

I can't think of any other questions to ask. Even if I did, it doesn't seem like he has the answers I'm looking for anyway. Maybe I'm being naïve, but my feeling is that Saleh is being completely candid with me.

"Thank you for talking to me, Mr. Saleh."

"It's Hamsah. And you're welcome," he says. "Please. Find Brad and his family. They are good people."

"I'm going to do everything I can," I say.

"If there is anything I can do, please call me," he says and hands me a burner phone. "My number is the only one programmed into it. You can reach me twenty-four hours a day."

"Actually, there may be something you can do. May I ask that you contact me if Mr. Keller reaches out and asks you to get him to Saudi Arabia?" I ask.

He hesitates for a moment—and that pause tells me he might not reach out immediately if Keller contacts him. His loyalty is to Keller, not me. And I understand that, but whatever is going on here is starting to feel important—and bigger than either one of us.

"Please, Mr. Saleh," I say. "My concern is for his young children. They have no part in all these spy games. They're innocent. I simply want to know that they are safe."

"If he reaches out to me, I will have him contact you—once I have gotten him and his family somewhere safe," he says. "That is the best I can commit to."

"That's good enough," I say, respecting his honesty. "Thank you, Mr. Saleh."

"Please. Call me Hamsah."

"Thank you, Hamsah," I say.

He gets to his feet and gives me a nod. "No. Thank you, Agent Wilder," he says. "Please find him."

"Call me Blake," I reply. "And I'll do everything I can."

I stand and shake his hand. His gaze is direct and penetrating, and I can feel just how much he wants me to find Keller.

"Until we speak again," he says.

"Until then."

CHAPTER TWENTY-FIVE

Rocky Mountain Inn & Suites Conference Room: Denver, CO

"AND WE'RE BELIEVING HIM?" MO ASKS. "WE'RE actually believing what he says?"

"I'm with Mo," Lucas says. "He's a spy. And an assassin. How trustworthy can he be?"

"Ordinarily, I'd say not at all. But I saw how much Keller means to him. And how badly he wants us to find him. I read it in his eyes."

"You saw that in his eyes?" Lucas frowns, his voice dripping with skepticism. "That's what you're basing your belief that he wasn't involved on?"

I turn to Lucas and give him a measured look. "When you've worked in the field for a while and have dealt with a fair number of suspects, you start to learn how to read people. You start to learn to hear the truth in their words and see it in their eyes. In their body language. In their facial expressions."

I'm doing my level best to keep from sounding preachy or condescending. But it's true. There are some things that you can only learn with experience in the field—something Lucas doesn't have. I also think having a degree in psychology gives me an edge. I've been well trained and have a solid understanding of the human brain. But the most important tool you have in the field and when dealing with suspects is experience. It teaches you things you'll never find in a textbook or sitting behind a computer terminal analyzing data.

"She's not wrong," Mo tells him. "I've learned a lot about reading a suspect in the time I've been on this team. It's something only experience is going to teach you."

"Blake's usually not wrong when she gets a read on people. I trust her when she has a feeling about somebody," Astra adds. "We call her the psycho whisperer."

Lucas grins. "Given my dating history, I thought that was my title."

Astra, Mo, and I all exchange a look then burst into laughter, his completely unexpected comment taking us all by surprise.

"Lucas, you made a joke," I say. "I didn't think you had it in you."

"I'm full of surprises, SSA Wilder."

"Are you ever going to just call me Blake like everybody else?"

"One thing at a time. Baby steps," he says with a smile.

"Fair enough," I say.

"All right, so if we're convinced the GID didn't have anything to do with Keller's disappearance, where are we at?" Astra asks.

"Unfortunately, that pushes us back to square one," I say.

"Well, we've been here before," Mo comments.

"We need to know what he was collecting evidence of," Lucas says.

"Agreed. But I have no idea where to begin with that," I tell him. "And I don't think we're going to know until we find Keller and he tells us."

"If we find him. And if he tells us," Astra says.

"Right. Lots of ifs to deal with."

"What about your buddy Kalfus?" Astra asks. "Do you think Keller might have told him what he was working on?'

I shake my head. "I already contacted Kalfus to ask. He didn't know anything about what Keller was working on."

"Isn't it strange that Keller wouldn't have told his handler what he was doing?" Mo asks.

I shrug. "Not necessarily. That's all part of the spy game," I say. "He might not have wanted to tip his hand before he had what he needed to do—whatever it was he was trying to do. At this point, we don't even know who he was investigating or what he was expecting to happen when he had what he needed."

"All right, so what's next?" Mo says.

"We need to find Keller and his family," Astra replies.

"We don't even know for sure that he's still in Denver," Lucas adds.

"We don't. Not for sure, but I have a feeling he is. With all the heat on him, I don't think he'd risk moving his family until he had a solid exit strategy," I reply. "We know he was looking to get to Saudi Arabia but not until he'd finished putting his case together—whatever that case is."

"Do you trust Saleh to tell you if Keller contacts him?" Mo asks.

"He gave me his word that he'll contact me once he's gotten Keller and his family to safety. I believe he'll keep his word," I say. "But the better path is for us to find him first. I'm feeling like whatever it is Keller's working on is important. And we need to find out what it is."

"Which brings us back to the problem of trying to find him," Astra says. "If the man doesn't want to be found, we're not going to find him. As a spy, it's kind of his thing."

"We could try rattling the CIA's cage again," Lucas offers.

"They're not going to help us," I reply. "Stone's already gotten us as much help as we're going to get by putting me with Kalfus."

I fold my arms over my chest as I pace the room, my mind spinning. There has to be a way to find Keller. I get that spies are trained to avoid detection, but there has to be a way to track him down. Mo, Astra, and Lucas are all sitting back in their chairs, the same thoughtful expression on all their faces as they work at the same knot I'm trying to unravel in my mind.

As determined as I am to find Keller and his family, I'm equally interested in learning what he's been working on. What could possibly be so sensitive, so important, that he needed to immediately leave the country after finding it?

The fact that he didn't trust Saleh or Kalfus enough to confide in either one of them makes me believe this is high-level stuff. It's not going to be something simple or some mundane crime. I have a feeling this is something that's going to involve some powerful people.

Given my own experiences with powerful people who are hunting you, I can understand why Keller's gone underground. He's playing a very dangerous game—one that could get his entire family killed if they catch up to him. It's understandable that he'd use every trick in the book to stay off everybody's radar. I know what it's like when you don't know who you can trust and fear that everybody will put a bullet in the back of your head. For Keller though, it's ten times worse, given that he's got a wife and two small kids in tow.

I make my third lap around the conference room, continuing to work the problem in my head. There's something I'm missing. Something I'm not seeing. I keep going over everything we've found to this point. But the list of evidence we've collected is meager, to say the least. And nothing points to where he might have gone or whom or what it is he's investigating. Keller is good. He covers his tracks well. He's a ghost. The Agency was right about his talent when they identified and recruited him.

It's then that my mind seizes on one of the few pieces of evidence we do have in hand. As I think about it, I gain a sense of clarity, and along with it, a growing buzz of excitement I usually only get when a case is about to break wide open.

"The passports," I say. "He left behind all his alternate IDs."

193

"And?" Astra asks. "We assume he left them behind because he knew they were burned."

"Right. Exactly," I say excitedly. "And he can't travel under his real name or his Agency-identified name. The names Brad Keller and Brad Hewitt are burned too. And he might not be contacting Saleh because he fears the Agency is tailing him—something Kalfus all but confirmed when I talked to him."

"I don't see how that helps us," Lucas says.

A slow grin stretches across Astra's face, and I can see she's picking up on my train of thought. She nods.

"If he can't go to Saleh to get him out of the country because the Agency is sitting on him, and he can't use any of his alternate IDs because they're burned, he's going to need papers. He's going to need clean passports they can travel on," I say. "Which means, we need to talk to local PD and somebody in the Denver Field Office and find out who the best forgers in the city are. We need to have a conversation with them."

The moment the words fall out of my mouth, I feel a rush of electricity burn through me. It's that feeling I get when we're on the right path and the sense of momentum on a case starts to swell. I'm positive that if we can find the forger who's putting his papers together, we'll be able to find Keller.

"All right," I say. "Let's get to work."

CHAPTER TWENTY-SIX

Boggs Photography Studio; Denver, CO

A FTER TALKING TO LOCAL POLICE AND THE FIELD OFFICE, we came up with the names of two dozen people in the greater Denver area who are known to forge papers on demand—and for a hefty price. But knowing these people are forgers and being able to prove it in a court of law are two separate animals entirely. Plus, having these people on the hook and living under the constant threat of arrest and prosecution is handy. They're more likely to help law enforcement in our time of need. And right now, we have a need.

We divided up the list, each of us taking six names, and I sent the others out to turn over the rocks and see what was underneath. I haven't heard anything from the team yet, which tells me they're having as much luck as I'm having so far. I'm walking into the shop of the fourth name on my list, feeling pessimistic about my odds of finding anything of value here.

"Snap out of it, Blake," I mutter to myself.

The small, one-story building is made of red brick, and there are two large, plate glass windows flanking the front door. The glass is smoked, making it impossible to see inside, and has the business name and logo imprinted on each side. The one thing this shop has going for it is that it's in the same neighborhood as Keller's firm, sitting just a couple of blocks down the street from it. That means Keller would have seen it every day and, if he's as good at his job as everybody says he is, would know Elliott Boggs, the owner of the studio, has a side hustle as one of Denver's premier forgers.

It's not much to hang my hat on, but it's something. I don't have a clue what we're going to do if none of these names pan out. But that's a battle we'll fight when we have to. Right now, I just need to focus on the man in front of me and hope he'll have something I can use.

I pull the door open and step into the studio. It's one large room with a raised desk to my right that is currently unoccupied. The interior of the studio is made of red brick and light wood. It's dimly lit and cool as if the air conditioner is going even though it's not warm outside. On the far wall to my left are several backdrops and stools sitting in front of them. A table with a computer setup and camera equipment stands about fifteen feet away from the backdrops, nearly butting up against one of the front windows. It's obviously where Boggs does his legit work.

There's a similar setup to my right, but besides the backdrops, there's a door set into the wall. It probably leads to storage rooms or an office in the back of the studio. There's another doorway directly across from me, but it's covered with a beaded curtain. Soft music plays from speakers mounted overhead, and as I stand there, a man pushes the beaded curtain aside and steps onto the main floor of the studio. He gives me a smile as he dries his hands off on a rag.

Boggs isn't a big man—five-six or five-seven at the most—and is stick thin. He doesn't look athletic. I doubt he works out much, if at all. His long, blond hair is pulled back into a ponytail that falls to the middle of his back, and he's got dark eyes. Dressed in blue jeans and a white T-shirt, he seems to have a casual nature about him, and his smile hints at a friendly demeanor. But it seems to be calculated. Though he tries to hide it, I can see he's a little twitchy and a little squirrely. I have a feeling that smile is about to fade.

"Elliott Boggs," I start.

"Yes, that's me. What's up," he replies. His voice is smooth and casual, like that of an aging hippie.

"Just hoping to ask you a few questions," I tell him.

"You got questions, I got answers," he chuckles, tucking his rag in his back pocket. "What ya in for? Headshots? Family shoot? Boudoir?"

He says that last word with more than a little bit of a leer in his voice. I roll my eyes and badge him. "Yeah, no thanks. SSA Wilder, FBI."

His eyes widen, and a flash of concern crosses his face. The smarmy smile drops instantly, which is gratifying.

"What the—I don't—what is this about?" he sputters.

I raise an eyebrow. "Just need to ask you a few questions about a customer of yours."

He licks his lips nervously and clears his throat, seeming to have finally calmed himself. "Um. Okay. Sure. How can I help?"

I look around his studio pointedly. "This is a nice place."

"Th—thank you," he says. "I'm proud of it."

"What can you tell me about forged passports?"

He shrugs, but there's a tension there that's such an obvious tell. "N—nothing. I don't know anything about forged passports."

I cluck my tongue and shake my head. "Let's try that again. Only this time, I'd like you to tell me the truth. I know you forge papers as a side hustle," I say. "I'm not here about that, and honestly, don't care what you do on the side. I need information about something going on that's bigger than you."

197

He clears his throat. "I—I don't know what you're talking about. I don't forge papers."

I sigh. "Elliott, let's not play games with each other. I don't have time for it," I tell him. "I'm looking for a man that you might have helped."

"Agent Wilder, I really have—"

"The more you deny what I already know, the more interested you're making me in your side hustle, Elliott," I cut him off. "Do you really want me to come back here with a warrant for your back rooms, and a team that will tear your studio—and your life—apart, when all you have to do is give me a little information? Because I'll do that if you make me. Or you can simply answer a few questions, and I'll get out of your hair."

He lets out a breath and lowers his gaze to the ground; he seems to be thinking about what I said and weighing out the pros and cons of cooperation. Ultimately, his self-interest wins out, and he looks up at me.

"What do you want to know?" he asks, his tone dejected.

I pull up the picture of Keller and hold it up for Boggs to see. He looks at it, and though he tries to hide it, I see the flash of recognition cross his face. It sends a shot of electricity through me I realize this is going to pan out after all. This is the key. This is the piece of evidence I need to blow this case open. And for the first time since this case began, I feel a spark of hope. I start to think that we might track Keller down.

"You know him," I say. It's a statement, not a question.

"I wouldn't say I know him."

"As I said, let's not play games. The sooner you tell me what I want to know, the sooner I'll be out of your hair," I say. "I told you, I don't care about you forging passports. That's not what I'm here about."

His jaw flexes as he grits his teeth. "Fine. Yeah, I kind of know him. Sort of."

"You made papers for him."

He nods. "I did. He wanted papers for himself, his wife, and his two kids," he says. "They all came in, and I took their pictures a couple of weeks ago. Said they wanted them because they were taking the kids overseas for a family vacation."

"All right," I say. "But I want to know about the fake papers."

"Yeah, that's the thing. He came back in the next day and told me he needed clean papers for everybody that were in different names than the ones they gave me the day before," Boggs explains. "I don't know how he found out about my side business, but he said he needed birth certificates, passports, driver's licenses, even a couple of credit cards in those names. He needed the full package."

"How much did that run him?"

"He gave me fifty grand for it all."

I whistle lowly. "Damn."

He nods. "That's what I said. It's way more than my usual rate. I couldn't afford to turn it down," he says. "But he was really demanding. Pressuring me to get them done. But like I told him, you can't rush perfection. The papers I provide are flawless. I pride myself on my work, you know? My mom always—"

"That's great. Your mom is wise. I get it, but I'm up against the clock here," I cut him off. "Has he been by to pick them up yet?"

"Yeah," he nods. "He picked them up yesterday. Why? What's going on? He must've done somethin' real bad to have the FBI looking for him, huh?"

"Mr. Boggs, I need the names you issued this man and his family on their new papers," I tell him. "And I need them now."

CHAPTER TWENTY-SEVEN

Rocky Mountain Inn & Suites Conference Room; Denver, CO

"THEY'RE USING THEIR FIRST NAMES, AND THE LAST name of Porter," I announce.

"Why are they using their real first names?" Lucas asks.

"Easier to remember," I tell him. "When you're undercover, the less you have to remember, the better. So, using your first name makes things easier."

Lucas nods. He still has a lot to learn about fieldwork, but he's starting to come around. It makes me glad. On the computer screen, Rick and Nina are waiting with bated breath for some instruction. Now that we have the IDs the Kellers are using, it should be a simple matter of tracking them down.

"How'd you come across the name?" Rick asks.

"Good, old-fashioned investigative work," I tell him. "No lines crossed, so Ayad shouldn't have anything to say about it."

"That was a great call with the passports," Nina says. "Smart."

"She's got her moments," Rick replies. "Horrible taste in music, but she has those moments of inspired brilliance."

I laugh. "Jazz is not horrible. It's among the best music ever created."

Rick rolls his eyes. "Yeah, maybe if you're over the age of sixty."

"Afraid I have to agree with Rick on this one," Nina says. "Jazz pairs well with the early bird dinner special down at Applebees, AARP cards, and senior discounts."

"Wow," I say. "You are both so fired when I get back to Seattle."

"So, as long as we're still gainfully employed, I'm assuming you didn't call just to chit chat," Rick points out. "Put us to work, boss. Give us something to do."

"There's that go-getter attitude," Astra says. "I didn't know you had that in you, Rick."

Nina laughs. "Is this something that could potentially get us fired—"

"—or thrown into prison?" Rick interrupts.

"No, on both. It's a routine search," I say. "No warrants needed."

"Sounds boring," Rick cracks. "But give it to us anyway."

"I need you to search for anything—travel documents specifically—related to the names Brad or Bridget Porter. Find anything you can that doesn't require a warrant," I say. "We'll apply for one to get the rest of their information if needed. I don't think it will be though."

"You got it," Nina chirps. "Simple enough."

"Perfect. Thank you," I reply. "Give us a call when you have something."

"Will do," Rick says. "What are you guys going to do in the meantime?"

"We are going to go round up some evidence," I say.

Astra and I pull to a stop in the roundabout in front of the Keller home, and I shut the engine off. Somehow, the house looks even more foreboding and imposing than it did the last time we were here. We get out of the car, and I look at the front door. Something about it doesn't seem right. It takes me a minute to figure out what it is, and when I do, a shot of adrenaline hits my system.

"Somebody's been here," I announce.

Astra looks from me to the door, and I see the surprise on her features.

"Dammit," she mutters.

We pull our weapons and head for the front door to see that it's been kicked in. The wooden jamb is splintered and cracked and there is a large boot print in the middle of the door. We both come in with our weapons up and at the ready, but it's a futile gesture since I'm sure the people who'd broken in are already gone.

We cross the threshold and spend about fifteen minutes clearing the house. It's just as I thought—nobody's here. But it looks like whoever was here turned the house over and shook it. Everything is in disarray. There are holes in the walls, picture frames lying smashed and in pieces on the ground, and couch cushions slashed open, their innards spread out across the floor. Rock stars don't trash hotel rooms this badly or thoroughly.

I walk into the kitchen, and all the cupboards are bare, all their contents on the ground. Plates, bowls, glasses—all of them are in pieces, the sun slanting in through the window glittering off the jagged shards. Books have been pulled off their shelves and lay spread out across the floor. Everywhere I look, something's smashed, broken, or torn to pieces.

I meet Astra in the foyer again and shake my head. "This place is trashed."

"Maybe it was the neighbors? Or some random group of kids just causing trouble," she offers. "Some kids like to trash vacant houses for sport."

"No, this was a search disguised as vandalism," I tell her. "Whoever broke in here was looking for something—but didn't want to make it seem that way. So, they staged a robbery."

"How can you be sure?"

"Because this doesn't look like random violence," I say. "The drawers have all been pulled out, the books on the shelves have all been looked through. Whoever was in here definitely searched everything. Then they trashed it all to cover their tracks, trying to make it look like teenagers just out to trash something."

We holster our weapons and walk through the ground floor again, and I point out what I interpret to be signs of a search. Astra finally nods.

"Yeah, you might be right," she says. "But whoever broke in here—what were they looking for?"

"Good question," I reply. "I'm going to assume it had something to do with this evidence Keller was trying to put together. It obviously made somebody nervous."

"That brings me back to the Saudis."

I shake my head. "I don't think so. I didn't get the sense that he was nervous about what Keller was searching for. It seemed like Saleh wanted to help him," I say. "I would bet money it wasn't the Saudis."

"Then who?" she asks.

"That's a good question."

"All right, can you tell if they found what they were looking for?"

I shrug slightly. "I don't know for sure, but I'm inclined to say no. Some of the mess here seems like it was done out of frustration. It's overkill."

"So, in theory, what we're looking for is still here?"

"In theory," I say with a shrug. "Only one way to find out."

"You want to search through this wreck of a house?"

I nod. "I do. It's the only way we're going to find out if my theory holds water."

"All right, so where do we start?"

"You take upstairs, I'll start down here," I tell her. "Search everything. Even places that seem like they're unlikely to hold anything."

"Like the bookcase back at his office."

"Exactly. Look for secret hollows and hidden compartments," I tell her. "The guy was a spy. He'll have some hidden nooks and crannies."

"That sounds as disturbing as it is distasteful," she says. "But your point is taken."

"Okay, then let's get to it."

As Astra heads upstairs, I start looking around on the first floor. I start in the foyer and walk around the room running my hands over the walls and kicking the baseboards, searching for a secret panel. I come up empty though. Nothing in the foyer. After that, I move into the living room and repeat the process. After that, I search what's left of the couch and coffee table and look behind the pictures that are left on the walls. Nothing.

I move to the kitchen and search it carefully, straining my eyes over every inch of the ruined countertops and inside the cupboards. Nothing. Nor is there anything stashed away in the refrigerator or freezer. The longer I go without a single whiff of anything that might lead me to the evidence, the more I start to worry that whoever was here beat us to it. I'm frustrated and kick a box of cereal across the kitchen floor.

Leaning against the center island, I fold my arms over my chest and rack my brain. There has to be a secret hollow somewhere. But that's the thing—I haven't seen any empty hollows. I haven't run across any secret compartments that have been opened. That realization settles me down some. It makes me think that maybe I was wrong and that whoever searched the house didn't find what they were looking for. That means, it's probably still here.

That's assuming Keller stashed his evidence here. There's a possibility he stored it down at the house in Hope. A search of records in the Keller name, as well as the names of his other IDs, didn't turn up any storage units or other dwellings. I suppose he could have stashed the evidence elsewhere, but if I'm a spy holding such sensitive material, I want to keep it close. Hidden, but close.

It's also possible he has the evidence on him, but something tells me that's not the case. I've thought about this scenario a thousand different ways and I keep coming back to the same thing.

There had to be an inciting situation that set Keller on the run in the first place. My guess is that somebody showed up here to take him out. Keller grabbed his family and split. That's the only thing that makes any sort of sense to me. A kill team showing up in the middle of the night, in my mind, is what put Keller on the run.

And if that's the case, if he had to suddenly take off in the middle of the night, he wouldn't have had time to grab clothing, let alone this mysterious evidence he'd turned up. No matter which way I think about it, I just can't see Keller taking the time out to get to his secret hollow and grab his evidence. That also explains why he's still in Denver. Well, that and getting clean papers.

On the other hand, he could have gotten clean papers anywhere. A guy like Keller, with his knowledge and skill, could have found somebody to dummy up some papers for him in any city in the country. I think he's still in town because he's waiting for the heat to die down enough that he can swing by and grab his evidence—evidence that's still here, somewhere in this house. But where in the hell is it?

I walk to the sliding glass doors and look out at the back deck. The fading sunlight is glinting off the surface of the pool, the fiery red and orange hues overhead reflecting off the water. Watching the gentle ripples that cross the otherwise smooth surface triggers a memory. I walk outside and over to the pool and start to look around. A long time ago, I worked a case where a murder suspect hid the knife he used to kill his wife in the filter basket. I know it's a long shot, but I'll take what I can get at this point.

I kneel down and slip my finger into the hole in the cover, then pull it off and set it aside. When I look into the filter basket, a smile stretches across my face.

"Bingo," I whisper.

Reaching into the basket, I pull out a plastic bag that's sealed with wax. I shake the water off and hold it up, my grin growing even wider when I see the six flash drives inside the baggie. Astra comes through the sliders and walks toward me.

"What is that?" she asks.

"With our luck? Probably not much," I say, but I already know that's not the case. "Or maybe—just maybe—it's what we're looking for."

205

CHAPTER TWENTY-EIGHT

Denver International Airport, Jeppesen Terminal, Gate C; Denver, CO

"**D**O YOU HAVE EYES ON THEM?" ASTRA asks.

I look around then shake my head. "I do not."

The terminal is packed with people, making it hard for me to pick anybody out of the crowd. After finding the flash drives, we were heading back to the hotel when we got a call from Mo alerting us to the fact that they got a ping on Bridget Keller's false ID. She and her two kids were booked on a flight to

London. We broke every speed limit getting here and arrived well ahead of their departure time.

My phone buzzes and I quickly connect the call and put the phone to my ear. "Wilder."

"Blake, it's Mo. Lucas and I are on-site," she says. "We're heading your way now."

"Good. Keep an eye peeled," I tell her. "We've only got half an hour before boarding, so she's got to be here somewhere."

"Copy that. We'll post up across from the gate and scan the crowd."

"Perfect. We're in the waiting area at the gate, but she's not here yet," I say. "Keep your phone on and keep your eyes peeled. There are a lot of people here, and it'll be easy to miss them if we're not on our toes."

"Copy that," Mo says. "I'll call if we see anything."

I disconnect the call, drop the phone into my pocket, and resume scanning the crowd.

"They're cutting it close, don't you think?" Astra asks.

"It's a countermeasure," I say. "Keller probably told them to hide out and arrive just as they begin boarding. Less time in the waiting area means—"

"Less time to get spotted and scooped up," Astra finishes for me. "Smart."

"The man is good."

"I just can't believe they've been married as long as they have and she never knew what he did for a living," she says. "How does that happen? How could she not know?"

"Because he's a master at compartmentalization," I tell her. "He had his work life and his home life, and never the twain shall meet."

"I don't know if that's more impressive or disturbing," she says.

"Probably a bit of both."

"Yeah, well, it's all come back to bite him in the ass now. I can't even begin to imagine what she must be going through right now."

"Yeah, it has to be rough," I say. "It's not the life she thought she was signing up for."

We fall silent for a moment and continue scanning the crowd. We're making the assumption she didn't know based on what Kalfus told me. But there's every chance that Keller told his wife what he does for a living. I'm curious about it. I want to know if she knew and if this was something she signed up for. It's purely an academic exercise, but this world, this life she's living—I want to know if she knew what she was getting into.

"Got her," Astra whispers.

I follow her gaze and see the woman coming our way. Her formerly brown hair is now blonde, and she's wearing a large, floppy hat to further obscure her face. She's got two kids in tow, both wearing baseball caps pulled low. The kids are shuffling along looking shell-shocked. I can't imagine what the past couple of weeks must have been like for them. Any pity I feel for them, though, I have to turn off. I have a job to do, and I can't afford to let my sympathy for her and her children override my logic and my sense of duty.

"Do you see him anywhere?" Astra asks.

I scan the faces in the crowd, searching for him. "No. I don't have him," I say. "And I have a feeling he's not coming."

"Another countermeasure?"

I nod. "He knows we'll be looking hard for him. Not them," I tell her. "So, he's going to try and get them out first then follow them on a later flight. But I guarantee he's here. He's somewhere in the crowd watching to make sure they get on the flight."

"The guy is good."

"That he is," I nod. "But not good enough. We finally got ahead of him for a change."

I pull the phone out of my pocket and call Mo.

"Hey," she says as she answers. "You got them?"

"We do, and we're about to snatch his wife up," I say. "Keep your eyes peeled. Keller is here somewhere. He's not going to let them out of his sight until they get on the plane."

"Copy that."

I disconnect the call and drop my phone back into my pocket. Astra is still looking around, searching through the sea of faces, trying to find him among the crowd like a live version of Where's

Waldo. I have a feeling we could sit here all day and never pick him out of the throngs of people.

"Let's go scoop her up," I say. "It might flush him out."

"All right, let's do it," she replies. "You go high, I go low?"

"Sounds like a plan."

I watch as Astra melts into the crowd and give her a moment to get into position behind them. When I see Astra pop up a few feet behind them, I step out of the crowd and put myself in her path. The woman pulls up short, her eyes wide and full of fear.

"Mrs. Bridget Keller?" I ask and show her my badge. "Blake Wilder, FBI. I need to ask you and your children to come with us."

She's trembling but is trying hard to keep it together in front of her kids. "I'm sorry, you have me mistaken with somebody else," she says, her voice trembling. "My last name is Porter."

I take a step closer to her and she recoils. "I'd rather not make a scene, Mrs. Keller," I say. "Please come with us."

Her kids are looking from her to me and back again, their eyes wide and shimmering with tears. The fear on their faces is painful to see, and I just want to scoop them up and get them somewhere safe. Bridget is looking around, undoubtedly looking for her husband. My phone rings, and I quickly answer it.

"Go," I say.

"We've got him. He's heading through the terminal and toward an exit," Mo tells me. "We're on him."

"Good. Pick him up and bring him back to the command post," I say and slip the phone back into my pocket.

"Is that—are you talking about Brad?" she asks, her face etched with terror.

"Yes, Mrs. Keller. My agents are going to pick up your husband and bring him where we're taking you and your kids. Someplace safe," I say. "I know the last couple of weeks must have been very difficult on you. Wouldn't it be nice to feel safe for a change?"

Her shoulders slump, and I watch a wide array of emotions cycle across her face. More than anything, though, what I see is relief. Exhaustion. She looks like a woman who hasn't slept in ages and is beyond weary. She kneels down and pulls her kids to her, hugging them fiercely. The crowd flows around us like a river flowing around a rock, the people all staring, expressions of annoyance on their faces at having to go around us.

"Mrs. Keller, are you ready?" I ask.

She raises her gaze and looks at me with tears streaming down her cheeks. She nods.

"Yes," she says. "I'm ready to go."

CHAPTER TWENTY-NINE

Rocky Mountain Inn & Suites Conference Room; Denver, CO

AFTER GETTING BACK TO THE HOTEL, I CALLED THE Denver Field Office and had them send over four agents. I put the kids in one of the rooms and gave Mrs. Keller a little bit of time to get them to sleep, leaving two agents on the door to guard them. Once they were down, I had the other two agents bring her to our makeshift command post, then stand guard outside the door.

She takes a seat at the foot of the table and seems to fold in on herself. She clasps her hands in her lap and looks down at them. She seems to be fighting back the waves of exhaustion and fear that are battering her, doing her best to keep as calm as she can. But she looks wrung out and emotionally spent. The past couple of weeks on the run have taken a real toll on her, and she looks like she wants to crawl into bed and sleep for the next month.

"I'm sorry to keep you up, Mrs. Keller," I start. "We'll let you go get some sleep with your kids as soon as we can, but there are some questions we want to ask you first."

Before we can begin, though, the door to the conference room opens. Mo and Lucas walk in, both wearing matching expressions of embarrassment on their faces.

"He gave us the slip, boss," Mo admits. "I'm sorry."

I shake my head. "It's not your fault."

It's not welcome news. But it's not totally unexpected either. Running down an experienced operator like Brad Keller isn't an easy feat. It's impossible really. He forgets more tricks of the trade than we're ever going to know. The chances are pretty high that they walked right by him and didn't even know it. We have his family though. Knowing that, I have no doubt he's going to be reaching out to me sooner rather than later.

I hand Mo the baggie with the flash drives in it. "I need you and Lucas to start going through the data on these. Maybe we can finally start getting some answers as to what this is all about and what's going on."

Mo takes the bag from me. "On it, boss. And again, we're sorry—"

"No apologies. There's nothing for you to be sorry about," I say. "He would have slipped by all of us. Don't worry though. We'll be hearing from him. Soon."

"Think so?"

"I know so."

I turn away and walk back to where Mrs. Keller is sitting and pull a chair closer to her. Astra sits down next to us as well while Mo and Lucas plug in and start working on the flash drives. Mrs. Keller sniffs loudly and wipes her eyes.

"Mrs. Keller, can I get you something to eat? Something to drink?" I ask.

She shakes her head. "No, I'm fine. Thank you."

"All right. Can you tell me what happened?" I ask. "Why were you getting on that plane to London under an assumed identity?"

"We were running. We had to get out of the country," she tells us. "There were men…. They broke into our house one night…."

Her voice trails off, and she's overcome by emotion. I glance at Astra, and she seems to be reading my mind. She gets up and walks over to a table at the side of the room, grabs a box of Kleenex and some bottles of water, then brings them back to us. Mrs. Keller looks at her gratefully and takes the box of tissues, pulling one out and dabbing at her eyes. She opens the bottle of water and takes a long swallow. Her hands are shaking so hard, she nearly drops it several times. But she manages to avoid spilling all over herself and sets it down.

"Mrs. Keller, I know this is difficult, and I'm sorry," I say. "But we need to know what happened. Can you walk us through it?"

She draws in a long, shuddering breath and tries to steady herself. Mrs. Keller's eyes take on a faraway look as she thinks back to the night her life was turned upside down….

"Get the kids and pack a bag, Bridge," he said. "We need to go."

Her eyes widened. "What are you talking about?"

"Now, Bridge. Get the kids and pack a bag. We need—"

The sound of the front door crashing inward cut off his words. He looked at her, and for the first time since she'd known him, Brad looked terrified.

"Oh, God. It's too late," he said and turned to her. "Forget the bags. Get the kids. Now, Bridge. Go. Now."

The sound of booted footsteps echo through the house as Bridget turned and ran toward the stairs. She caught a glimpse of her husband moving toward the sound of danger. Her heart leaped into her throat, and she shook with fear. As she got to the second-floor landing and was moving toward the kids' rooms, the sound of fighting echoed up to her. Bridget heard something that sounded like a muffled pop that was followed by the sound of a man crying out in pain.

Bridget didn't know what was happening. A home invasion robbery? But that didn't explain Brad's reaction. He seemed to know who was coming for them. Even worse, it seemed like he had been expecting it. But why would he be expecting somebody to come crashing through the door? Brad was an architect. He wasn't involved with crime or drugs or anything like that. What was happening?

Her heart racing, her mind filled with fearful, frantic thoughts, Bridget pulled the kids out of their beds. They were bleary-eyed, fussy, and still half-asleep as she grabbed their hands and pulled them toward the stairs. Brad seemed to appear in front of her out of nowhere, startling her, and she let out a yelp of fear and surprise.

"Brad, what's going on?" she demanded fearfully.

"Not now. I'll answer all your questions later," he said. "But right now, we have to get out of here. There's more coming."

"Brad—"

"Not now, Bridget. If we don't go and go now, we're going to die. Do you understand?"

He'd never snapped at her like that, and it frightened her. It also told her how serious the situation was. Brad grabbed hold of Cole and picked him up. She carried Lyssa on her shoulder down the stairs. Her heart nearly stopped dead in her chest when she saw the bodies on the floor. Dark pools of blood were spreading out around them, and she had to stifle a cry to avoid scaring the children any more than they already were.

"Brad, did you—did you do that?" she asked.

"Not now, Bridget. I swear I'll explain it all when we're safe."

"Who are those men?"

"Bridget, please," he snapped. "Not now."

She followed close behind him, her heart thundering in her chest, feeling like she was about to collapse under the weight of terror. Brad loaded them all into the Suburban, and Bridget let out a scream when a man grabbed Brad from behind. The man was dressed in black from head to toe, and a balaclava covered his face, leaving only his eyes exposed. Bridget watched in horror as Brad spun around, his movements fast and fluid as he grabbed the intruder's arm and twisted it viciously.

The intruder screamed as the sound of his arm snapping filled the air. Brad plucked the gun out of the intruder's hand and swiftly pivoted, putting it against the man's head. She heard that muffled popping sound again as Brad pulled the trigger. The intruder's head snapped back, and Bridget watched a mist of red spray into the air. The man fell to the ground, limp and boneless.

He lay there, unmoving, and she opened her mouth to scream, but no sound came out. All she seemed able to do was stare at the dead man in the driveway—and her husband standing over him with a gun in his hand.

Brad turned and climbed into the Suburban and pulled the door shut. With a look of grim determination on his face, he started the car, and with the kids in the back crying, he threw it into gear and roared around the roundabout, nearly clipping the other cars parked in the driveway. Bridget heard the hard thump of something slamming into the side of the car. She looked and saw more men coming out of the house, saw the muzzle flashes of their weapons, and knew it was bullets that were hitting the SUV.

"Brad—"

"Not now, Bridge. Please. Not now."

He had become a man she didn't know. He didn't look the same. Sound the same. It was Brad, but it wasn't. And she was suddenly terrified of the man behind the wheel of the Suburban. Without a word to her, Brad put the SUV in gear and roared down the hill then through the open gate at the bottom of the hill. He turned the wheel sharply and slammed on the accelerator, their SUV rocketing off into the night....

Silence descends over us when she finishes relaying her story. Bridget slumps back in her seat, a haunted look in her eyes. I can't possibly imagine what it's like to see a man you've been married to for so long turn into a cold, calculating killer. I can't imagine what it has to be like to see the world you've spent your life building fall to pieces when the man you've devoted yourself to reveals himself to be a ruthless and efficient killer. Astra and I exchange a look as the weight of it all presses down on us. It's a heavy story.

"And you had no idea your husband worked for the Agency?" Astra asks gently.

She shakes her head. "Not until that night," she says. "Once he got us into a hotel and to safety, he explained everything. He told me those men showed up to kill him because he had been gathering evidence against them. And we've been on the run ever since. He said he has friends in Saudi Arabia who can protect us—who can help us rebuild a life over there."

"Evidence of what?" I ask.

"He never said," I reply. "He just said it was his duty to make sure these men went down. Said it was his duty to expose the corruption."

"Okay, what about the attackers?" I ask. "Did he say who they were?

She shakes her head again. "He didn't."

"Did you happen to see the attackers?" Astra asks. "Did you see anything that might help identify them?"

"I didn't. But they were speaking English."

"All right, that's good," I say. "Did they have accents?

"No. Not that I heard. They sounded normal. Just like us."

So, the attackers are possibly American. But that makes me wonder why American spies would show up to kill one of their own. If they even were American. It's entirely possible they were foreign but were fluent in English. Not all spies have a distinguishable accent. Unfortunately for us, the answers Bridget is giving us only lead to more questions.

We question her for another half-hour or so, but she doesn't have many more answers. And by the end, she looks even more wrung out than before.

"All right, I think we can end this here for now," I say. "We'll pick this up again in the morning after you've gotten some sleep."

She nods wearily. "Thank you. But I don't know any more than I've already told you. I don't know what my husband was doing or why people would want him dead. I don't even know who he really is."

She looks away, and I see the sadness in her eyes. The realization that her husband isn't who she's thought he was all these years has got to be a heavy burden on her heart. On her soul. I've had just a taste of that sort of burden when I learned that Mark Walton was inserted into my life to spy on me—and take me out if necessary—courtesy of the Thirteen. But what Mrs. Keller has endured far exceeds my own experience with this sort of betrayal. And it sucks.

"Astra, can you escort Mrs. Keller up to her room?" I ask.

She nods. "Of course."

I watch as Astra takes her out of the conference room and catch sight of the two agents I'd stationed on the door falling into step behind her. When the door closes, I turn to Mo and Lucas; the air in the conference room is heavy.

"That's quite the story," Mo says. "Can't help but feel bad for her."

Lucas nods. "That is one twisted story. How could he do that to his own wife? How could he hide who he is?"

"Because he thought he was protecting her," I reply. "Tell me you've gotten something off those flash drives."

"I've got quite a bit," Mo says. "According to these emails, Keller tumbled onto somebody selling arms and information to hostile countries—China and North Korea just to name a couple."

"Who was he building a case against?" I ask.

"Unclear at this point," Mo says.

"Lucas?"

"Same. I've got surveillance photos, emails, even voice and video recordings," he says. "But it's not clear who Keller was building a case against. Not from what I have here on these drives so far."

"That must be the last piece of evidence he needed to find," I muse. "He told Saleh he needed to finish putting together his case and turn it over before he could leave."

"But things were getting too hot for him, so he decided to send his family on ahead of him?" Mo asks.

"That's my guess," I nod. "I'm also guessing he's targeting somebody in the Agency."

"Stands to reason," Mo says. "Somebody he's worked with."

And then a light goes off in my head and the picture finally becomes clear.

"It's Doyle Kalfus," I whisper. "Oh my God, it's Kalfus."

"His handler?" Lucas asks. "What makes you say that?"

"Who inserted himself into our investigation from the start? Who's the one who fed us the Saudi angle?" I ask. "And who's put us on a false path every single time I talked to him?"

Neither Mo nor Lucas says a word. They don't need to though. I don't need them to say anything to make me feel like a bigger idiot than I already do. I can't believe I swallowed down everything Kalfus fed me. He played me for a fool. Played me like I was a damn Stradivarius. I run a hand through my hair, trying to understand how I missed it. How could I not see that he was playing me like a mark? And I fell for it—hook, line, and sinker.

"I should have seen this," I mutter.

"He's a spy," Mo offers, but it's not much comfort. "He's trained to lie. Trained to make you believe his lies."

"And I'm supposed to be trained to see through the lies. He put us onto the Saudis to buy himself the time to search Keller's house—and kill him if he'd been able to find him, no doubt," I say. "Please tell me you can find something in there that will link Kalfus to this scheme to sell arms and information."

"Not so far," Mo says. "But we'll keep looking. There are loads and loads of information on these flash drives we haven't looked through yet. We'll keep looking."

"Good. That's good," I say.

My phone rings and I glance at the caller ID. The call is coming from a blocked number, and I have the notion that it's Kalfus. As if thinking about him made him call me. I snatch up my phone and connect the call.

"Wilder."

"Agent Wilder," says the man. It's not Kalfus—but thankfully, it's someone I've been wanting to speak to all the same. "You have my family."

"Mr. Keller, your family is safe. They're resting right now," I reply. "We've been looking for you. You've had a lot of people worried about you."

"I've had a lot of people trying to kill me and my family too."

"You're building a case against Doyle Kalfus, aren't you? He's the one who's been selling arms and information to the highest bidder, isn't he?"

"You're as good as your reputation says you are," he says.

"Why don't you come in? Let's talk about this."

"There's a parking structure across the street from the Downtown Aquarium," he says. "Meet me there at midnight. And come alone."

"Mr. Keller—"

The click of the call being disconnected tells me that he's gone. If I have any chance of closing this case and bringing Keller in, I'm going to have to meet him. And that's exactly what I intend to do.

CHAPTER THIRTY

Park Place Parking Structure, Level 5; Denver, CO

THE NIGHT IS COOL AND DARK. A THICK BLANKET OF clouds is blotting out the moon. The lights of downtown Denver provide ample lighting to see by, but the night has a dim, fuzzy quality to it. There's something ominous in the air. It's a tension that's infused in every muscle that makes my entire body tighter than a piano string. It's as if the entire world is holding its breath waiting for something to happen.

The top level of the parking structure is about three-quarters full. Judging by the lack of foot traffic, I assume it's overnight parking. It's well past midnight, and I've been sitting here for what feels like hours. He's late. I'm sure it's purposeful. He wants to ensure I'm alone and that it's safe to come out of hiding. I can't blame him for exercising caution. Not with everything that's happening and the men who are hunting him still running loose.

The sudden rapping on the passenger side window makes me nearly jump out of my skin. I turn to see Brad Keller standing there. He'd somehow managed to come up from behind the car without me noticing him. There's a loud click as I disengage the locks. Keller opens the door and looks in at me for a long moment, his expression caught somewhere between fear and rage.

"Out of the car," he says.

"Why don't we talk in here?"

He says nothing but raises his hand to show me the Sig Sauer P220 pistol he's holding. It looks like a match to the handgun we found in the secret hollow in the base of the bookcase in his office.

"You do like your Sigs, don't you?" I remark.

"They're reliable," he replies. "Now, get out of the car."

"All right, let's just take it easy," I say as I raise my hands to show him I'm unarmed.

In the time it takes me to open the driver's side door, Keller has moved around and is standing in front of me.

"So, is ninja training required at the Agency?" I ask. "Or is it just a hobby?"

He shuts the Yukon's door, removing the last barrier between us, then steps closer, the barrel of his Sig trained on my chest. His eyes are still burning with that mix of anger and fear. My Yukon is parked in an open space. Two slots over on the passenger side is a Porsche, and the nearest car on the driver's side is a BMW three slots down. I have no cover and nowhere to run if this all goes sideways.

Keller is an ordinary-looking man. Like Kalfus, there's nothing exceptional about him. He's probably a tick under six feet tall with sandy brown hair and dark eyes behind a pair of round, black-framed spectacles. He's got high cheekbones, a patrician nose, and a deep cleft in his chin. He's also grown a mustache and beard that are neatly trimmed and flecked with gray. No doubt an attempt to alter his appearance.

Keller is lean but athletic. The black turtleneck he's wearing displays his toned chest and biceps but doesn't do much to make him look less like a math teacher than the highly-trained spy and assassin he is. Although, with that hand cannon he's holding on me and that murderous gleam in his eye, he looks plenty dangerous to me.

"Is my family safe?" he demands.

"Yes, they're safe. I've got my team as well as four agents from the local field office watching them," I reply. "Nobody's getting near them."

"Underestimating the Agency is your first mistake," he tells me. "They can get to anybody, anywhere, anytime they want."

"The Agency isn't omnipotent, Mr. Keller," I say. "They're prone to the same mistakes and political pressures we all are."

"They're uncomfortably close to omnipotent, Agent Wilder," he says. "In fact, I have a feeling you're going to find out just how close they are to all-powerful. You've put a target on your back by meddling in Agency matters."

As if I didn't have enough to worry about. As if there aren't already enough shadowy figures lurking in the dark wanting to destroy and/or kill me, now I have to worry about the CIA coming after me. That's awesome. Yeah, good times.

"I want you to bring my family to me. I need to get them out of the country," he presses.

"We're not going to do that, Mr. Keller. We can protect them. And you," I tell him.

"You can't protect us. Nobody can."

"You need to come in," I say. "We know everything."

"I somehow doubt that."

"We found the drives you put into your pool filter basket, Mr. Keller," I tell him. "Clever place to hide them, by the way."

There's a brief flash of surprise on his face, but he quickly masters it, his expression returning to one of cool neutrality.

"I have my techs going through everything as we speak," I continue. "We know you uncovered a mole within the Agency—that somebody is selling arms and information to foreign buyers. And I believe it's your old handler, Doyle Kalfus, that you're investigating."

His gaze lingers on me, and even though he makes no outward gestures, his silence tells me that I'm right. It's Kalfus. That feeling of embarrassment over being duped by him washes over me again. I stuff it down though. Now is not the time to deal with my bruised ego. The important thing—the only thing that matters—is that we've figured it out and I'm standing before the man I've been searching for. Now all I have to do is convince him to come back with me. It won't be easy to do.

"Did you find the last piece of proof you needed to tie Kalfus to the plot?" I ask.

He says nothing, but his gun hand remains steady, the large, looming barrel of his Sig looking even more ominous to me. Keller's eyes are completely blank. They're flat and dead. It's like he flipped a switch inside of him that turns all his emotions off.

"I can help you," I say. "I know you don't know who to trust, and you feel like you're all on your own out here. But you can trust me, Mr. Keller. I only want to help you."

"You can't help me."

"I can," I reply. "I know you feel you can't trust the Agency. I know you're scared that whoever you report this corruption to is going to be the wrong person and you'll wind up catching a bullet for your trouble. I've been in your shoes, Mr. Keller. In many ways, I still am."

"There is no way you can relate."

"But I can," I reply.

I know there's a crack there I need to exploit if I'm going to get Keller to trust me. So, I tell him a condensed version of my saga with the Thirteen. I tell him about the numerous attempts on my life as well as the reshuffling within the Bureau, making sure to emphasize the point that I don't know who I can trust, proving that I can relate to him. Keller listens, and when I'm finished, he nods and surprisingly, lowers his weapon.

"I take it back. Apparently, you can relate," he says with a wry grin.

"I can."

"Then you know how dangerous my situation is."

"I do."

He blows out a long breath and looks away for a long moment. I can see he's grappling with the string of decisions that have led him to this point. That has put the lives of his family in danger. It's a heavy burden. I can't think of a burden that could be heavier. To know that your wife and your kids could be killed because of decisions you made has to be a crushing, smothering weight.

"What happened, Mr. Keller?" I ask. "How did you get here?"

"I was in Marrakesh doing... a thing. I wasn't scheduled to be there—I was supposed to be rotating back home. But I was following a lead on another pressing matter," he says. "Anyway, I saw Doyle there. He didn't know I was there—he was supposed to be rotating home as well. But I saw him meeting with two SVR agents. I watched them make an exchange of something—Doyle gave them a flash drive, and they gave him a bag I assume was filled with cash."

"Jesus," I gasp. "Kalfus was selling information to Russian Intelligence?"

"I didn't want to believe it at first. I've known Doyle for years and always knew him to be a good man. A patriot," he says, his tone mournful. "But I started to dig into things, behind the scenes of course, because seeing him with SVR agents continued to nag at me. If anything, I wanted to prove that I was wrong—that I didn't see what I saw. I wanted to believe there was a perfectly reasonable explanation for Doyle to be meeting with intelligence agents from a hostile foreign nation."

"And you didn't find that."

He shakes his head. "No. I investigated for about a year, collecting information and documenting my findings. That's what's on those six drives you found. But Doyle is smart. Clever. He knows how to hide his tracks and keep his fingerprints off everything," he says. "But I finally got surveillance photos of him with those same SVR agents. They were meeting in Baltimore, and I witnessed another exchange."

"He sold more secrets?"

"False ones. I wanted to force the issue, so I baited him with some false intelligence I knew he wouldn't be able to resist passing on," I say. "He bit and met with them. I'd intended to get my family out after that, but Doyle found out about my sting quicker than I anticipated and sent a kill squad to my house. He tried to murder my family, Agent Wilder. So, I've done what I've had to do to keep them alive. To keep myself alive. And, of course, to expose Doyle and his team for the traitors they are."

"How many of them are there?"

"From what I've been able to find, Doyle has a core crew of four. They supply him with intel, facilitate arms transfers, and work out those logistics," he tells me. "And he finds the buyers—of which, there is no shortage. From what I've been able to find, they've made tens of millions of dollars. Maybe more. There are statements from offshore banking entities on those six drives you found."

There's a heavy silence between us as I process his tale. It's quite a story. It seems more like the sort of thing you'd see coming out of Hollywood than in real life. The weight of it all seems to be catching up with Keller, and he suddenly looks exhausted. He's got that look of soul-deep weariness about him.

"I'm tired of the corruption, Agent Wilder. I joined the Agency to serve my country. To protect it," he growls. "And to have people around me who are actively undermining and exposing this country to danger is unconscionable. They have to be stopped."

"I agree. Let me help you, Mr. Keller," I say.

He shakes his head. "You can't help me. You'll only get yourself killed if you try."

"If that's the price of doing the right thing, so be it," I reply. "I made my peace with the possibility that I could die in the line of duty long ago. I'm not afraid. Let me bring you in. Let me bring you to your family."

That wry smile touches his lips once more. "It's going to take a little more than marriage counseling for Bridge to get past this, I think."

"She's strong. And she loves you, Mr. Keller. Don't underestimate her."

He shakes his head. "I don't. But we'll never be safe in this country," he says. "We have to get out. Build a new life."

"Mr. Saleh going to help you with that?"

He gives me a gentle smile and nods. "You're good, Agent Wilder."

"I wish I could take credit for finding Mr. Saleh on my own," I say. "It was Kalfus who turned me onto the Saudis."

He pales as he looks at me. "You spoke with Doyle?"

I nod. "Yeah. My boss put us together when this case started changing early on," I say. "I didn't see through Kalfus's deception and—"

"When did you speak with him?" he asks, his tone tight and nervous.

"A few days ago," I say. "We met at the—"

"Wait, he's here? In Denver?"

"Yeah, you didn't know?"

He shakes his head, the fear on his face thickening. "He usually doesn't get his hands dirty. He spins stories and sends people to do his dirty work. If he's here—God, we need to go. You need to go, Agent Wilder."

Keller extends his hand, and as we shake, he presses another flash drive into my palm and closes my hand around it. The gleam in his eyes tells me to not mention it. To just act natural and pretend we're doing nothing more than shaking hands.

"I have to go. I'll come for my family when it's safe to do so," he says. "Until then, lock them down like Fort Knox. Please, Agent Wilder, protect my family. Please."

"Come in with me. We can protect you—"

"You can't. If Doyle is here, the situation is worse than I thought. And if you spoke to him face-to-face, he's probably tracking you. And if he's tracking you ..."

His voice trails off, but he doesn't need to finish the statement. I know what he's thinking. And there is a primal fear etched into his features that pulls at my heartstrings.

"Nobody followed me, Mr. Keller—"

"You'd never know if he did," he says, then gives me a weak, watery smile. "It's that ninja training you mentioned earlier."

He steps away from me and scans the darkness around us nervously. Keller licks his lips and turns to me again.

"Keep your head down, Agent Wilder. I'll contact you as soon as it's clear to—"

Keller never finishes the sentence. A shot rings out of the darkness, echoing off the buildings around us, making it impossible to know which direction it came from. I watch in horror as Keller's body jerks. His eyes widen and his mouth falls open as another shot tears through him. Blood erupts from his back as the round passes through him. He hits the ground with a sound like wet meat slapping the pavement, and red, viscous blood immediately starts to pool around him.

I pull my weapon and frantically scan the darkened buildings around us, already crouched low to the ground. My heart is thundering in my chest, and my stomach is in knots as I wait for the next shot to rip through my body. But the shot never comes. Hunched down, trying to keep my eyes moving, searching for the shooter, I scoot over to Keller. There are two crimson blooms in the middle of his chest. The tight grouping tells me it was a professional who took the shot.

Bracing myself, expecting to take a bullet at any moment, I hold my weapon in one hand and press my fingers to his neck, searching for a pulse. It's faint, but it's there. Moving quickly, I holster my weapon, waiting for the next shot to come. I grab Keller's hands and use all my strength to pull him across the concrete, leaving a wide, scarlet swath in our wake. I get him behind the Yukon, and not knowing where the shot came from, I'm left to hope and pray I picked the right side to shelter behind.

A thin rivulet of blood spills from the corner of Keller's mouth and his eyes are glassy. I grab hold of his hand and give it a tight squeeze as I fish my phone out of my pocket.

"Hang on, Keller," I tell him. "Hang on. Stay with me."

I call 9-1-1 and press the phone to my ear, reporting the situation and our location when the dispatcher answers. Keller squeezes my hand, pulling my attention to him. Tears are spilling from the corners of his eyes, and I know the ambulance isn't going to get here in time.

"Save my family," he whispers, his voice raspy and fading. "Protect my wife and my children. Please."

"I will," I tell him. "I promise I'll make sure they're safe."

His face goes slack but he's wearing an expression of relief. Brad Keller dies in the darkness as the sound of wailing sirens draws closer.

I look at the darkened buildings around us, wondering if Kalfus is watching me. Wondering why he didn't shoot me too. Maybe he didn't want to add the murder of another federal agent to his list. Maybe he knows the game is up, and just wanted to kill Keller as an act of petty revenge before he makes his escape.

And he will make his escape. Guys like Kalfus always have an escape plan.

EPILOGUE

THE NEXT COUPLE OF DAYS AFTER THE DEATH OF BRAD Keller were a buzz of activity. It seemed to be an endless parade of questions, interviews, statements, and rehashing the shooting. I spent hours with Agency spooks who grilled me on every aspect of my story. I gave them the flash drives with all the information Keller had collected. The final drive he gave me provided the conclusive link between Kalfus and the SVR agents; it was the final nail in his coffin.

And all the while, it seemed like the fact that Bridget had lost her husband and Cole and Lyssa had lost their father was forgotten. She endured it as best as she could, but it wasn't difficult to see the toll it was taking on Bridget. My heart went out to her. I don't know how she and her kids are going to recover from this and suspect they'll always bear the scars. Especially Bridget, who not only has to cope with her husband's death but the reality that her husband had an entirely separate life she never knew about.

Once all the formalities were done—at least, our part of them—we were able to turn Bridget and the kids over to the Marshals service. I had been in contact with them from the start and made sure the Marshal who was assigned to their case was somebody I know and trust. I did everything I could to make sure Bridget and her kids are buried as deep under the bureaucratic red tape and behind as many walls as they can be.

Now, all I can do is hope that they're buried deep enough that not even the Agency will be able to find them. My hope, though, is that Kalfus will decide the damage has been done and go underground—and never surface again. I want to believe that's going to be the case, given the fact that he didn't kill me when he had the chance. He could have easily taken me out when he murdered Keller. But he didn't. I hope that's a sign that he got his revenge, and he'll leave Bridget and her children alone.

A day after getting back from Colorado, I'm sitting in Ayad's office. It's apparently time for Bossman here to take me out behind the woodshed. He sits on the other side of his desk, leaning back in his chair, staring at me, a smug smirk upon his lips. Ayad is trying to see deep into my soul. It's a classic intimidation tactic that is wholly ineffective on me. I couldn't care less how long we sit here having this stupid staring contest.

Content to wait him out, I cross one leg over the other and fold my hands on top of my knees, leaning back in my seat to return his stare right back at him. His goal here is to make me uncomfortable enough that I'll just start talking to fill the silence. What he doesn't realize is that silence doesn't bother me. And frankly, I don't like him enough to either give him the satisfaction of breaking first or wasting my breath on him.

Ayad sighs and sits forward again, and I have to suppress my smile as an expression of annoyance crosses his face.

"You got a good result in Colorado—"

"Before we begin here, I'd like to know if I'm allowed to speak freely or if you're going to put everything I say down on the record so you can punish me for it later."

"You are permitted to speak freely."

"Good," I reply. "Then in response to your initial statement, I don't think Mrs. Keller or her children think it's a very good result."

"It's an unfortunate circumstance, of course, but you closed the case," he says. "And for that, you and your team are to be commended."

"There's the velvet glove," I say. "Here comes the iron fist."

"The iron fist wouldn't be necessary if you weren't so insolent and dismissive of my authority," he fires back.

"Did you stop to think that maybe my insolence is because of the way you use your authority?" I snap. "If you weren't so busy micromanaging me and questioning every decision I make and let me work a case without interference, you might find I can be a pretty nice person. And that I can do my job more effectively."

"As I've told you before, part of my job is making sure you do your job without crossing lines that shouldn't be crossed. If you break a law, you taint the entire case."

"Do you think I'm stupid?" I demand. "Do you believe that I'm a moron, Chief Ayad?"

"Moron? No. But I think you let your ego and attitude get in your way sometimes," he says. "You also have a habit of running right up to that line of legality—"

"Yes. I may run up to the line, but I have never crossed it," I growl. "And if you can show me one instance where I've broken the law, I'll turn in my badge right now."

"Let's not be dramatic."

"You're accusing me of endangering cases by breaking the law. You're assailing my reputation and my character," I say. "I'd argue that's a pretty good reason to be dramatic."

"Look, that didn't come out right. I admit I spoke too hastily," he relents, trying to adopt a calmer tone. "I apologize. I didn't mean to imply that you have broken the law. But you tread so close to that line, I fear one of these days you're going to cross it."

"Chief Ayad, I know exactly where that line is. I'm very aware of it," I tell him. "And when you're in the field, you sometimes have to get close to that line to make a case. But I challenge you to look at my record—go as far back into my career as you want—and find one single instance where I've crossed the line. Where I've tainted a case by doing something illegal. Just one. I dare you."

He winces like I just slapped him across the face. Alluding to the fact that he hasn't been in the field for some time as he chases a higher seat at the leadership table is a soft spot for him. Good to know. I'll file that nugget away for later use.

He clears his throat and regroups. "I'm not going to do that—"

"Because you can't."

"Perhaps. But that doesn't excuse your insolence. That doesn't excuse your disrespect," he says. "As I said before, I know you think you're special and the rules don't apply to you, but I'm here to remind you that they most certainly do."

"This unit would run a lot smoother if you spent less time focusing on what I do or how I do it and more time focusing on the crimes we need to solve," I say, my voice growing more heated. "Micromanaging people doesn't have the effect you think it does, Chief. It runs down morale, strips them of their confidence, and builds resentment toward you."

"Well, thank you for that lesson in leadership," he says sarcastically. "I'll be sure to take it under advisement."

"Let's all take a deep breath and calm ourselves."

Ayad and I both turn to see Stone standing in the doorway, his overcoat draped over one arm and his newsboy cap atop his head, obviously knocking off for the night. He walks in and leans against the wall to the side of Ayad's desk, standing roughly between the two of us. Stone looks from Ayad to me, an expression of disapproval on his face.

"You two kids need to learn how to get along," Stone says. "You're two of my brightest stars, and it's on your work I plan to rebuild the rapid response program. But that's going to be impossible if you two can't find a way to work together."

"ADIC Stone, I don't know that I can work with her," Ayad tells him. "She's impudent, insulting, and has zero respect for my authority."

"Respect is earned, Chief Ayad. Do you think you're entitled to her respect simply because you sit in that chair?" Stone says.

"I'm her superior officer," Ayad argues.

"That doesn't mean SSA Wilder should grovel at your feet every time you step into a room," Stone points out. "Your title doesn't entitle you to anything. If you want her respect, earn it. Stop micromanaging her. Let her run her team the way she sees fit. Unless and until she crosses a line, there's no reason to be breathing down her neck. And I can assure you that I've read her jacket back to front and there is not one single accusation of misconduct."

"I understand," Ayad protests. "But there are rules and protocols—"

"Those rules and protocols are crap. To make a case, you sometimes have to walk that line. You sometimes have to get so close to it that it feels like you're breaking the law. It's how I built my career. I got close to that line, but I never crossed it. And I made a lot of cases as a result. That's what she's doing," Stone says. "And what allowed me to have the success I've had in my career is having people who support me and didn't micromanage me. Stop breathing down her neck and give her some room to do her job. Do you understand me?"

Ayad clenches his teeth but nods. He doesn't like being told how to run his unit—especially in front of *me*—and it shows on his face. I have to physically stifle my grin.

"The relationship between you and SSA Wilder needs to be symbiotic," Stone continues. "You two need to find a way to work together. I can't have you at each other's throats. I won't."

I'm glad to hear that Stone is defending me against Ayad's overreaching. I'm glad to see Stone putting Ayad in his place. It's about time somebody does.

But then he turns to me.

"As for you, SSA Wilder, I understand your natural inclination is to buck authority, but that needs to end. Now. Chief Ayad is correct when he says that he is your superior officer, and you should have a level of deference," Stone tells me. "All this little snark, all this constant friction and escalation, is completely uncalled for. It's out of line, and you know it's out of line because you'd hate it if anyone under your command stepped up to you that way. It's counterproductive, and frankly, it's beneath you. This petty bickering is ridiculous. You're a rising star in the Bureau. You're an excellent agent and you have a bright future ahead of you. I truly believe the sky is the limit for you, but if you bog yourself down in these pissing matches, you're going to throw that all away. Act like a grown-up, Blake."

I look down at my hands, feeling my cheeks burning with embarrassment. I'm not used to being dressed down like this, but I know Stone is right. I have been acting like a child, and my feud with Ayad has been petty. I haven't risen above like I normally do. Stone looks from me to Ayad and back again.

"You two need to work this out. I have big plans for both of you and this unit as a whole. But for us to reach the goals I have, you two need to find a way to work together," he says. "If you can't, I'll get rid of one of you—if not both of you. I refuse to let children who can't work and play well together in my unit. So, figure it out."

And with that, Stone turns and walks out of Ayad's office, leaving both of us sitting there staring at each other, the directive to figure things out hanging in the air between us. I'm not sure what to do with it. And judging by the look on Ayad's face, neither is he. We stare at each other for a long moment, neither of us seems to know what to say. I run my fingers through my hair and try to gather myself. It pains me to admit, but Stone is right about everything he said.

"All right," I say. "Is there anything else?"

He shakes his head. "No. I think ADIC Stone said everything that needs to be said."

"Yeah, I think so." I get to my feet. "Before I go, I want to apologize. ADIC Stone is right. I've been petty and childish and haven't handled this transition well. I give you my word that I'll do better."

"And perhaps ADIC Stone is right that I've been a little too hard on you—that I have micromanaged you. I recognize your talent and know that you're a good agent. I suppose you don't need somebody breathing down your neck. I see that now."

Ayad gets to his feet and extends his hand to me. I take it and give him a firm shake.

"Hopefully, we'll find a way to work together more effectively," he says.

"We will. If for no other reason than neither of us wants to be fired."

"That's a very valid point."

I share a smile with Ayad and think I feel a slight thawing in the wall of ice that exists between us. Very slight. I doubt he and I will ever be on each other's Christmas card lists, but perhaps we can find a way to work together without killing one another.

"Good night," I say.

"Good night. I'll see you in the morning."

I turn and leave his office, feeling slightly better about everything that's happened. All except for Keller's death. That's a sting I don't think will fade anytime soon. The bullpen is empty as I walk through; everybody has already gone home for the night. I head toward the office to grab my bags, anxious to get the hell out of there for the night. There is a hot bath and a glass of wine in my immediate future.

When I step into my office, though, I see a newspaper on my desk. I know wasn't there when I went into my meeting with Ayad. I pick it up and see the note attached to it. It's Astra's neat, precise handwriting, and it says: *The spy game sure is a rough business, huh?*

I pull the note off the paper and look at the story underneath. The headline grabs my attention immediately: *Veteran CIA Agent Killed In Car Accident.* Embedded into the story is a picture of Doyle Kalfus.

"That was quick," I mutter. "Quick but well deserved."

I drop the paper and grin to myself as I turn and walk out of my office and head for the elevator, feeling a bit lighter than I did when I got here today. Things sometimes work out well. They sometimes work out the way they're supposed to, and some cosmic injustices are set right.

Or in the case of Brad Keller and his family, as right as they can be.

The elevator chimes and the doors slide open. I step out of the elevator and into the underground parking garage, heading for my car. My footsteps thump dully on the concrete beneath me. Shielded by a row of cars, I round a corner and stop in my tracks. My heart leaps into my throat, and I feel the knots in my stomach pull tight. I duck behind the wide pillar to my right and lean around it, peering out at the two figures standing about twenty yards away from me.

"What the hell?" I whisper to myself.

Standing near an idling black Town Car, I see Senator Kathryn Hedlund standing with ADIC Stone. They're talking softly; all I can make out are hushed murmurs. I strain my ears, but between the sound of the car idling and how low they're speaking to one another, I can't hear any individual words. But they seem to be chummy. Very chummy. I can see Stone throw his head back and laugh at something she just said. Hedlund is laughing along with Stone and puts her hand on his arm with an unexpected familiarity.

I didn't know that Stone knew Hedlund, and as I think back to what SAC Locke told me about the Senator having a large role in the Bureau's reshuffling, it sends a cold chill sweeping through me. As I watch them from behind the pillar, a thousand questions flash through my mind. What on earth could she be talking to Stone about? What is a Senator from West Virginia doing in Washington? What are they planning together?

What in the hell is going on?

Before I can even begin to think up answers to those questions, the shrill shrieking of my phone echoes throughout the garage. I duck back behind the pillar, press my back against it, and try to will myself into invisibility. I fumble my phone out of my pocket, nearly dropping it twice before I'm able to mute it. My heart is racing, and I clutch the phone to my chest, my breath shallow and ragged.

I stand there expecting Stone and Hedlund to come around the pillar, find me standing here, and give me the CIA treatment.

Instead of catching a bullet, though, I hear the sound of a car door closing, followed by the rev of an engine that shortly speeds off into the night. A moment later, I hear the sound of a second car starting and the squeal of tires on the pavement as it rumbles away. Leaning out from behind the pillar, I see that Hedlund and Stone are gone. I'm alone again.

"Jesus. What is happening?" I whisper to myself.

I hate the fact that a thousand conspiracies are firing through my mind, but I can't stop them from coming, one after another. I can't stop thinking about my suspicions, that Hedlund is part of the Thirteen. But if she is, does that mean Stone is too? If he wasn't, why would she come across the country to speak with him? There are so many conspiracies and scenarios flashing through my mind all at one time that when my phone rings again, I let out a sharp yelp of surprise and nearly drop my phone again.

My hands are trembling, but I manage to control myself enough to look down and see the call is coming from a restricted number. For a brief moment, I consider sending the call to voicemail. But they've called twice in less than a minute now which makes me think it's important. So, I connect the call and press the phone to my ear.

"Wilder," I say.

"Blake?"

It's a woman's voice I don't recognize. "Yes, this is Blake Wilder. Who's this?"

"I'm a friend of Kit's. I—I'm sorry to call you out of the blue like this," the voice says. "But she asked me to call you if anything happened—"

A dose of ice water floods my veins, and my heart nearly stops. I stand there with the phone pressed to my ear, trembling with fear. Time seems to slow to a crawl, and I feel myself choking on emotion as my eyes well with tears.

"What happened?" I ask, my voice cracking. "What happened to my sister?"

"Blake, Kit's been shot."

AUTHOR'S NOTE

Thanks for reading *The House on the Hill*, book 11 in the *Blake Wilder FBI Mystery Thriller series*. I hope you enjoyed the new characters. It took me a long time drawing up each of them - their look, back story, and personality. I scrapped up Nina's character again last minute before publishing, so I hope it turned out well!

My intention is to give you a thrilling adventure and an entertaining escape with each and every book. Being a new indie writer is tough. However, your support has helped tremendously. I don't have a large budget, huge following, or any of the cutting edge marketing techniques.

So, *all I kindly ask* is that if you enjoyed this book, please take a moment of your time and leave me a review and maybe recommend the book to a fellow book lover or two. This way I can continue to write all day and night and bring you more books in the *Blake Wilder series.*

By the way, if you find any typos or want to reach out to me, feel free to email me at egray@ellegraybooks.com

Your writer friend,
Elle Gray

P.S. I'm working hard and there's more Blake and Olivia to come :)

ALSO BY
ELLE GRAY

Blake Wilder FBI Mystery Thrillers

A Pax Arrington Mystery

ALSO BY
ELLE GRAY | K.S. GRAY

41506366R00135